I0647507

POPULAR PUBLICATIONS  FACSIMILE EDITIONS

Dime Detective Magazine #13 (November 1932)

Dime Detective magazine was the flagship detective pulp in the Popular Publications stable, running for almost 300 issues over twenty years. The November 1932 issue contains stories by Carroll John Daly, Erle Stanley Gardner, and Frederick Nebel, and includes installments in the Cardigan, Cass Blue, and Vee Brown series.

Authors:

Carroll John Daly, Frederick Nebel,

Erle Stanley Gardner, John Lawrence, Howard E. Morgan

Illustrators:

William Reusswig, John Fleming Gould

Contents originally appeared in the November 1932 issue of *Dime Detective* magazine. Copyright © 1932 by Popular Publications, Inc., and assigned to Steeger Properties, LLC. This edition copyright © 2025 by Steeger Properties, LLC. All rights reserved. "Dime Detective" is a trademark of Steeger Properties, LLC.

NOTE: We have attempted to restore the original page scans in this facsimile in order to provide an enjoyable reading experience. However, in some cases there can be text loss due to damage to the original pulp, tight bindings, or other reasons.

DIME DETECTIVE MAGAZINE

10¢

EVERY STORY COMPLETE **EVERY STORY NEW**

Vol. 4   CONTENTS for NOVEMBER, 1932   No. 1

THREE GRIPPING MYSTERY-ACTION NOVELETTES

THRILLING BOOK-LENGTH HORROR NOVEL

TENSE DETECTIVE SHORT STORY

Watch for the December Issue   On the Newsstands November 15th

Published every month by Popular Publications, Inc., 2256 Grove Street, Chicago Illinois. Editorial and executive offices 205 East Forty-second Street, New York City. Harry Steeger, President and Secretary, Harold S. Goldsmith, Vice President and Treasurer. Entered as second class matter Feb. 26, 1932, at the Post Office at Chicago, Ill., under the Act of March 3, 1879. Title registration pending at U. S. Patent Office. Copyrited 1932 by Popular Publications, Inc. Single copy price 10c. Yearly subscriptions in U. S. A. $1.00. For advertising rates address Sam J. Perry, 205 E. 42nd St., New York, N. Y. When submitting manuscripts, kindly enclose sufficient postage for their return if found unavailable. The publishers cannot accept responsibility for return of unsolicited manuscripts, although all care will be exercised in handling them.

JACK "PUTS ONE OVER" ON HIS BOY FRIEND!

BILL: Say, Jack, look at that he-man's physique that Bob has! He makes us look like a couple of scarecrows!

JACK: I wonder how he did it? Six months ago he was just my size. He sure has made a hit with Helen!

HELEN: Hello, Skinny! How are you? Did you see Bob since he took the George Jowett course?

JACK: Oh! So that's how he did it?

JACK: Yes, Bill, I took Helen's tip and sent for Jowett's course, two weeks ago. Look what it has done for me already!

BILL: Well you have to show me!

(Two Months Later)

HELEN: Why Jack! I wouldn't know you... You certainly are a new man!

JACK: Don't forget our date tonight.

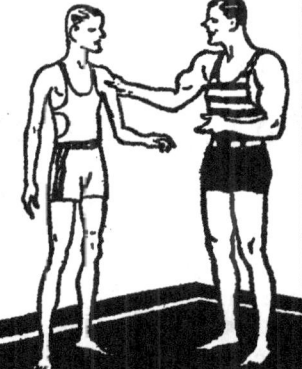

BILL: Gosh, Jack, you don't mean to tell me George Jowett did this for you?

JACK: Yes, sir! He added three inches to my chest and two inches to my biceps!

BILL: Well, here goes the coupon. What George Jowett can do for others he certainly can do for me!

Yes Sir, I will add 3 INCHES TO YOUR CHEST
2 INCHES TO YOUR BICEPS
... or it won't cost you one cent!
Signed: GEORGE F. JOWETT

TWO solid inches of tough, sinuous muscle added to your biceps... 3 inches added to your chest... or it won't cost you one penny! That's my unqualified guarantee!

If I hadn't accomplished this for thousands of others... If I wasn't absolutely sure that I could do it for you... I wouldn't dare make such a startling guarantee!

You will not only increase your biceps and chest, but every part of your body will be developed proportionately... I'll give you lithe, muscular legs that will be columns of power for speed and endurance... I'll make your whole body vibrate with muscular energy, pep and health!

Take my full course and I will guarantee to add 3 inches to your chest and 2 inches to your biceps or it won't cost you one penny!

Try one of my test courses NOW... prove to yourself that you too can get a sixteen inch bicep!

Send for "MOULDING A MIGHTY ARM"
A Complete Course for only 25c

It will be a revelation to you. You can't make a mistake. The guaranty of the strongest armed man in the world stands behind this course. I give you all the secrets of strength illustrated and explained as you like them. In 30 days you can get an unbreakable grip of steel and a Herculean arm. Mail your order now while you can still get this course at my introductory price of only 25c.

Try any one of my test courses at 25c. Or, try all six of them for only $1.00.

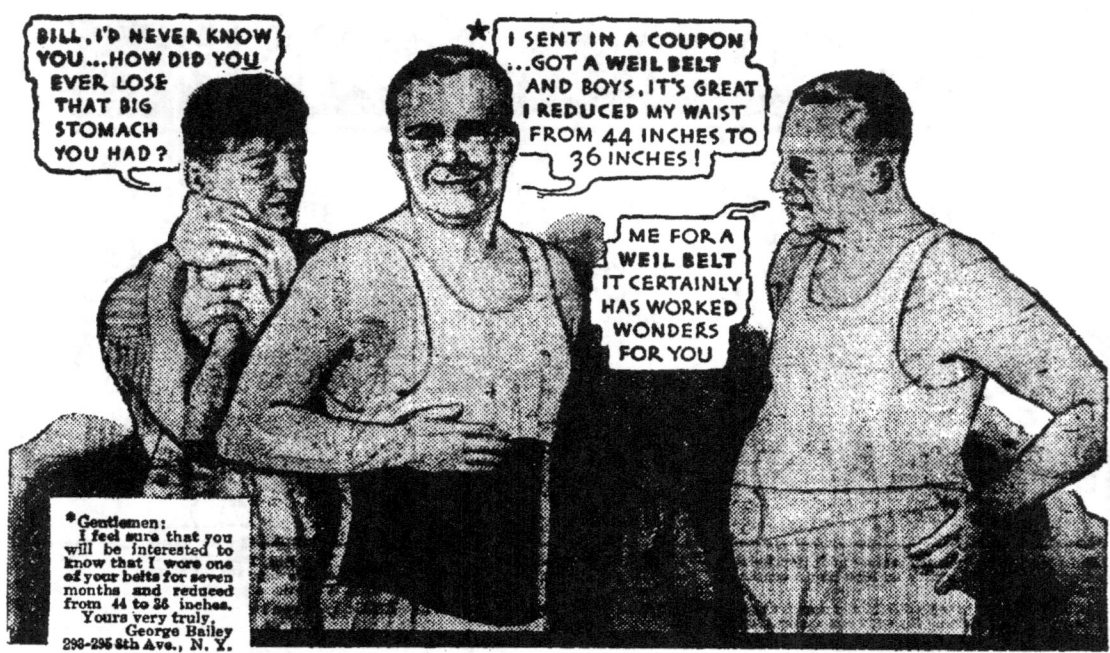

Yes Sir! We absolutely **GUARANTEE**
to REDUCE your **WAIST 3 INCHES** in **10 DAYS**
. . . or it won't cost you a penny!

YOU will appear **much slimmer** at once, and in 10 short days **your** waistline will actually be 3 inches **smaller**—three inches of fat gone—or it won't cost you one cent. For 12 years the Weil Belt has been accepted as ideal for reducing by men in all walks of life...from business men and office workers who find that it removes cumbersome fat with every movement...to active outdoor men who like the feeling of protection it gives.

IT IS THE MASSAGE-LIKE ACTION THAT DOES IT!

Now there is an easy way to reduce without exercise, diet or drugs. The Weil Health Belt exerts a massage-like action that removes fat with every move you make.

NO Drugs
NO Diets
NO Exercises

It supports the sagging muscles of the abdomen and quickly gives you an erect, athletic carriage. Many enthusiastic wearers write that it not only reduces fat but it also supports the abdominal walls and keeps the digestive organs in place—that they are no longer fatigued—and that it greatly increases their endurance. You will be more than delighted with the great improvement in your appearance.

DON'T WAIT—FAT IS DANGEROUS!

Fat is not only unbecoming, but it also endangers your health. Insurance companies know the danger of fat accummulations. The best medical authorities warn against obesity, so don't wait any longer.

You Can't Lose—Either you take off 3 inches of fat in 10 days or it won't cost one penny! Even the postage you pay to return the package will be refunded!

Send TO-DAY for details of TEN DAY TRIAL OFFER

THE WEIL COMPANY, 10211 HILL STREET, NEW HAVEN, CONN.

Gentlemen: Send me FREE, your illustrated folder describing
The Weil Belt and full details of your 10 day FREE trial offer.

Name————————————————— Address—————————————————

City————————————————— State—————————————————

4

To those who think Learning Music is hard-

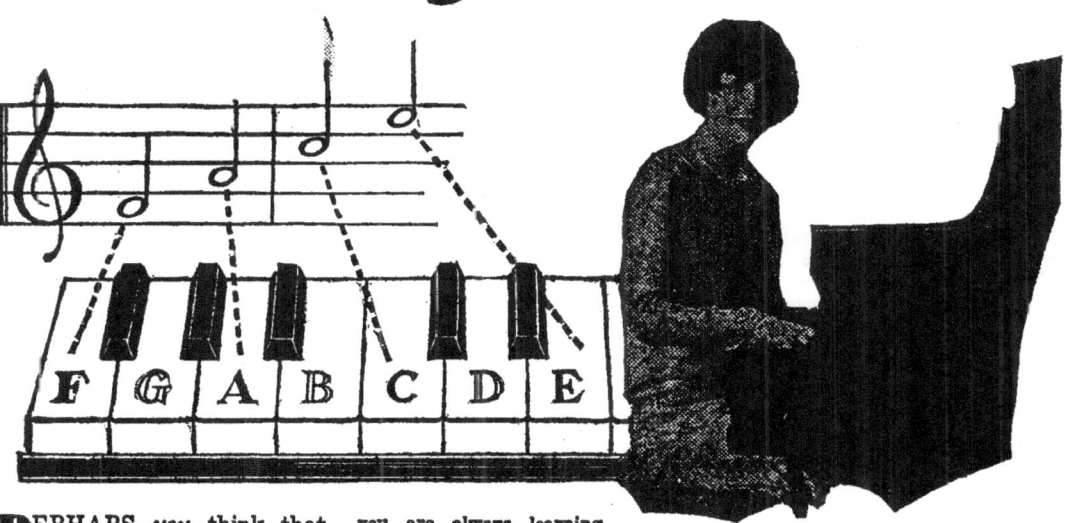

PERHAPS *you* think that taking music lessons is like taking a dose of medicine. It isn't any longer!

As far as you're concerned, the old days of long practice hours with their horrid scales, hardwork exercises, and expensive personal teacher fees are over and done with.

You have no excuses — no alibis whatsoever for not making your start toward musical good times *now!*

For, through a method that removes the boredom and extravagance from music lessons, you can now learn to play your favorite instrument entirely at home—without a private teacher—in half the usual time—at a fraction of the usual cost.

Just imagine . . . a method that has made the reading and playing of music so downright simple that you don't have to know one note from another to begin.

Do you wonder that this remarkable way of learning music has already been vouched for by over 600,000 people in all parts of the world?

Easy as Can Be

The lessons come to you by mail from the famous U. S. School of Music. They consist of complete printed instructions, diagrams, and all the music you need. You study with a smile. One week you are learning a dreamy waltz—the next you are mastering a stirring march. As the lessons continue they prove easier and easier. For instead of just scales you are always learning to play by *actual notes* the classic favorites and the latest syncopations that formerly you only *listened* to.

And you're never in hot water. First you are *told* how a thing is done. Then a picture *shows* you how, then you do it yourself and hear it. No private teacher could make it clearer or easier.

Soon when your friends say, "please play something," you can surprise and entertain them with pleasing melodies on your favorite instrument. You'll find yourself in the spotlight—popular everywhere. Life at last will have its silver lining and lonely hours will vanish as you play the "blues" away.

New Friends — Better Times

If you're tired of doing the heavy looking on at parties—if always listening to others play has almost spoiled the pleasure of music for you—if you've been envious because they could entertain their friends and family—if learning music has always been one of those never-to-come-true dreams, let the time-proven and tested home-study method of the U. S. School of Music come to your rescue.

Don't be afraid to begin your lessons at once. Over 600,000 people learned to play this modern way—and found it easy as A-B-C. Forget that old-fashioned idea that you need special "talent." Just read the list of instruments in the panel, decide which one you want to play and the U. S. School will do the rest. And bear in mind no matter which instrument you choose, the cost in each case will average the same—just a few cents a day. No matter whether you are a mere beginner or already a good performer, you will be interested in learning about this new and wonderful method.

Send for Our Free Book and Demonstration Lesson

Our wonderful illustrated Free Book and our Free Demonstration Lesson explain all about this remarkable method. They prove just how anyone can learn to play his favorite instrument *by note* in almost no time and for just a fraction of what old slow methods cost. The booklet will also tell you about the amazing new *Automatic Finger Control*.

Read the list of instruments to the left, decide which you want to play, and the U S School of Music will do the rest. Act NOW. Clip and mail this coupon today, and the fascinating Free Book and Free Demonstration Lesson will be sent to you at once. No obligation. Instruments supplied when needed, cash or credit. U. S. School of Music, 3871 Brunswick Bldg., New York City.

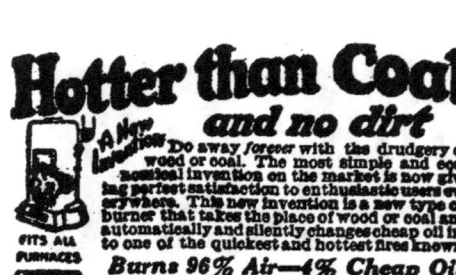

6

7

THE RED DEATH

A Vee Brown Story

by

Carroll John Daly

Author of "As Midnight Strikes," etc.

The D. A. heard of Brown's threat to drill Louie Mandozza through the back—so he took him off the case. But Brown didn't care. If he couldn't get "King Louie" legally from behind a copper's shield— Well, there are more ways than the guillotine to kill a king!

The figure of the pirate disappeared.

CHAPTER ONE

The Figure in the Doorway

I WAS nervous, of course; maybe I was irritable with Brown, which was strange. But perhaps stranger still was the fact that he put up with it. After all, he had his own troubles as a detective assigned to the district attorney's office. He had told the district attorney, Mortimer Doran, that the super-racketeer, Louie Mandozza, would never be back in the city. And now that the income-tax fraud evidence that Brown had given to Mandozza in order to save my life and that of Una Coles was gone, Mandozza was running things in the underworld again. And Una Coles! There was nothing now to protect her from Mandozza. That was what I was discussing with— or rather, hammering at Vee Brown.

"You're in love with the girl, Dean," he said, "and it dims your mental vision and magnifies your imagination. After all, I haven't made a bad job of it, considering everything."

"Considering everything!" I repeated

those words a little bitterly. "I know that it was my fault. But I was trapped because I wanted to save Una Coles. You saved my life and hers, of course—but what good has it done her?"

"You forget," he said, "that I also made her a widow. You'll admit that opens up possibilities for you, Dean. Even in your wildest fancies, you're too conventional to attempt bigamy."

It seemed an ill-timed joke. I said: "There's nothing to protect Una from Mandozza now. She sold him out and saved your life. Mandozza must hate her, will even kill her unless—"

"Unless someone kills him." Brown shook his head and smiled. "Good old Dean. You weren't, perhaps, thinking of a bit of murder. But don't look so shocked. You'd have to get a search warrant to locate your gun, while Mandozza was shooting you to death. You mustn't play another man's game."

I didn't smile with him. I simply picked up the evening paper.

"Seriously, Dean," he was across the room, his hand upon my shoulder, "there would be nothing for Mandozza in the death of Una Coles but vengeance. I know he's strong for vengeance, but for vengeance that would also strike you and me; put the girl in a position where I would be helpless to protect her. Mandozza isn't afraid of me. He fears neither man nor devil. He'll plan to strike in some horrible way; is planning to strike now."

"How did you discover that?" The paper fell to the floor. I forgot my grouch toward Brown. Just one thing then. Una was in danger—immediate danger.

"Inspector Ramsey."

"He told you! He knows who Una Coles is, knows she's the girl whose life you bargained against Mandozza's freedom!"

"Not so fast, Dean. He doesn't know yet. He has never seen her—at least, to place her. But he does know there's such a girl, and he would sell his soul to find her. Especially since that night he searched my apartment for the Mandozza evidence and got himself all tied up for his troubles. I rather rode him about that, you know. No—he didn't tell me he knew her, but he told me enough to convince me that he thinks he will very soon. He believes, if he gets the girl he'll get the solution to my bargain with Mandozza. And he hopes that that will break me as a first-grade detective. That's why I'm going out now. To find out just why he believes he will have Una Coles tonight."

"How will you find out? How will you protect her?"

"Department leaks!" he told me. "Or I will buy my information just like I would buy any other commodity. Clever sleuthing is all too often worked on a cash basis. That's why I work alone." And suddenly, "Don't touch anything in the music room, Dean. I've got a rather sentimental puzzle in there, that only needs fitting together. And above all— don't go out!"

And he was gone, whistling out the door. An unfamiliar tune. Probably one of his new ones, for which, as the Master of Melody, Brown received a princely income.

THERE was no doubt that I was in love with Una Coles. Una, who had been married to a murderer, a man that Brown had killed in a gun fight in Mandozza's billiard room. And Mandozza! He held enough over the girl's head to command her every move. She hated him but she feared him; more for her parents than for herself. Her parents had no knowledge of Una's marriage, or her criminal connections. But who were her parents? I thought a moment and then began to pace the room. It wasn't who her parents were that bothered me. It was—who was Una Coles?

It was close to one o'clock. I didn't go to bed; I couldn't. Brown had said not to go out. That must mean he would need me. What was keeping him so long? What had he gone out to learn? And the phone rang.

"Hello. Hello!" I was talking into the mouthpiece almost before the bell had stopped ringing. Brown's voice came back to me. I had never heard him so excited.

"Listen, Dean." His words fairly crowded each other over the wire. "Go at once to—" and he gave me an address in the upper Seventies. "If Una Coles hasn't already gone in the house, watch for her and stop her. If the trap is sprung, why—"

"What trap?" I cut in.

"Never mind that. If you don't see her come along within a few minutes, she's already in there. Then—do everything to help her. Keep Ramsey busy until I can get there. Tell him anything, but keep him from searching the house."

"But—" I started again.

"Don't you see? I can't tell you any more; I don't know any more. I only know that Una is in danger if she has entered that house. . . . No, no—not in danger from Mandozza. In danger from the police; from Inspector Ramsey. You'll have to work it on your own, Dean. But don't let Ramsey see Una tonight."

A receiver clicked onto a distant hook. For a moment I stood, dazed. Then I snapped back to life and dashed toward the door.

THE taxi was almost at the number Brown had given me when I called sharply to the driver. The car pulled to the curb. Getting out, I paid him and watched the car start away. Then I looked up and down the block. There

was not a soul in sight, though a bit down the block a big touring car was parked by the curb, lights extinguished.

What would Brown do? Would he go down the block and inspect that car? I thought not. My orders were to watch for Una Coles and prevent her from entering that house. I did walk by the house, but not as far as the parked car. But for a single light that flashed from beneath a drawn shade in a first-floor front room, the place was in darkness. Maybe I was in time. Maybe Una had not gone in yet. But if she had— Then what? For nights I had lain awake and planned how I would help Una. Fantastic ideas, full of self-sacrifice and heroism, but senseless. Now that I had the chance, what would I do? What should I do?

I stopped dead before that house. The light in the front room went out. For perhaps a minute I stood so, looking up at that darkened window. Then my eyes switched. There was a distant click. I looked at the front door. It had opened. A figure was framed there. I couldn't be sure, but I thought it was a woman.

Moving back against the iron fence in front of the house, I waited. The figure moved, came through the open door—then stopped. Clearly I heard a bell ring —an insistent, steady ring. It was a telephone.

The dim outline in the open door hesitated, turned quickly and passed back into the house as the door closed softly. No light went up in that front room again. The house remained in darkness.

I jerked erect. Out of the corner of my eye I thought I saw a moving figure. A figure that, even as I looked, ducked back into the vestibule of the house to my right. Was it just fancy? Overexcited nerves? Or had a human form disappeared in the blackness?

Two lights suddenly flashed down the street. A car had turned the corner and was coming along the block toward me. Was this Una Coles after all, or was the figure in the doorway Una? I was almost certain it was a woman.

I acted quickly and, I thought, cleverly. Avoiding the steps to the basement entrance, I vaulted that low iron railing and dropped into the areaway below. From there I could watch both the street and the stone steps leading to the house. And I could watch too, the approach of that car and see if Una Coles alighted from it.

I landed, half crouched, straightened, lost my balance, and putting out my hand to protect my body from the hard stone, felt something soft and yielding. A human body.

Spinning around I stretched out my hands to grapple with the man, then dropped them to my sides. A gun was shoved hard against my stomach; a face was thrust forward close to mine, and a voice was saying: "Easy does it, brother. You wouldn't want me to mess up other people's property with you."

I could see his face raise in the darkness. A low whistle came from the sidewalk above us. And the voice said: "That'll be the inspector. Get going up them steps."

"You're—you're the police!" I gasped.

"Exactly." He swung me around and prodded the gun against my back. "You didn't expect to pounce on the Salvation Army after just robbing a house, did you?"

"Robbing a house! I'm here to prevent—" I stopped short, suddenly remembering Brown saying that Una's danger came from the police. "I do some work for a newspaper. The Evening Globe."

"Never read it." The big man laughed. "Take it up with the inspector. On your way!"

And the first man I bumped into as I came up those steps was Inspector Ramsey.

"Says he's a reporter." The man spoke behind me. "Evening Globe. That's a new one, inspector."

INSPECTOR RAMSEY stared at me a long moment. Then he reached out and jerked up my slouch hat. "Condon— Dean Condon." He scowled. "Vee Brown's little playmate."

"Then he is on the paper." The man behind me lowered his gun, and pushing his mouth close to my ear, whispered: "My name's Finnigan. Detective Frank Finnigan. Give a guy a break if the story's a big one."

"What are you doing here?" Inspector Ramsey asked me in his best official manner, which was abrupt and threatening.

I hesitated a moment and looked to his left with surprise. A couple of plain-clothesmen and a uniformed cop were on the sidewalk. Another man was standing by the alley. A lump came into my throat. Inspector Ramsey was there with a vengeance. Was—was Una inside? "Trapped" was the word Brown had used, and now I was to delay Ramsey.

"I saw a man run from this house and dash into the alley across the street and—"

"When?"

"Just a few minutes ago."

"How about that Fiester?" Ramsey turned to a big double-chinned man who was chewing a match.

"Not a chance. No one has come in or out of the house since the dame went in and—"

"Never mind that." Ramsey snapped him off, but not before I had heard enough to convince me that Una Coles had already gone into the house. "What brought you into this neighborhood at this hour?" Ramsey was at me again.

"Nothing. I was just— I was just visiting a friend."

"Where?"

"Look here, Ramsey," I straightened and tried a little dignity, "if you want to question me, arrest me. I know my rights. I work for a newspaper."

"Yeah." He sneered. "Write bedtime stories about Vee Brown." And turning to the fat-chinned Fiester, "All right, sergeant. I've been around to the street behind. A rabbit couldn't get through the back. Cohen's in the alley?"

"Right! She's sewed up tighter than a drum. I could'a got a look at her face if you hadn't made me stick in the vestibule."

"You'll get a look at it now," Ramsey said with satisfaction. "Not over tall, was she?"

"Oh, so-so," said the sergeant.

"Great description," Ramsey growled. "They'll be calling you 'camera eye' after a while. Come on!"

As Ramsey started up those steps I grabbed him by the coat. "If you want," I said, "I'll show you the house where I was visiting, and——"

"I'm not interested in you." He turned on the first step and looked down at me. Then he stretched out a hand and jerked me toward him. "On second thought you'd better come along," and probably remembering The Globe and the influence behind it, added, "if you want to, of course. You're not under arrest, you know."

"But the man I saw running, went——"

"To hell with him." Ramsey was smiling now. "It's a woman I want, Condon. Maybe you'd like to get a look at her too." And roughly, "Maybe you'll enjoy seeing her with bracelets on. You and that boy detective, Brown, have a peculiar sense of humor about seeing people tied up."

"You did look funny, Ramsey." I stopped. Not because he had closed his fist or of my memory of the last time he had closed it, but because of Una.

If trouble were ahead for her, there would be no use in further antagonizing Inspector Ramsey.

He turned suddenly and mounted the steps, paying no more attention to me.

CHAPTER TWO

Inside That House

INSPECTOR RAMSEY entered the vestibule, turned the knob, rattled it once or twice, then leaned out and pushed the bell.

"It'll be a surprise to Vic." He laughed when he spoke to the sergeant. "Imagine anyone shaking him down in his own home. We're giving the girl plenty of time to slip out the back."

"Who's the girl?" asked the sergeant.

"You'd be surprised." Ramsey seemed rather pleasant now, as he looked at me. "And you, Condon; and Vee Brown will be simply amazed."

"Yeah?" was the best I could get off. Then, "Who is Vic?"

"You don't know?" I think his eyebrows went up in the semidarkness. "Victor Marks."

"The pawnbroker!" I gasped.

"Exactly—and fence." He tried to peer through the glass above the door, then pressed the bell again—viciously. The buzz sounded far back in the house. "Understand he's getting ready to do a squeal. You know that, don't you?"

"Me?" I said.

"No wonder Brown shines, going around with such a dumb partner. This is Vee Brown's little side-kick, sergeant."

The sergeant smiled amiably. "Yeah. Great guy, Brown. Wish I had his nerve with a gun, and his pull after he uses it."

"Never mind that!" Inspector Ramsey cut in, with a glare. It was evident he hadn't taken others into his confidence about his suspicions of Brown. Then, "Damn that bell. Damn Vic!"

He jerked the doorknob, shook it violently, pounded on the glass, put his weight against the door, and said: "It's the servant's night out, I know. But Vic must be sleeping like a log." A moment, and then, "Come, sergeant! Give me a hand with this door." He threw his weight against it again.

"You want it busted in, eh?"

"No, no." Ramsey was sarcastic. "I'm just scratching my shoulder against it. Come on! We're going in."

Sergeant Feister muttered something under his breath, grabbed hold of the knob and hurled his body against the door. The door shook and the wood groaned. The second time that huge body crashed against it, wood splintered and cracked. The door sagged, and then with a final snap crashed in, dragging the sergeant with it.

"That's done." The sergeant climbed from his knees. "I thought—"

We all paused and listened. There was the distant creak of loose boards. We raised our heads. Footsteps were going up stairs. Hurrying, light feet.

"Well—we're in," I said loudly, and Ramsey cursed me.

"Will I follow those steps?" Sergeant Fiester had his flash out, was shooting it along the hall, onto the well-worn stairs that led above. There was a click and the sudden glare of electric globes almost directly above me as the sergeant found the light button.

"We won't go above yet." Inspector Ramsey rubbed his hands together, then called out the front door. "Wilson, come in here. Find the kitchen and stand by the back stairs. At the bottom of them; don't go up. We'll try the front room on the left, here, sergeant—where the light came from. We'll see who was interested in this room. No, no—you needn't watch the front stairs. We can

see them from the room here. If she wants to dash out the front way, there's a couple of lads waiting as a reception committee." He parted heavy curtains and tried to peer into the room on the left.

The sergeant's flash shot between the parted curtains and almost at once lighted on an open safe. Then it crept about the room. Onto the desk—loose papers, a pen and an open inkwell. Down the side of the desk that small circle of yellow went, picked out a spot on the rug, a queer patch of red that— I drew in a quick breath. The queer patch of red was blood.

Almost the instant I saw the blood, the circle picked out something else—something white. It was a face; a sharp, beak-like nose; thick yellow lips; gray eyes. Staring eyes that did not blink in the sudden glare; glassy eyes that could not blink. The light hovered a moment, came back to that face and stayed steadily on it—on the eyes that could not blink. They were the sightless eyes of a dead man.

"Victor Marks." Sergeant Fiester just breathed the words as he found the electric button and the tiny circle of light was merged in a sudden flood of brightness.

INSPECTOR RAMSEY stood, grim-faced, over the body. Sergeant Fiester was kneeling beside him, looking closely at the dead man. At length he came to his feet and said: "Someone held a gun close behind his ear and let him have it." And with a shrug of his shoulders, "Is this what you were looking for?"

"No, no," said Inspector Ramsey. "I got a tip it was to be a robbery only." And suddenly turning on the sergeant, "You don't think I'd of stalled around if I knew a man was to be murdered while—"

"While we waited, eh?" the sergeant cut in. "Well—he's dead enough to bury, and he won't be overmissed. He double-crossed a lot of crooks. He just tried it on the wrong guy this time."

"It was a woman. That's my tip. She wanted something he had. She got it out of that safe. Then she let him have it behind the ear."

"She never did that. She couldn't do that." I just blurted out the words.

"Who?" They both swung on me together. There was elation in Ramsey's face; simply surprise in Fiester's.

"Who?" I stammered. "Why—any woman."

Ramsey grinned. "It seems like you know who did it, Condon. Or, at least, you know who should have done it."

"A child could have done it." Fiester nodded. "Just the closing of a finger on a trigger. A thirty-two, I think." He was on his knees again. "It wasn't done long ago. The body's still warm. While we were outside, waiting for—"

"Since when did you become the medical examiner?" Ramsey snapped. "He's dead, and that's that. I couldn't know murder was planned. Now—" he looked toward the hall and the stairs—"the murderer is still in the house."

"That's right." Fiester came to his feet. "We better close in."

"We!" Ramsey thrust him back as he started toward the stairs. "You stay here, sergeant, at the foot of the stairs. I'll go above and search the upper rooms."

"Alone!" Fiester gasped.

Ramsey looked at me. His lips were hard and grim. "No, I guess not. This lad, Condon, seems interested. I'll let him go with me. What do you say?" He turned to me.

I simply nodded. I thought of the figure I had seen in the vestibule; of Brown's message that Una Coles might already be in the house. Of the light feet upon those stairs, which I had tried to drown out with my voice; and of the

dead man in the library with the bullet in his head.

I hesitated there at the foot of the stairs, waiting for Ramsey to precede me.

"After you, Condon," Ramsey said. "Get going!"

Mechanically I got going.

Fiester was talking below. "You're not letting him lead the way, inspector! The party above might be desperate and—"

"My business!" Inspector Ramsey snapped in. And then with a half chuckle, "Don't worry, sergeant. This woman wouldn't shoot a pretty boy like Condon here."

WE WERE at the top of the stairs now. A flash in Ramsey's hand was picking out the landing, throwing the bannister into weird shadows. He hesitated; then spoke. "Give her a call, Condon. Tell her the game's up. Tell her to come out and face the music."

"Who?"

"The girl."

"What girl?"

"Try any name," Ramsey sneered. "You'll probably hit the right one. But try one that will best protect yourself. She mightn't recognize your voice and start shooting."

"I won't." I said loudly. I was in a panic. Maybe, as Brown had told me, I was trying to delay Ramsey. Maybe I was just warning Una, if it was Una, that we were coming. There were wild ideas in my head of turning suddenly on Ramsey, snatching the gun from him and— And what? Simply playing into his hands, making a fool of myself. But I did nothing.

For a long moment we stood there in the upper hall. Then I heard it. Down that hall a door closed. Ramsey heard it too. His breath sucked into his mouth. He shoved me roughly aside.

"We've had enough play-acting for one night," he said briskly. "There's one chance in a thousand I'm wrong. I can't have another death to explain. And I'd like to hear what she says when she sees you and me together."

He was down the hall and his flash had picked out the closed door. His hand was on the knob. If Una were in that room I couldn't save her from the police, but I could help. I could shout out for her not to talk; not to say a word. Then see what Brown could do.

I saw the black police automatic in Ramsey's hand; saw the flash in his left hand, and heard him call out as he flung open the door—"Come out, young woman! The game's up."

A second or two of silence, then Ramsey had slipped his hand in that open door and pressed on the light.

He was looking into the lighted room cautiously, from the side. As I reached him he stepped quickly over the sill. No one was in that room. It was a bedroom. Ramsey bent and looked beneath the bed; he walked to a bureau and glanced behind it. With a grin at me he turned to the only other hiding place. A closed closet door. Walking rapidly toward it he grasped the knob and jerked it open.

Swaying suits greeted our eyes, and back of them—simply darkness. It was a deep closet.

"Come out!" Ramsey raised his voice and there was elation in it. And when there was no answer, "You don't want to be dragged out or shot out, do you?"

"There's no one in there, Ramsey," I told him.

"No—" he said. "Then there'll be no harm in scattering a few bullets inside, eh?"

"You wouldn't do that." I half stepped between him and the open closet door. Then, when his eyes narrowed and he took a step toward me, "I'll look."

I swung quickly and entered the closet, felt along the coats. Maybe, after all, it was empty. Maybe— And I stood still. Cold fingers had gripped my wrist, a damp palm was against mine. A soft voice, that I barely heard, whispered: "I'm here, Dean. Vee Brown telephoned that I was not to leave."

"Stay there," was all that I said as I turned quickly from the closet. Inspector Ramsey was looking at me.

"See!" I tried hard to convince him. "There is no one there."

"You were talking to yourself, eh?"

"I was talking to you. I said the closet was empty."

"You're a fool and you take me for a bigger one. Stand aside!"

I tried desperately to block his passage. His left hand tossed the flash to the bed and gripped me by the shoulder; his right swung up. His gun cracked against my chin, knocking my head back. I staggered slightly as he darted past me toward the closet.

Then I gasped. Was it in warning to Ramsey? Was it simply surprise, or perhaps even fear that rattled in my throat? I don't know. But I was staring straight at the open door that led to the dark hall. And through that open door a white hand came. Groping fingers were moving along the wall, searching for the light button; finding it even as the whistling sound came from my throat.

CHAPTER THREE

Dead-End Getaway

INSPECTOR RAMSEY heard me of course. He half swung sideways, then spun toward that door as the light went out, throwing the bedroom into blackness.

There were rapidly running feet, a peculiar thud, the stifled cry of a man and the jar of a heavy body falling to the floor. I raced toward the door and the light button, crashed against a chair, spun nearly lost my balance, regained it, then tripped over something soft and yielding. The body of a man! And I was on my knees.

My fingers touched a human face, a thick neck, the softness of hair. I came to my feet, found I had lost all sense of direction, and stretched out a hand. Almost at once I felt the bed, remembered the flash Ramsey had tossed there. I hunted frantically for it in the blackness.

Perhaps ten seconds; perhaps longer before I found it. I don't know, but it seemed a long while. I pressed the button. There was the open closet door, the chair that I had bumped in the center of the room, the door to the hall. And between that door to the hall and me was the body of a man.

I didn't turn the flash on the face then. I turned it into the closet, ran to it frantically, threw aside the clothes, splashed every bit of it with light. The closet was empty. Una Coles had gone.

I ran quickly to the light button, looked now at the man upon the floor. He was moving his right hand slowly, the fingers opening and closing. It was Inspector Ramsey. There was a welt on his forehead. He was breathing heavily.

Going into the hall I looked up and down, played my flash along the floor, then called out: "Fiester. Sergeant Fiester! Quick. Something has happened!"

For my flash was shining on a figure that half lay, half sat against the bannister. His face seemed very white, his eyes were closed, and his chin hung down on his chest. I knew him of course. It was Vee Brown.

There was someone else there; someone beside Una in the house! The murderer, of course. In his frantic effort to escape he had struck down Inspector Ramsey and Vee Brown. Brown! How did he get there? Was he badly hurt? Was— I put the flash on his face again as I knelt beside him. Heavy feet were

pounding up the stairs. Fiester was beside me, wanting to know what happened.

"It's Brown. Someone struck him down in the hall here." My words stuck in my throat. I forgot all about Ramsey. And then, in surprise, "How did he get here?"

"Came from the district attorney's office," Fiester told me. "Finnigan let him in and I let him up. Gawd—I didn't think anyone would knock him over that easy. Don't be so excited. He isn't hurt much; just knocked out." And suddenly, "Where's Ramsey?"

"In there." I pointed to the open door. "Got him too."

"Cripes!" Sergeant Fiester stiffened. "Why the hell didn't you tell me?" He stood at the door, looking down at Ramsey. Then to me, "You turned out to be a lot of help." And he strode into the room.

Despite what Sergeant Fiester said about Brown not being badly hurt, he was very still. I put a hand beneath his coat, trying to feel his heart.

Then I raised my head. I don't know if I heard a tiny creak of loose boards or not. Anyway, I raised my head, jerked up the flash I still had in my hand and sent a pencil of light to the top of those stairs. My breath stopped. That light lit smack on the white face of Una Coles.

I ALMOST called out; would have, maybe, but for a hand that suddenly shot across my mouth. Another hand covered the light from the flash. A low voice whispered: "Easy does it, Dean. Out of the room isn't out of the house, you know. There's a lot to do yet."

"Brown," I gasped. "You're not—not—"

"Not dead." He laughed now, as he came to his feet. Then in a lower voice, "Not even hurt. I just laid down for a rest. I've had a busy night, you know."

"Then it was you who struck Ramsey;

who found Una. It was all just a fake. Now—how will you get her out of the house?" And I whispered hoarsely to him how well the place was guarded.

"Of course—of course." Brown was alert now as he whispered there in the hall. "Did you get names? Who is by the kitchen door and who in the alley? Finnigan's out front, I know, and the harness bull on the beat. Also another quiet-clothes man."

I told him, after a moment's thought, that Cohen was in the alley and a dick called Wilson by the kitchen steps.

"And the basement?" Brown questioned. "The outside steps from the basement? Who is there?"

"Why—no one is there. At least, I don't think so, now." And I told him that Finnigan had been there. "But the man in front can watch that."

"Finnigan is in front now." Brown nodded. "That will be her exit, and my car her escape. The alley will do for a decoy. Stick close here."

JUST then Fiester appeared in the door. Brown rubbed a hand across his head.

"There you are, young fellow." Fiester looked from me to Brown. "Your pal thought you were dead. Never seen such a look on a lad's face!" And jerking his thumb back over his shoulder, "His nibs is coming around. He'll be raising hell in a minute or two. The one who crowned him must be in the house, and it don't seem like it's a woman."

"A woman! Nonsense. I'll check up below and have one of the boys in. You stay here with Fiester, Dean." And with that twisted smile, "Help soothe the troubled brow of the inspector when he comes out of it."

Brown turned. We heard his feet descending the stairs.

"I don't know," said Fiester, tugging at his chin, "if I should stay here or—"

"I won't stay alone with him," I blurted out. "I wouldn't be surprised if he blamed me for the whole thing."

"Knocking Brown about too! Well—" he shrugged massive shoulders—"he would hang around here, waiting for the dame to go in and shoot up Marks. He'll have more explaining to do down at headquarters than you or me'll have. I'd rather see Brown in charge of things any day. Then—"

"Yes, sir?" Fiester straightened and set his lips tightly. Inspector Ramsey was sitting up, leaning heavily upon his right hand.

"What's this about Brown?" Ramsey ran a hand across his forehead and sort of rubbed his eyes. And then suddenly, "Was that Brown you were talking to in the hall?"

"Yes, sir—it was. He's taking charge below."

"Taking charge!" Inspector Ramsey climbed to his feet, wabbled slightly. "What the devil do you mean? Who let him in here?"

"Why—he came in." Fiester's eyebrows went up. Brown was a big shot in police circles and worked straight from the district attorney's office. "Said he was sent here."

"I see." Ramsey steadied himself, felt again the lump that was rising on his forehead. Then he walked to the closet, went inside it, pawed about and threw clothes out into the room. "She's gone," he said.

"Who?" said the sergeant.

"Never mind who, you fool." Ramsey cursed. "Tell me about Brown. What happened? How long have I been out?"

"You've been out only about five minutes or so. Brown wanted me to come upstairs with him but I said I had orders to stay down there. Then he went up. Condon, here, shouted for help and for me. And you were stretched out, and so was Brown."

Inspector Ramsey hesitated. "So was Brown? You say Condon, here, called for help!" And to me, "What were you doing? What became of the girl in the closet?"

"Why—why—I told you there wasn't any girl."

"Hell!" he said. "Hell!" He rubbed his head, then snapped his fingers and turned toward the door. "Where's Brown now? Damn it, man!" He almost shouted the words. "I tell you Brown did it."

"Brown!" Fiester actually gasped. "That wallop on the head must have knocked you bow-legged, inspector. Brown's gotten more criminals than—"

"Where's Brown now?" the inspector demanded. His eyes blazed; his chin shot forward. He shook a huge fist in the sergeant's face.

Sergeant Fiester stepped back a bit. "He's taking my place downstairs. Damn it, inspector, someone had to be here with you!"

"Someone did, eh? And you were picked. I'm not able to take care of myself! That's what Brown told you, I suppose. Well—"

He stopped. We all straightened, listened. A single shot had come from somewhere in the house below. Just for a split second, maybe, we stood so. Then another shot and the falling of glass.

Fiester said: "The shot came from downstairs, where Victor Marks was killed—or in the alley."

Ramsey wasn't listening. With a single movement he picked up his gun that lay on the floor, pitched forward so that I thought he was going to fall, then dashing from the room tore down the stairs.

Someone shouted something below. A voice that might have been Brown's called for Wilson, and we were down those front stairs and in the lighted hall.

Figures peered through the glass of the front door, pushed against it. It was partly open. Then I saw that a chain was slipped across it. Fiester tore the chain from its bolt. Two officers crowded in. A third, Finnigan, peered from the vestibule.

Then Brown stepped from the lighted room where the body of Victor Marks lay. "Did you get him?" He looked at the excited faces.

"What happened?" three voices asked at once.

Brown explained it to Ramsey. "I was taking Fiester's place at the foot of the stairs. I heard a shot; then another, as if someone out in the alley had—"

"What are you doing here?" Ramsey cut in as the detective, Wilson, appeared on the scene.

"Why—I heard the shot, and someone called me. I thought it was you, inspector."

"Back to the kitchen!" Inspector Ramsey ordered. And then, "Who's covering the front of the house now?" A sharp look from Brown to Wilson. "Who's covering the basement?"

"Me!" said Finnigan from the vestibule, then faded suddenly back onto the length of stone that served as a porch.

I was almost directly in the doorway when Ramsey started out. He drove me with him, stumbling out onto the stoop.

I guess I was the first to see her, for I was thrown hard against the stone support just above the basement entrance. There was only her flying shadow as she was up those basement steps and running like a frightened rabbit along the sidewalk. Ramsey shouted something and jerked up his gun. Then he careened against me, almost knocking me to the stone below. His gun roared. A window cracked across the street.

RAMSEY straightened and fired again. Then he was down the steps and on the heels of the pursuing Finnigan. The girl had reached the big touring, passed it. Ramsey was gaining on her, Fiester was a poor third, and I had joined Brown in the rear.

And I saw the roadster just beyond the touring. Ramsey called out hoarsely and fired again.

Brown panted in my ear: "If he was any kind of shot I'd have to shoot him in the leg. But she's in, Dean. The motor's running, and with luck she's clean away. Easy does it now; we'll join the chase."

And we did, piling into the back of the big touring car with Fiester and Finnigan. Ramsey climbed into the seat beside Cohen, who had joined the chase from the alley. There were some quick orders from Ramsey about searching the house from basement to attic.

Then Brown spoke. "You're letting the murderer get a good start on you, Ramsey. You're not fool enough to think that girl did it."

"I'm not fool enough to think a lot of things." Ramsey spoke back over his shoulder to Brown as the car jerked away in pursuit of the roadster. Then, "What the devil are you doing in this car anyway?"

"My own has been stolen," Brown said. "You can see it just turning the corner ahead of you if you look closely."

Then the shriek of a police siren on the big touring drowned out further conversation between them.

"She's a good driver," Brown shouted eagerly in my ear as the roadster swung the corner at terrific speed. And then, "But Cohen's a better one, Dean," as we took the corner and roared down the block.

Brown shook his head as the roadster doubled in and out of blocks.

"She should have hit for the Drive," he told me. "That boat's got speed. We're gaining on her now. That was a nice little row I staged below."

"Make believe Ramsey doesn't know it," I said.

"Of course he knows it. But then, he knows a lot of things he can't prove, just as you and I do. We know Mandozza to be a murderer many times over, for one thing—but he still commits murder."

"Ramsey will make it hard for you."

"I don't think so. I—By God! She's trapped herself now. This is a dead-end street, because the street beyond is under repair."

It didn't seem to matter. Cohen was an expert driver. He gained at every corner. Now he was closing up on her quickly.

THE siren no longer shrieked as we tore down that street. The roadster ahead pulled to the curb. We were so close that I heard the tires screech their protest as the brakes were jammed on.

But I was watching Una. She had dashed from that car and up the steps of a pretentious stone house with a massive wrought-iron fence about the grounds. And they were really grounds; one of the city's few remaining mansions.

Then we all gathered on the sidewalk before the house.

"She went right in the front door, didn't she?" Ramsey demanded of Finnigan.

"I couldn't rightly say," said Finnigan. "It seemed like she passed along the side of the house."

Brown said: "Finnigan's right. She went along the side of the house. Better get around the block and head her off."

"I didn't ask your opinion," Ramsey snapped.

"Crooks don't hang out in houses like that," I said.

"Crooks that are Mandozza's friends do. Come on!" Ramsey started toward the front steps when Finnigan spoke.

"Don't you know whose house this is, inspector?"

"No!" said the inspector. "And I don't care."

"Well," said Finnigan, "it's the home

of Coleman Parker, the banker." And very slowly, "He's like *that* with the commissioner." Finnigan held the index and second finger of his right hand close together "The Parkers are giving that masquerade ball for charity next week. My missus read all about it in the paper."

Brown whistled softly.

Ramsey stood for a long time on the sidewalk. I think it was Brown's laugh that finally decided him.

"Cohen," he said in a determined voice, "you watch the front of the house. Finnigan, try that side entrance you're so sure the girl took, and look over the outside of the house. Fiester, you and me will go in." And when Fiester just looked at him, "We are serving Coleman Parker as well as the city. I'm fairly sure the girl went in this front door."

Without another word Inspector Ramsey stuck out his square jaw and followed it up those massive stone steps between the two bronze dragons.

"You wait here," Brown told me. "Ramsey can't very well keep me out. But you—" he spread his hands. "On the level, Dean, how did it look to you?"

"I'm almost positive she went right in the front. They'll find her hiding in there now."

"I don't think so." He shook his head.

"You don't think they'll find her?"

"I don't think they'll find her—hiding." And Brown was up the steps on the heels of Ramsey and Fiester.

CHAPTER FOUR

Glassy Doyle

COHEN proved dull company. He had a one-track mind. His job! He just stood and watched that house, leaning against the car. Finnigan had already disappeared along the side. I saw the lights go up a minute after the bell rang. Then the front door opened and the out-

line of a head appeared. I even heard Ramsey's sharp, rough voice.

Then Ramsey, Fiester and Brown passed into the house. Lights appeared to the left of that door, then across the hall, and finally in the front windows of the second story. For a good ten or fifteen minutes there were plenty of signs of activity inside that house. The night air grew chill. I paced up and down. Then Fiester appeared and beckoned from the doorway.

"Not you, Cohen," he said. "I want Condon." And as I went up the steps, Fiester said: "Both Mr. and Mrs. Parker are out of town, and it's a good thing for the inspector, I guess. No girl went in there. But Miss Parker is home, and she's class. Come inside."

"What for?" I was nervous. What of Una?

"Brown told Miss Parker you were outside, and cold. It seems she's been reading your write-ups in the paper, about him. Anyway, you're invited in. And I'm telling you they ain't people to overlook."

I followed Fiester into the great entrance hall, passed through a high arched doorway and into a brilliantly lit reception room. From the end of it a laugh came. I recognized it at once. It was Brown. Then I saw him. He was standing in another room. I saw comfortable leather chairs, books along the wall. He called to me.

"Miss Parker has ordered some hot coffee." He made way for me to pass into the library at the end of that big room. "She's got a heart of gold, Dean, and when I told her how susceptible you were to chills, she— There, there—don't be overwhelmed with gratitude." He was laughing again.

And I saw "Miss Parker."

The woman—the girl—just a blurred picture of the slender, graceful figure that came toward me. Then black eyes, a slightly tilted chin—and I knew the truth. I tried to smile, too, as that cold little hand crept into mine and red lips parted. Maybe I rubbed a hand across my eyes as Brown said I did. I don't know. I only know that I was holding the hand and looking down into the big black eyes of Una Coles.

"Miss Una Parker," Brown was saying. "Come—come, Dean. I was making you out quite a Don Juan, now— Why, Sergeant Fiester will be ashamed of you."

We were talking after that. All three of them were talking, I mean. I was sitting in a leather chair, drinking the coffee and watching Sergeant Fiester perform miraculous juggling feats with his cup and saucer. And I was wondering, too, just how long it would take the sergeant or Inspector Ramsey to find out that the girl was an impostor. The servants, of course, would tell him. Then my eyes went wide and my brain began to work. Coleman Parker—Una Coles. And I realized that the girl was not an impostor. That Una Coles was really Una Parker. That was what Una had meant when she told us of her parents; that she would rather die than have them know the truth of the life she had been dragged into. That was what Mandozza held over her head, which she feared above everything else. Not exposure to the law, for she had said she would gladly face that. But exposure to her parents. The Coleman Parkers; the name which meant as much in the financial district as it did in the social register. The truth about Una Coles—Una Parker! And tonight Mandozza had planned and very nearly succeeded in trapping her for murder in the house of a notorious receiver of stolen goods.

INSPECTOR RAMSEY pounded through the outer room and stood by the door. "So you're here, Fiester," he said, and then to Una, "I'm sorry, Miss Parker, I made a mistake. Let me assure you the police had only your best interest at heart."

"No apologies are necessary, inspector." Una stretched out her hand and took Ramsey's, "I appreciate your interest and your zeal. I know the commissioner, and will certainly see that he hears how well we are protected when you conduct things. And sergeant— The sergeant, too, of course."

Ramsey bowed a bit stiffly and his lips parted. It wasn't often that he smiled. He liked it, but he didn't speak. Fiester, however, did not neglect the opportunity. He said: "The name is Fiester—Sergeant Fiester." He tried to make his voice low, but Inspector Ramsey heard it and scowled.

As the others passed out the door I hesitated and turned to Una. The next instant she was in my arms. The smile had gone from her eyes; lashes were wet against my cheek; lips were close to mine and she was crying softly.

For a short instant I held her so. Then the phone rang. It was low and soft, yet it jarred us apart as if it were the blast of a siren. Una stared for a moment at the telephone upon the desk. Then it rang again.

She lifted the receiver and said: "Yes, this is Miss Parker. . . Yes, he is here . . . I understand . . . Oh—you wouldn't do that. You . . . Tomorrow night at seven." A long minute this time, and I saw her upper teeth clamp down heavily on her lower lip. "Yes, I'll be there of course."

She turned to me, and her voice shook. "That," she said, "was Louie Mandozza. He failed in trapping me tonight. Perhaps it would be better if he succeeded. No one else knows my real identity; none of his friends know it. Now he has decided to bring his association with me into the open. I am to dine publicly with him tomorrow night in the Gold Room at the Fenmore Tower Hotel."

"But you won't—you can't go."

"But I will. I must go. I must obey him." She stood there facing me, her little hands clenched at her sides, her black eyes sparkling through the film of tears. Then Brown returned. He took me by the shoulder.

"We can't stay behind the others," he whispered. "Inspector Ramsey has no suspicions of Miss Parker. Don't give him any."

When Brown and I descended the wide front steps, Inspector Ramsey was saying to Fiester: "If more moneyed people were like that we'd have fewer Reds damning the rich." And seeing us, he went over and laid a finger against Brown's chest. "You aided and abetted in the escape of a murderer. Even the D.A., when he hears the story, will have to act." There was elation mingled with the disappointment in Ramsey's voice.

"What story, and who's to tell it?" Brown said quietly

"I'll tell it." Ramsey shot his face close to Brown's.

"All of it?" The corner of Brown's mouth twisted. "You'll begin with your being tipped off by someone unknown. Then you'll tell how you surrounded the house, waiting for some poor, inoffensive girl to walk into a trap. You'll tell that, of course, inspector. But will you tell that while you waited outside, with the house surrounded by your men, a murder took place inside—took place before the girl got there? Oh, there'll be no dispute about that, Ramsey. The medical examiner will place the time of death. And will you tell that, through personal jealousy of me, you chased a girl about the city, while the murderer, who was still hidden in the house, escaped? You're only guessing about me." Brown's voice was soft now. "No one would believe you, and when I turn in the murderer your story will fall flat."

"You know who the murderer is?"

"Absolutely!" said Brown. "I'm pretty busy. I was thinking of letting you make the pinch. Do you want to play ball?"

THERE was more of course. Ramsey's face went through more tricks than a movie comedian's. But he did want to make that pinch and cover his blunder. At length Brown got the whole story from him. Ramsey had received a telephone call that "the girl whose freedom Brown had bought from Mandozza by turning over evidence" was to be in the house of Victor Marks for the purpose of robbery. Ramsey had acted on that anonymous information. The idea of murder never entered his head.

"I'll have to make my report as things happened." On that point Ramsey was stubborn.

"That's fine!" Brown nodded as he looked straight at Ramsey. "Just don't embellish your report with personal opinions." And suddenly, "The name of the man who killed Victor Marks is 'Glassy' Doyle."

"Glassy Doyle! Mandozza's partner before Mandozza became a big shot?"

"And now his enemy. I know they seem very close to outsiders. But Glassy hates Mandozza and Mandozza fears Glassy's knowledge and ambition. You can be sure he knows that Mandozza double-crossed him and had you tipped off."

"But if I had searched that house and caught Doyle, he would have talked if he suspected Mandozza crossed him."

"Not Doyle. He'll never be taken alive. He's a killer. Remember that, when you put the finger on him, Ramsey. He has only one eye, but sees straight and shoots straighter. If you leave him alone he may kill Mandozza and save the Department a lot of trouble and the State a future electric bill."

"And that," said Brown to me as we climbed into his roadster which was still parked at the curb, "is force of habit, of duty. The mechanical action of a crime machine. You see, in letting Glassy Doyle go free there is a probability, or at least a possibility, that he'll knock over Mandozza for us."

"But how did you know the murderer was in the house?"

"I didn't know until Una told me. I got a few words with her alone. She saw Glassy at Victor Mark's house and recognized him. It was a lovely trap of Mandozza's that failed. Una Parker taken in for murder! The Coleman Parker name dragged through the mud! A failure for me in protecting the girl who saved my life! I discovered that Ramsey was planning a raid tonight. I won't say that I expected murder, but I will say that I wasn't surprised at it. Now—what did Una have to say to you?"

"Nothing much." And then, "That was Mandozza who called her on the phone. He's to have dinner with her at the Fenmore Tower. People'll recognize her there."

"I see," said Brown. "I think I see. He's through with Una Coles. From now on it's to be Una Parker. Mandozza is going to force his association with the girl into the open."

"Why—that will ruin her and her family."

"Maybe. Maybe not. Mandozza, the gangster, is far in the past. Mandozza, the racketeer, is a figure in the underworld. If the police were to arrest him tomorrow on any one of twenty-five crimes which they know he either committed or directed, he would be free in twenty-four hours. He has offices in the center of the city; he does a tremendous volume of business with the banks. His credit is good; his account a source of pleasure to harassed bankers. Visibly he is a business man of wealth. His power lies in that invisible empire."

"What good will this do Mandozza?"

"To be associated with the Coleman Parkers! Mandozza has his pride, Dean, just as you and I have ours. It may not show on the surface, but down deep it festers. He may meet big financial men in their offices; do business with a bank president. But he is forbidden their clubs, their homes, their social activities. He is an outcast. He knows it and resents it. The Coleman Parkers, now—" And Brown stopped short. His lips set grimly; his dark eyes focused on the road ahead as he drove straight to our apartment.

IT was close to morning when I awoke to hear Brown pacing back and forth in the living room. For a while I listened to the soft, yet steady tread of his slippered feet. Then I got up and went in to him.

"I tell you, Dean," he raised his head quickly, "so far, I can see no other way. If it wasn't for Una I'd be dead now." A long pause as he faced me, his legs spread far apart, his shoulders hunched slightly, his piercing black eyes fixed on me. Then he said quite calmly: "There is no other way. I'm going to kill Mandozza."

I started to speak—and stopped. He turned suddenly and, going into the music room, closed and locked the door behind him. A moment of silence, and then the piano. Hard, slow, gripping notes. I knew it was the new piece he was working on. Nothing of sentiment in that. It was called *The Death March*.

But Brown was different at breakfast. He laughed and talked, mostly of his music.

"What of Una?" I asked him when he was at the door preparing to leave. "What of—of the thing you said last night?"

"Oh—that." He smiled. "I've figured out another solution to Una's problem." The smile went and he frowned. "At least I think I have. It's built on my own pride and my belief that the fear of death is often quite as serviceable as death itself." And just before he closed the door, "I forgot to tell you that we're dining out tonight. Meet me at the Fenmore Tower at ten minutes of seven exactly."

I just stood there with my mouth hanging open. Then he was gone.

CHAPTER FIVE

In the Gold Room

THERE is no doubt that I entered the Fenmore Tower with some misgivings. I had no more than checked my hat and coat when Brown greeted me. His dress clothes gave a distinguished air to his wiry body. His black eyes sparkled and he laughed as he saw my face; the whiteness of it, maybe.

Those sharp eyes darted up and down the hall a moment, then his left hand came up and the thumb flipped back his jacket. Just for a split second the soft whiteness of his shirt sleeve showed, but I saw it plainly. The hard, blue steel against the whiteness; the snub nose of a heavy automatic in its shoulder holster.

"Brown—" I gurgled the words in my mouth as I laid a hand on his shoulder, "what do you intend to do tonight?"

"Always the reporter, eh, Dean?" he joked as he twisted his shoulder free and tapped his armpit suggestively. "You've written many things about me. Tonight may be the climax of your career as a feature writer." He jabbed a thumb into my side. "What a story it would be if a man were to be shot to death in the Gold Room of the Fenmore Tower."

"Brown! You can't—you don't mean Mandozza."

"Maybe not. But if it weren't Mandozza, the alternative would be most unpleasant. That is, to me."

"You're going to shoot Mandozza?"

"In self-defense only, Dean. It's well known that Mandozza fears neither man

nor devil. Now we're to see if he fears— Vee Brown."

We were at the door of the Gold Room. A waiter was bowing. "Reservations, sir?" he asked.

"For three!" Brown nodded as we followed the waiter down the room.

"Three! Who is the other?" I asked.

But he took my arm and whispered: "This is drama, Dean. Real drama. There's Mandozza at his table there. Watch his face."

And I was watching his face. That is, after assuring myself, with a little sigh of relief, that Una was not of his party. But others were there. I recognized the man to Mandozza's left. It was Sampson Kleige, head of a well-known brokerage house; and rumor had it that his house was saved from crashing by Mandozza's money. Then there was "Big Ed" Flannigan, a power in city politics. To top that off, I spotted a nervous little man whom I knew as a lawyer slated soon to become a city magistrate.

But it was Mandozza whom I watched. I think he saw us the very moment that I saw him. His huge shoulders jerked slightly and the fingers of his great hairy hands drummed upon the table. Then he pushed a hand through his black oily hair, and that peculiar pink ran in and out of his eyeballs just before he settled their black points on us.

He was surprised all right. Not that he showed it, but I sensed it from his eyes that were suddenly hard and cruel, like his mouth.

Brown didn't seem to notice him as we followed the waiter to an adjoining table and took our seats.

"We'll wait." Brown dismissed the waiter. "We are expecting a third party." And to me, "Mandozza has the stage set for quite a little publicity, Dean. You see, it would all work naturally into his scheme of things. Kleige is rather well known socially. I think, at one time he handled some investments for Una's father, Coleman Parker. It might very easily look like his party. The others—" He shrugged his slender shoulders. "They're hardly more than a block and a half ahead of the sheriff; but then, the man on the street doesn't know that. I suppose Mandozza is buying the lawyer his position on the bench. It's quite the thing, you know."

"And what—what are you going to do?" I leaned across the table toward Brown, but my eyes stayed fastened on Louie Mandozza.

"What am I going to do?" Brown laughed. "I am simply the man who sets the stage. Mandozza must choose the part he is to play. It's for him to make it a comedy, a melodrama, or a tragedy. I am quite ready to fill any role he elects to play." He straightened suddenly. "Now for it!" he said, and although his words were light, his voice was grim.

I FELT the tenseness even before I raised my head and saw her. It was Una—dazzlingly, radiantly beautiful in evening clothes. Her wrap was thrown well back, so that I could see the soft whiteness of her bare shoulders, the slender, delicate throat above them. But it was her eyes that held me. Even at that distance I caught the hunted look in them, the fear—and suddenly, the surprise and the uncertainty when she saw us.

Mandozza leaned across the table and said something to his companions. His queer eyes, with their peculiar shading of pink, flashed toward us. His thick lips parted. And Brown was suddenly on his feet, his boyish figure slipping quickly toward Una.

I followed him of course, was almost at his side when he passed Mandozza's table, reached the girl and had her by the arm. The waiter, who was escorting her, was already pulling out the chair beside Mandozza.

"You're late." Brown's voice was cheerful, the laugh that followed it, easy and seemingly natural. "There! No explanation is necessary If I lack manners, Dean would have waited gladly the rest of the night for you." Then something low, that I didn't get, and he was pushing Una past me.

Mandozza was on his feet now, and reaching out a hand took Vee Brown by the shoulder.

"Take Miss Parker to our table, Dean." Brown actually thrust the girl into my arms. "And under no circumstances let her leave it. I suppose I'll have to apologize to the big Wop." And he swung quickly, almost bumping against Mandozza; at least thrusting his hand out with enough pressure to force Mandozza back into his chair.

For a moment my final impression was of Mandozza sitting there, his eyes popping, the tinge of pink gone entirely, the cruel points of black focused upon Brown.

I know I must have thrust Una into the third seat as roughly as Brown had Mandozza. I know that Una nodded her head when I asked her to promise to stay there. I know that her face was very white and that her voice shook when she said: "What is he going to do?"

And I answered without thinking, and in a hushed, frightened voice. "I think— I think he's going to kill Mandozza."

Then perhaps mechanically, or perhaps with some purpose that I can't recall now, I crossed again and stood close to Brown at Mandozza's table. My breath was coming hard and fast, like a man who has run a great distance. And so was Mandozza's; his face was red with anger. Brown was talking calmly, addressing Sampson Kleige.

"It may be quite possible, Kleige, that

you didn't know this tramp," he jerked a thumb contemptuously at Mandozza, "was going to join your party when you invited Miss Parker. Fortunately she had a previous engagement with me."

"I—" Kleige had trouble in getting out his words. "It's not my party."

"Your apology is accepted." Brown grinned evilly. Mandozza had come to his feet again.

"So—" Mandozza had difficulty in keeping his voice low and controlling his rising temper—"you come here with your bulldozing tactics and expect to glare me down." His chin shot forward; his head bent as, towering above Brown, he stared down at him. "Out of my way! Miss Una Parker is coming back to this table whether you like it or not. She's coming, and she'll want to come; be glad to come. You thought I wouldn't make a scene here, eh?" He glanced quickly down at both of Brown's empty hands, and his own right hand crept across that white shirt front, toward his left armpit.

Brown sneered up at him.

"Mandozza, the business man; Mandozza, the financier, is slipping away tonight, eh?" and every word was one of goading sarcasm. "We have in his place the real Mandozza. The Wop. The gangster of earlier days. Just slipping back into the old rut. Dirty Louie, the greaseball who never takes a bath."

I KNEW the danger, but I didn't move out of the line of fire. I was frozen there by the hatred in Mandozza's face; the conflict that was taking place inside the man who had risen from street peddler to a power in the half world of a great city. Brown was acting a part. He was goading Mandozza into drawing a gun. He was chancing that well-known draw of Mandozza's against his own. He wanted Mandozza to be found dead with a gun in his hand. Vee Brown was—

And Mandozza's fingers were beneath his coat now, close to his gun. On his gun.

The lawyer, who was soon to be a judge, spoke. "Careful, Louie. He's trapping you to your death." And whether the words were spoken to save Mandozza or to save himself from political oblivion were he in on such a death, I don't know. But I do know that his words broke the spell. Just once Mandozza's glance fell to Brown's empty hands; just one single moment of hesitation as he raised his eyes and looked straight into the eyes of Brown, then his hand slipped slowly back along his stiff shirt bosom. Fingers finally appeared. Empty fingers. And Brown spoke.

"Yellow, eh? I half suspected it. No guts. Big words; big mouth; Big Wop!" But it was useless now, and I guess Brown knew it the moment I did. Mandozza's pride was hurt of course. But the lawyer's words had done the trick. Though his eyes still blazed and his cheeks remained a vivid red, Mandozza's hands fell to his sides and he tried to smile when he spoke.

"The Crime Machine; The Killer of Men now plays a new part. The world's greatest bluff!" Mandozza waved a hand about the room. "Already people are looking toward our table. You feel safe with the crowd around and a tin badge in your pocket. Now— we'll start where we left off. Miss Una Parker is dining here as my guest. It will be a simple matter to escort her back to my table."

Mandozza seemed quite himself again as he started past Brown and toward the table where Una sat.

"Don't do that, Mandozza," Brown said very steadily. There was something ominous in his words; something deadly cold and fear inspiring, that even got me down in the pit of the stomach.

"Why not?" Mandozza was surprised

or startled into stopping—and turning.

"Because," said Brown, and although his voice was very low, the three other men at the table must have heard it, "it will be the first time in my life that I ever put a bullet through the center of a man's back."

"That—that," said Mandozza, "would be—be murder."

Brown nodded his head. His voice was very steady. "That's why," he said, "I don't wish you to do it. The fact that it would be murder would trouble my conscience for some time, but certainly it would not bring you back to life."

"You're crazy!" Mandozza looked down at Brown for a long time. "Or you think I am." His eyes drifted over the half-filled room.

"We're not discussing that. We're discussing your life and my conscience. Here's the lay of it, Mandozza. If you ever so much as talk to that girl again; ever say anything that will hurt her, I'll shoot you to death the first time I see you. Don't grin like that. You've never known me to break my word. I'm giving you my word now. I'll shoot you to death whether we meet in a back alley at midnight or on Fifth Avenue in broad daylight."

"That's a threat!" Mandozza looked at his three friends now. The red had gone out of his cheeks, leaving them a pasty white, with great yellow blotches. "That's a threat!" he said again as he licked at his lips.

"That's gospel!" said Brown, and then in a resigned voice, "You don't believe me, eh, Mandozza? Well—get it over with! Go over and speak to Miss Parker now."

FOR a long minute the two men looked at each others' eyes. I don't know if Mandozza believed Brown then, but I do know that I did.

Mandozza took a step toward Una. I looked at Brown. His hand never even moved; he didn't speak at once. He just looked at Mandozza. Then he said: "She saved my life, you know."

Mandozza stopped and swung quickly. And he was right. Those simple words, low and barely audible, like a spoken thought, were more terrifying in fact than anything Brown had yet said; any threat of death he had made. It was as if he were excusing himself for—for murder.

Mandozza's laugh was like a shovel across dry pavement.

"Tomorrow's another day," was all that he said as he dropped back in his chair.

Then Brown turned, and I followed him to our table and to Una. People were looking at us. They sensed something wrong, but certainly did not have the slightest idea of the drama they had witnessed. If they had—well, the room would have been cleared by now. For perhaps five minutes longer, occupants of tables here and there continued to start from our table to Mandozza's. Then they lost interest.

"I don't know," Brown said to Una, after a bit, "whether your reputation is more at stake sitting here with Vee Brown, the detective, than it would be with Louie Mandozza, the rat." And despite his smile there was real viciousness in those last two words.

"I think," said Una, and in my opinion sensibly, "I had better return home. I don't know what you said to Mandozza, Vee Brown. I don't know if you threatened or promised. But it would be foolhardy to stay here and antagonize him further. I heard his last words to you and I am afraid. He said, 'Tomorrow is another day'."

"And why do you think he had you

come here tonight?" Brown asked her.

"To put the Coleman Parker stamp of approval on himself." She answered without a moment's hesitation. "He telephoned me again this afternoon. He has demanded an invitation to my home. He insists upon meeting my people. He told me that I had proved a very daring and valuable woman, that I was too brave and too useful to die. That—that—"

"That—" Brown encouraged her.

"I think—" she tried to control her voice—"I think that he intends to marry me."

"Marry you!" I gasped. "Mandozza! Why—he must be out of his head. What did you tell him?"

"It is not for me to tell him. I asked him to wait while I thought. But I didn't tell him what I wished to think." She paused a long moment, avoided my eyes and looked straight into those of Brown. "I must think of my parents. I must think which would cause them the least unhappiness. My arrest and imprisonment as an associate of murderers and an accessory to a murder, and the knowledge that I am the widow of such a murderer; my marriage to Mandozza; or the final—" her lips set rather grimly—"my death."

"Only cowards die like that," Brown said. "Think of another alternative. The death of Mandozza!"

"I've thought of that for a long time." She was coming to her feet now, pulling her wrap about her. "But it's useless. I almost did it once. And now—I guess I am a coward."

"It's a man's job," Brown told her. "It's all through the lower city today, that Glasy Doyle's one ambition is to get Mandozza before the police get him." Then turning to me, "Take Miss Parker to her car, Dean."

CHAPTER SIX

Enter—the D. A.

THERE was no subterfuge about Una's real identity that night. Outside, a long Rolls Royce was waiting, with a liveried chauffeur behind the wheel. I leaned far into the car and held her hands. She bent forward and kissed me.

"It may be the last time I will ever see you, Dean. Mandozza has forbidden it."

I took her by the shoulders then, held her and tried to make her promise to see me just once again anyway.

At length she said: "Just once. In some way that Mandozza won't know or can't resent. I was always spoiled, Dean, given everything I wanted; took orders from no one. And now—Mandozza has only to snap his fingers and I must obey. Don't try to encourage me in a false hope. There can never be anything for us; for me, until Mandozza is dead."

"All men die. With this Glassy Doyle out to kill Mandozza, with Vee Brown to protect you, things will turn out all right, Una."

"No!" she shook her head. "The longer I fight against it the more danger I put you in, put Vee Brown in. Mandozza would think nothing of murder." And just as the car drove away, "You don't know Mandozza."

Standing on the curb as the tail-light passed me I muttered to myself: "And you don't know Vee Brown." And I thought, "I guess I don't know Vee Brown either."

While I was still standing there watching Una's car disappear up the street Brown joined me. We hailed a cab and drove to the Park Avenue apartment in silence. But back in the penthouse once more Brown talked.

"He wasn't yellow, Dean. Not Mandozza. He was just careful, and he knew the truth. He hates me. I thought I could goad him into drawing a gun. I'd be safe then, if I lived. There would be plenty of witnesses to see him draw first. But he knew it; remembered seeing me kill Major Hisdale, and will wait his time."

"But you saw him kill a man, or order the man killed. That night Una thrust the gun into your hand and saved your life. Can't you hang that over his head?"

Brown shook his head. "I thought of that, of course. There would be the fact that I had evidence against him which I suppressed and later gave up to release you and the girl. Now, I'd hardly make a pretty witness for the State with such delayed accusations. Besides, there is the girl. It would end everything for her. Respectability—freedom. Bring disgrace to her parents, whom she values above everything else."

"But your threat to kill him. You've killed many men, Dean. That should make him leave Una alone."

"Not after Mandozza thinks it over quietly. And even if it did, the relief would be only temporary. My threat to take Mandozza's life is only a threat as long as I live. No—I was a fool to make it, Dean, but I thought he would act on it then. I thought that well-known temper of his would turn the trick. But he has learned to control that temper. I made a mistake. Mandozza, I'm afraid, will act in some way that will surprise us. After all, it was more or less of a public insult," and slowly stroking his chin, "And a public threat."

THE next morning I rushed in to Brown with the mail. He too had received a large square envelope, the same size as mine. And mine was an invitation to the Coleman Parker's masked ball, the beginning of the following week.

And there was more to mine. A little slip of paper clipped to the heavy card. I read aloud the penciled words upon it.

"It will be the last time you can see me. Come dressed as a Pierrot, and be sure and leave before the unmasking.

Una."

"But why a Pierrot? There will be a dozen dressed like that! There always are," I complained to Brown. "And why go before the unmasking? I don't understand that."

"I do." Brown nodded. "It will not make you conspicuous, for one thing; and for another—" He paused and then, "They haven't caught Glassy Doyle yet. There's real hope for Mandozza's death in that."

"What will you dress as?" I was thinking of the masked ball and of seeing Una again; and perhaps convincing her that she should see me—always.

Brown smiled. "I think," he said, "I should go as the king's jester—a fool. But we'll see if there's any reason why I should go at all."

That afternoon we had a visitor. Mortimer Doran, the district attorney, stood in the center of the living room. His broad shoulders were bent forward, his legs spread far apart, his cane swinging back and forth in his hand as he spoke to Brown.

"I'd have hard work even keeping you on as a detective if the truth came out," he said and meant it. "Talking like a common gunman! Threatening to shoot a man down on the street! Do you deny it or not?"

"It's the truth, of course." Brown shrugged his shoulders. "You know that the man was Mandozza."

"Yes. How does that help matters? You made a public threat to take his life. You—a representative of the law, the most trusted man in my department. I couldn't believe my ears!" And in a kindlier tone, "It's not going to become public. I made a bargain with them."

"With whom?" Brown's eyebrows went up.

"Flannigan spoke for the others, though they were all there in my office."

"And how did Flannigan and the 'others' explain their presence with Mandozza?"

"They didn't have to explain it. Legally, Mandozza's an honest man. Flannigan's a politician and Mandozza gets out the vote. There isn't a single legal action I could take against Mandozza tomorrow and not see him walk from the court a free man."

"And your bargain?" Brown was very quiet.

"You're off the Mandozza case, Brown. Off it for good. Don't look at me like that. I'd have taken the same action even if they didn't suggest it. And another thing." The cane came forward and pointed at Brown. "You stay clear of Mandozza. Don't threaten him; don't bother him in any way. At least, while you work for my office."

"And if I do, I won't work any longer for your office. Is that it?"

"That is just it. I like you. I want you. I need you. But you brought this on yourself. Personal hatred has no place in police routine. At least, to the extent you used it. Why—damn it! Don't you see? It was nip and tuck whether they'd have a warrant out for you or not. You're off the Mandozza case—off Mandozza!"

"Anything else?" Brown asked, his sharp eyes on Mortimer Doran. He must have sensed, as I sensed, that there was more to come.

MORTIMER DORAN coughed. "In a way, yes. You've been working pretty hard. You've overstrained, and it's gotten you. In plain words, Brown, you need a rest. A few week's vacation will do you good."

"It's a suspension from duty, eh?" Brown said very quietly.

"No, no. A vacation with pay."

"For long?" Brown's lips were very tight.

"Oh—that doesn't matter. Just till you feel right again."

"Indefinite suspension, until the Mandozza affair blows over. That it?"

"Something like that." Mortimer Doran nodded. "It's not influence, Brown. It's not politics. I never played either, and you know it. It's your own fault. You let yourself go, and you made a fool of yourself." He hesitated a moment. "To be perfectly frank, I don't think Mandozza wants it to come out any more than you do, at this time. But his friends were really angry. It put them in rather a bad light, if nothing were done."

"Mandozza doesn't want it out! What do you mean—'at this time'?"

"I don't know That is, not for sure. But I gather that he's thinking of getting married."

"To whom?" I just blurted out the words.

"How should I know?" Doran turned and snapped at me. "But it's class, I guess, for Mandozza's making a sudden bid for social recognition. He's to dine at the Kleige home tonight. There'll be talk of course. Some mighty prominent people will be there."

Brown said nothing as Mortimer Doran walked to the door. He just stood and watched him. Hand on the knob, Doran paused, turned and walked back to Brown.

"You think I'm letting you down." He held out his hand, and when Brown didn't take it, "There's two sides to that, of course. Did you ever think that when you publicly threatened Mandozza's life, you let me down; let the whole Department down?"

"You wanted Mandozza." The words seemed to stick in Brown's throat. "You wanted him dead."

"Yes. And I want him now. I want him dead, now. You never failed me before. You're slipping, Brown. It's the first time I ever heard of your trying to talk a man to death. And, remember, you have no official connection with the Department now. If you shot Mandozza to death, I'd have to prosecute you like any other citizen."

He turned and pounded out the door.

"What do you think of that?" was all I said to Brown. "You'll resign, I suppose."

It was some time before he answered me. Then he said simply: "He was right, Dean. Absolutely right. I let him down. I forgot, for a while, that I was the Crime Machine operated by the State. No, I won't resign. Not under fire, anyway."

"What of Una?" The words slipped out mechanically.

"I forgot my duty to the State. I mustn't forget my duty to the girl who saved my life." He picked up his hat and started toward the door.

"Where to now?" I didn't like his attitude. It was a dead calm that was foreign to him.

"About the masked ball. I must look up a suitable costume." And he was gone, almost on the heels of Mortimer Doran.

After dinner that night he was in a different mood. I stayed away from the subject of Mortimer Doran's visit and spoke about the masquerade ball. Then I said: "I think I'll ask Una to skip the country with me. She loves me. We could be married secretly, and gone before Mandozza ever suspected. What will you wear to the ball?"

"Me?" Brown jarred out of a dream. "I'm not going. I thought it over, and it would be absurd. Inspector Ramsey will be on duty there and would recognize me. I don't think the district attorney would approve, at this time. Mortimer Doran will want me to stay out of the

public eye for a while. A person can't afford to offend him, Dean. At least, not a first-grade detective in disgrace." And his smile now was not whimsical, but bitter.

I had never seen Brown like that before. Was it possible that he was a beaten man?

CHAPTER SEVEN

King Louis

THE night of the masked ball came, and Brown acted like anything but a beaten man.

"You make a wonderful Pierrot, Dean." He walked about me in mock admiration. Then he shook his head. "It's lucky I'm not going. I wouldn't have the legs for it."

"But," I said, "Una may need you. I haven't heard a word from her. There might be something you could do; advice you could give her." And when he still shook his head, "Why—you might even urge her to run away and marry me."

"Urge her to do that after she saved my life? What an ingrate you must think me, Dean!" And then, but without seriousness, "How could a suspended and disgraced detective help Coleman Parker's daughter? But there, Dean, don't scowl like that. You can tell me all she says, and if necessary I'll advise her about Mandozza."

"If necessary!" I fairly gasped. "What do you mean?"

"I didn't tell you because I didn't want to spoil your evening. Glassy Doyle was seen this afternoon and recognized by half a dozen people. He was in the act of emptying a gun into a car that Mandozza had left less than a minute before. The police are combing the city for him now. But he means business, Dean. Mandozza will be looking for him too. He won't hesitate to draw a gun on Glassy as he did on me, given the proper opportunity."

"But why didn't you tell me before? What do you mean—it would spoil my evening?"

"Why—that Glassy missed, of course. It would be funny, Dean, if the bullet of a rat and a murderer ended the career of Mr. Louie Mandozza, just at a time when I threatened his life. It would be quite a coincidence, wouldn't it? I wonder if the police; if Mortimer Doran would look on it as quite a coincidence too."

Brown shrugged his shoulders.

"Have a good time," he said. "As for me, I must work on my music, *The Death March*. It goes like this, now. You'll see where I've changed the chorus a bit." And his low, untrained, but not unpleasant voice was chanting those weird, eery notes again.

"Can't you feel it, Dean?" He paused a moment. "Can you perhaps recognize in it the faltering steps of a huge body? *The Death March*. The death march of Louie Mandozza."

Then I departed, my long coat wrapped tightly about my costume; my black mask sunk deeply in my pocket.

Brown seemed to have forgotten Una. And only a week before he had sworn to kill Mandozza if he so much as spoke to her again. Was the detective Brown as a simple citizen of the State a different man than assigned to the district attorney's office? Was he, stripped of his official standing, just Vee Brown, Master of Melodies, and no longer Detective Vee Brown—Killer of Men?

Then just one thought. Una! I was going to see Una again.

COLEMAN PARKER'S palatial home put on a much different appearance the night of the masked ball. Even the men on the door, who so carefully collected the invitations, were in costume—the black satin knickerbockers and white wigs of the Colonial period. Two uniformed policemen were on the sidewalk; several plainclothesmen, one of whom I recognized as Finnigan.

Guests alighting from cars were adjusting their masks as they climbed the broad stone steps. There was laughter and talk, and an apparent attempt to disguise voices. Coleman Parker, stepping from a side room, greeted me.

He was dressed as George Washington. He was unmasked, rather bored, and a little self-conscious of his appearance. I recognized him at once from newspaper pictures.

"Good evening, Pierrot." He took my hand and peered hard through the slits of my mask. "Your number," he said, "is legion, and I must admit my failure to recognize you." And as he turned his head and followed my gaze to the broad stairs and the staggering figure of a Louis XIV being helped up them by a bull fighter and a Roman gladiator, "You know, of course, that that's Charlie Wentworth, and drunk again."

And as I left him and started toward the stairs, "I don't know why we tolerate him." Coleman Parker shook his head. "He'll be down again in a few minutes, to annoy the guests some more."

A Spanish dancer, in white satin, red slippers and a crimson rose passed close to me. A soft voice spoke, very low, but I got it.

"You, Dean!" It was Una.

"Yes." I turned and gazed at the face beneath the white lace mantilla. But her mask left only her lips to view.

"I'll find a chance to talk to you later," she said. "But if I can't find you, be sure to leave before the unmasking at twelve."

The cold hand that gripped my wrist was gone. The girl passed down the hall toward the ballroom.

When I reached the gentlemen's dressing room on the second floor, Louis XIV had already been taken care of. I caught a glimpse of him as the bull fighter and Roman gladiator stepped from between the drawn curtains of a little side room. He lay on a couch, apparently fast asleep. His right hand hung at his side, his black mask dangled from limp fingers. Just for a second I saw his face. Fat, pasty, flabby, yet with a kindness to it that might account for Society's good-natured acceptance of Charlie Wentworth's dissipations.

I went below.

In the rear of the house was the ballroom, which I had not seen a few nights before. I pushed my way through milling, masked humans. A harlequin, a Turk with his ladies of the harem, a Chinese mandarin, an Indian chief, a shepherdess, dancing girls from the Far East, a sturdy Egyptian prince, Venus, Cleopatra, Nero with his fiddle, Arabs, Dutch girls, and as Coleman Parker had said, multitudes of Pierrots.

I reached the end of the ballroom and slipped out on the balcony behind it. It was long and narrow, with a stone balustrade, and below it, perhaps ten feet, was a sloping grass terrace and a stretch of green lawn. Even a garden. And that is something in our big city. Closing the glass doors behind me I went back into the ballroom. The night air was damp, rather cold. There was the feel of rain in it.

Try as I might I could not get in a word with Una. Two or three times I saw her with little groups. Half a dozen times she whirled by me on the dance floor. Yes, I danced. The little plump shepherdess, whom I more than suspected of being Mrs. Coleman Parker, saw to that. She was everywhere among the guests, urging this one and that one to dance.

I saw Inspector Ramsey. He was standing by the door of the ballroom, watching the dancers and talking to Cole-man Parker. He was dressed in a plain, gray business suit and chewed on a cigar. "Police Officer" was stamped all over him. But this was just police routine. A fortune in jewels was there tonight. On the enormous bosom of a Mary Antoinette, alone, diamonds hung like a display in a jewelry store window.

I gave Ramsey a wide berth and fitted my mask tighter.

Eleven; eleven-thirty, and still no talk with Una. Once I tried desperately to attract her attention, even pointing toward the balcony, which was now completely deserted because of the light drizzle that had started.

So I took up my position not far from that balcony door. It would soon be twelve. People would be unmasking, and for some reason or other, Una didn't wish me to be recognized. What did she fear? But one thing, I thought. That Mandozza would hear that I was there.

WHEN she finally did whirl by me, that slim little vision in white, with the touches of crimson, I was too surprised to try and attract her attention. She was dancing with Louis XIV. He had come to with a vengeance. Yes, it was the same figure; straighter, consequently taller now. But I knew the resplendent and expensive outfit. The buff knickerbockers, the plum-colored velvet jacket, with its priceless lace ruffles at wrists and throat, the powdered white wig and the shining silver buckles on the dancing pumps. Just one change in his appearance. He must have lost the black mask, for now he wore a red one that covered even his mouth.

There was our Louis XIV, light upon his feet, dancing easily, and holding Una close to him—very close to him. Coleman Parker had been right. Charlie Wentworth had returned to annoy the guests —or at least, one guest; for certainly I was annoyed.

And Una! Why didn't she seek me out? Why didn't she give me some sign? Why wouldn't it be just as simple for her to dance with me, slip unseen to the deserted balcony and talk. She must have known that there were a dozen things I'd like to know. She must—I looked down at my wrist watch. It was exactly eighteen minutes to twelve o'clock.

I lost Una in the surging mass of people. Confetti was being distributed, gayly colored balloons and tiny tin whistles. Through the rooms I wandered, and again saw Louis XIV. He was standing in one corner of the library, peering through the slits of his mask at an oblong bit of paper he held in his hand. Once he almost shoved it into his pocket, thought better of it and read it through again. Then he crumpled it up in his hand, half glanced at the waste paper basket; and finally, still holding the paper tightly in his closed left fist, strode quickly back to the ballroom.

He had received a note. Well—Charlie Wentworth would be quite a man with the ladies. But it gave me an idea. I could write a note to Una. There was paper there on the desk—a pen. Hastily I pushed aside the pile of invitations that had been left on the desk and scribbled off a few lines. Just the suggestion that the anxious Pierrot would like to talk with the Spanish dancer on the balcony.

I folded up the sheet and went to the ballroom again. No sign of Una. Still, she could very easily be there in that crowd and I not see her.

But I saw the huge, elaborate back of Louis XIV. He was opening a glass door at the rear of the room, edging through it and out onto the balcony. A thought struck me. Everybody liked Charlie Wentworth; perhaps Una had entrusted him with a note for me. A note saying that she would wait for me on the balcony. The old rake! He was old enough

to be Una's father. He had read the note, and he was taking my place on the balcony.

But where was Una? There were only a few minutes now before the unmasking. Was she on the balcony? It would be very easy for me to find out. And I was pushing along the wall, bumping dancers, apologizing to those I jarred. Louis XIV had disappeared onto the balcony, closing the door behind him.

I reached the glass doors to the balcony, thrust one open, half stepped across the threshold—and stood still. Faintly, above the music, a distant clock in the city struck the hour of twelve. And I was staring straight at the broad back of Louis XIV. Staring at it and beyond it.

THE light through the closed glass door shone upon the stone balustrade of that balcony; shone upon two white hands that gripped it; upon the red sash around the waist; the black mask and the three-cornered hat with the white skull and cross bones that labeled the wearer a pirate. The figure must have come from the terrace below.

Then the pirate raised his head and looked straight at the red mask of Louis XIV. Things happened with lightning-like speed after that. Louis XIV thrust his hand quickly beneath that plum-colored coat, to reappear almost immediately with something square and black in it. There was a sudden quick stab of orange-blue flame and the roar of a gun, followed by a hard laugh deep in the shooter's throat.

A split second I saw the whiteness at the pirate's shoulder; a whiteness that suddenly was spotted with red; a spot that was growing larger before my staring eyes.

Then both the pirate's hands left that balcony rail. He hung so for a moment, suspended in midair. His white hands didn't seem to move, but from one of them a spurt of flame came; two roars, I thought, as Louis XIV fired again.

The figure of the pirate disappeared. The great bulk of Louis XIV whirled suddenly; then hurtling backward, crashed through those glass doors as if they were papier-maché. And Louis XIV, in all his splendor, lay beneath the white glare of the ballroom lights.

CHAPTER EIGHT

The Red Death

THERE was excitement then. Women screamed; some fainted, I think. The music stopped dead. Ramsey was shouting across the room; two policemen were pushing through the crowd. And I —I was standing there, stunned. Looking down at the red mask; the tiny hole in the center of it, just above the eye slits. The red mask. I shuddered slightly. The red mask of death!

Then I saw the tightly closed left hand and remembered the note that had been gripped in it.

I was thrust roughly back. Inspector Ramsey was there. A uniformed policeman and a plainclothesman behind him. Ramsey was chewing viciously on his cigar. I realized that many people were around me.

"It's Charlie Wentworth." A baldheaded cupid spoke far back in his throat.

"Nonsense!" said one of Cromwell's soldiers. "Charlie's upstairs, out like a light."

"We'll soon settle that," said Inspector Ramsey, and kneeling down he tore the mask from the dead man's face.

At first I saw only a blue-black hole almost in the center of the dead man's forehead. Then I saw the thick, cruel lips; the eyes; the glassy eyes, with the semblance of pink back of them

"Louie. Louie!" I gasped.

"Yeah—" said Inspector Ramsey. "Not Louis XIV though. Simply Louie Mandozza."

And he was right. I was staring straight down at the dead face of Louie Mandozza.

Something in my voice must have attracted Inspector Ramsey, for he rose suddenly and faced me. I didn't wait for his order. I jerked off my mask and faced him.

"It's you, eh?" Then, "Where's Vee Brown?"

"He didn't come," I said. "He's home." Then I told Ramsey of the shooting, and the escape of the pirate.

Ramsey nodded, and a cop said: "The stiff's got a note in his hand, inspector."

"Good! Keep these people back." Ramsey dropped quickly to his knees and tore open the fingers of Mandozza's left hand. Instinctively I leaned over his shoulder as he smoothed out the crumpled mass. With some difficulty I made it out.

> Louie—
> Glassy Doyle knows you're here tonight. He'll bust in as a pirate. He's coming by the balcony behind the dance hall, at 12:00.

After that there was much talk, quick orders from Ramsey, and the information from a plainclothesman that one of the attendants at the door had taken in a note to Mandozza. Later it turned out that the note was delivered by a messenger boy.

"Will we hold these people?" a pockmarked detective asked.

"Don't be a fool," Ramsey snapped. "What would they be doing, shooting Mandozza? You heard Condon's story. It rings true. If the man's badly hurt, they'll find him on the grounds. Mandozza shot at the wrong guy for once— just once." Ramsey's lips clamped tight. There seemed a certain satisfaction in it. And then, "But how did Mandozza get in here without an invitation?"

THEN I saw Una. In fact, I felt her before I saw her. She was standing there clutching my arm; seemingly forcing herself to look down at the dead face of the racketeer who had so long held her in a grip of horror. But, surprisingly, there was nothing of elation in her face; not even relief. She just seemed struck with the horror of it all.

"How did he get in, Una?" I asked as I led her away through the somber, quiet gathering.

"He was invited. He made me send him an invitation, Dean. And he was going to make me introduce him——"

I wasn't listening any more. I was hurrying Una through the reception room and into the library in the rear. The invitations! They were there. I ran hastily through them, missed the name; tried again and found it. The invitation that had brought Louie Mandozza there. It was hardly tucked away beneath my loose blouse when Ramsey came in with the pock-marked detective.

"There are the invitations," he said, "just where Mr. Parker said they'd be. See if you find his name." And to Una, "It's too bad such a thing had to break up your party. But there's nothing else to do about it. We won't keep him lying there a minute longer than necessary. Your father's seeing the thing through in great shape. You stay out of it. Mandozza wasn't invited here, was he?"

Una looked at me, and then: "Of course not."

"No offense," Ramsey said. "This Mandozza's been pushing his way up in society lately for some purpose." And jerking a thumb toward me, "What's he doing here?"

"Why—you introduced him to me, inspector; or at least, brought him here the other night. And," she smiled up at Ramsey, "Dean turned out to be such a nice boy."

"He did, eh? He did." Ramsey stroked his chin. "When we look for a criminal in your house, she ain't here. But when we come to protect you from annoyance, the biggest criminal in the country gets himself knocked over right in your ball-room. But it's cut and dried. This Mandozza gets his warning and decides to get Glassy Doyle before Glassy gets him." He spread his hands far apart. "Like lots of things we plan in life, it don't always work out that way." And with a shrug, "But you wouldn't be up on such things, miss. Doyle was wounded, like Condon said, for there's blood on the balcony. Men are combing the block now, and——" Someone called him from the hall and he left us.

The man by the desk was pawing over the invitations, studying each one carefully. The reception room was empty; voices came faintly in as the last few guests departed. For a brief moment I held Una close in my arms.

Una said softly: "It's all right now, Dean. That is, if you still want me."

And the man by the desk swung around suddenly, and seeing us said: "Excuse me. What the hell!"

Upstairs in the cloakroom a pale-faced gladiator and a trembling bull fighter were getting a slightly dazed and gesticulating Louis XIV to his unsteady feet.

At the foot of the stairs Coleman Parker, erect and steady of voice, if slightly white, bade me good night. "So you're Dean Condon," he said. "Una has spoken of you often. Now that we've met, I hope to see more of you."

"You don't need to worry about that, Mr. Parker," I said.

There was more I was going to say to him. For a moment I held his hand, then I dropped it and dashed from the house. I had to find Brown. He'd given me many a thrill and now I was to give him one. Maybe his biggest one. I could describe everything in detail. I was there on the balcony when Mandozza was killed.

STRAINS of music came to me as I opened our door, high above the street. It was the dull strum of the piano behind the closed music-room door, as if Brown beat out the notes upon it with but one hand. Halfway across the living room I paused. The notes grew louder. Weird, uncanny, in their somber, eery, deathlike rhythm. For a long moment I stood so. It was *The Death March*. Mandozza's death march. But Brown did not know that yet. I stepped across the room, clutched the knob and threw open the door.

He swung to his feet and faced me. His face was white and heavily lined, his cheeks sunken, and his black eyes burnt feverishly far back in their sockets. It had gotten him, then, even more than I suspected; this suspension from his work.

"Brown." I just blurted it out. "Una's troubles, my troubles, your troubles— they're all over." And going to him and shaking him by the shoulder, "Don't you understand? Mandozza is dead. He was shot to death tonight."

Then I gave him the whole story, and when I finished, asked: "How do you suppose Glassy Doyle knew Mandozza would be there, and what he would wear?"

"Possibly in the same way that I knew. Maybe he suspected it as I suspected it. That's why I made the rounds of the costume-renting and theatrical shops, and finally visited Mandozza's tailor. A twenty-dollar bill furnished me with a wonderful description of the Louis XIV outfit that Mandozza would be wearing."

"Then you did know Mandozza was going. That's why you didn't go?"

"I did know he was going—yes. But what makes you think Glassy Doyle shot him?"

"Why—the note, of course."

Brown looked at me. "Mandozza was killed, you say, at twelve o'clock. Less than ten minutes ago I got a telephone call that Glassy Doyle was killed by the police in a rooming house in Brooklyn, while resisting arrest. And the time of his death was exactly eleven-fifteen."

"Then the note— It— Let me tell you exactly what happened."

Brown shook his head, and his dressing gown dropped open as he pointed to the corner by the piano. I forced my eyes from the freshly dressed wound upon his shoulder and riveted them upon the white silk of a pirate shirt; the white that was stained with red. Then I looked back at Brown.

The corners of his mouth twisted up in that whimsical, crooked smile, and he said: "I sent that note to Mandozza. Mandozza wouldn't draw on me, but he would on Glassy Doyle, or the man he thought was Glassy Doyle. No, Dean, you don't have to tell me just how it happened. You see, I know. I was there. And I shot him."

The Bloodstone

by
John Lawrence

Author of "The Torso Trap," etc.

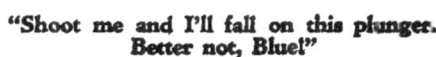

"Shoot me and I'll fall on this plunger.
Better not, Blue!"

It was a house of horror where the Kyle family dwelled. Murder stalked for no apparent reason, struck at random from the shadows. Yet behind all these killings was a blood-red motive. And the answer could be read only in a dead man's palm!

CHAPTER ONE

The Mysterious Mr. Kyle

THERE was a picture of me in The Sentinel, and a nice little blurb, giving me a hand for knocking off Joe Cirofici, as dirty a gun, incidentally, as had prowled New York for some time. I was giving the item my undivided attention when my office girl—Tam Cotter her name is—came in and laid the card on my desk. "He's old, and he looks like money."

I fingered the card. The *Mr. David Kyle* was engraved. "Send him in," I said.

He had on expensive clothes, and two diamonds. One in the tie, and one on a skinny, shrunken hand. He had a limp, and a stick to work it with. His face was wrinkled skin, tight over razor-edged cheek-bones; his lips were moist and vermillion, like a girl's and his little red tongue kept licking them. His frame looked as though it had shrunk. His eyes were brown, but there was a red smoldering light behind them. Dirty white hair stuck down over one eyebrow. He didn't take off his hat. There was a folded newspaper in his free hand. He looked at it, then at me.

"If you're Cass Blue," he cracked suddenly in a harsh voice, "this don't look much like you."

He had The Sentinel too. I said these half-tones never look much like a person. His eyes kept darting up and down, all over me. "All right," he snarled finally, "I've been swindled by every other crook in town. You might as well have your cut," and sat down.

I warmed up under the collar right away. Things were breaking just about right for the Blue Inquiry Agency at this point. I couldn't see where this drooler got a call for language. "If you've got something to say, suppose you get going on it," I said. "I've not got much time."

His eyes got narrow. "Oh, you've got time all right!" he snapped. "I've got the money to pay for your time. Listen—there's a man—maybe more than one—trying to murder me!"

I said was that so?

"He's an Italian. Name's D'Aguido. He's in New York now. I live out at Pine Lake. He's trying to find me to kill me."

"Why?" I said.

"That's none of your business, is it?" he blurted—and I got him then. He was frightened half out of his wits, and trying to bluff it out. "You don't have to know that, do you?"

"Depends. What do you want me to do?"

"Find him! Arrest him—have him deported! Anything—only keep the devil away from me!"

"How do you know he's here?"

"I saw him!" The bluff wasn't holding up. His face was strained and a vein was bulging in his forehead. "I saw him in the—in the street."

"What's he look like?"

"He's an Italian—a big man, an enormous man—with brown eyes. And black hair. He's always snarling."

"Well," I said, "there's probably not over twenty-five or thirty thousand Italians in New York would fit that."

"But this man's name is D'Aguido!" he raved. "He's been after me for fifteen years! Everywhere I go, he pops up. I see him everywhere—snarling, showing his teeth at me, like—like a dog!"

"There's no law against that."

"But my God! He's going to kill me!"

"Do you live alone?"

"Alone!" He laughed gratingly. "Alone but for my family and any alley cats they can drag in!"

I was getting a little fed up with this. "You want a bodyguard. I'll supply one for twenty-five dollars a day, and—"

"No! I don't want a guard! I want you to find this man, keep him away from me—arrest him!"

"For what? If he's been in the country for fifteen years, you can't deport him. And in the first place, unless you can give me a far better description, I couldn't find him anyway. If he's looking for trouble, as you say, he won't be using his own name. What am I supposed to go on? How many people are there in your establishment?"

"That doesn't matter. Ten maybe, but—"

"Does he know where you live?"

"He'll find out! He always does. Now, mind you, I'm willing to pay, Blue—pay well."

I shrugged. "I'm just as willing to be paid, but there's nothing to it, unless you'll hire a bodyguard. If you're certain you're in danger, you can watch yourself, and with your family around—"

He got up. "It so happens," he said in a hollow voice, "that I can expect anything but protection from my family. They— but that's something else. I've told you what I want. If you won't do it, someone else will. Will you or will you not, look for this man for me? For a substantial—"

"I will not," I said disgustedly, "and if I were you, I'd hire a psychoanalyst, not a detective."

"Oh," he showed broken teeth again in a snarl. "So you think I'm crazy!"

I shrugged again. "I didn't say so. The fact remains, I'm not going to take your money when I haven't a prayer of producing."

He stood there a minute, a funny succession of expressions running over his face. "Well," he bit off finally, "I suppose I owe you something for even talking to me."

"No," I said.

For another half minute, he didn't move, kept looking at my face. Finally he turned on his heel, muttered something like a surprised "Well!" and limped out.

When the outer door closed behind him, Tam came and put her head into my office. "What the hell?"

"Nut," I said.

That was three years ago, the first and only time I had ever seen David Kyle.

I HADN'T forgotten a word of it, either. But the atmosphere around banks makes me a little fidgety. And when I'm fidgety I get pretty cagy. So I wasn't broadcasting when this curly-headed ex-football player started the conversation by asking did I know a man named David Kyle. I just said I didn't seem to recall the name. He frowned, took up a long, wax-sealed manila envelope, started tapping it on the triangular, brass, desk sign that read—*Mr. Ryan— Assistant Trust Officer.*

"Well, no matter," he said finally. "He —they—seem to have heard of you. I— we—have been acting for Mr. Kyle for some years. He is a very eccentric man —or was, possibly I should say. This envelope—" he stopped tapping—"he left with us, sealed. We were instructed to deliver it to you, should anything happen to Mr. Kyle. You, in turn, are to deliver it to Miss Louise Kyle, his daughter, unopened, at the earliest possible moment. Also, you are expected to remain at their home—it's in Oakville, Pennsylvania— for not less than forty-eight hours. You are to investigate the theory of foul play, regardless of any official decision to the contrary, and endeavor to make out a case against the perpetrator. Certain conditions—"

"Wait a minute," I said, "What happened to him? Is he dead?"

"Dead? No. He's disappeared."

"When?"

"Why, why—I don't know exactly." He reached for a clip of papers, thumbed through them. He located a telegram, handed it to me. "Possibly you'd better read this."

As I glanced at the telegram I noticed it was dated that same afternoon.

Trust Department
Century Bank & Trust Co.
New York City, N. Y.

David R. Kyle, my father, missing from home. I was told some time ago to get in touch with you in this eventuality. Please advise.

Louise M. Kyle,
Oakville, Pa.

I handed it back to him. "When did you say he left these instructions with you?"

"About a year and a half ago."

"Who pays my retainer—if I take the job?"

"Eventually, the amount will come out of the estate. Temporarily, Miss Kyle has wired a thousand dollars for that purpose." He cleared his throat. "There is also a reward offered for the conviction of his murderer."

"His murderer? How do you know he's murdered?"

"We don't. I am only quoting from the instructions Mr. Kyle left. Let us say, if there is one. Five thousand dollars reward."

"And a thousand in hand."

He nodded. I held out my hand. "How do you get to this Oakville?"

"I would suggest you charter a plane. There is an emergency landing field ten miles from the town. I called the airport to find out. The trip will take around two and a half hours."

I looked at my watch. "That means I'll arrive there about nine o'clock."

"Just sign this receipt, will you?" he said. "I'll wire Miss Kyle."

THE air was hot, heavy, humid, even three thousand feet up. And the plane could have been wrapped in black velvet—for all I could see from the windows. I'd gotten myself into a dull, uneasy frame of mind. The picture I kept

getting of a dead man, pulling the strings to start the man-hunt for his killers, from beyond the grave, seemed kind of horrible, somehow, and the storm and the state of my stomach didn't help any.

It was six minutes to nine when the plane started to dive at an orange postage stamp of light completely framed by wet, smothering darkness. We straightened out for a little while. Then the pilot leaned forward, fumbled with a gadget, and the nose of the plane dipped. The frame of light angled up at us, grew larger and larger, was suddenly a field. It rocked once from side to side—then we hit—bumped up again—came down to stay, sped across the soggy ground, little spurts of water flying up from the wheels.

There were flare-lights around the field. Big puddles reflected the glare. We stopped fifty yards from the northeast corner of the field, where long, low sheds were dimly outlined.

I took out my handkerchief and mopped my face. Three figures, dim in the blanket of fog that was steaming up from the ground, detached themselves from the shadows and tramped toward us. I hoisted out my bag, climbed down.

Two of the men were mechanics, the third a tall man with a tan polo coat and no hat. As he came nearer, I made out a smooth, thick thatch of dark hair, and a leathery, seamed face. Then his eyes were looking into mine.

"Mr. Blue?"

I said I was. He didn't offer to shake hands. "My name's Crane—Harold Crane. Miss Kyle asked me to meet you. My car is behind the sheds."

I picked up my bag. "Fair enough."

He turned and led the way, across the lighted field and into the darkness. Around the corner of the shed, headlights were visible.

The car was a big coupé, the rumble open. I put my bag in the rumble, walked around and climbed in as he started the car. The headlights lit up a narrow, tree-lined dirt road.

"Any news of Mr. Kyle?" I asked.

He looked straight through the windshield. "Yes. In a way. You'll see when you get there."

He spoke abruptly, almost hostilely. I didn't like that. He seemed like a reasonable party. "You're a friend of the Kyle's?" I asked.

"Yes."

"Mind telling me what you know about—this?"

"Mr. Kyle disappeared some time during the night. He didn't appear for breakfast, or for lunch. Miss Kyle had instructions from her father as to what to do in such a case. She wired the trust company. They informed her that money was necessary. I lent it to her. She sent it to them, and they sent you. There are other facts, of course, which you can best learn at the house."

I got out cigarettes, lit one, looked at the side of his face a couple of times. His jaw was tight, and there was lots of worry in the blue eyes he kept on the road.

"What's the matter?" I said finally. "Don't you like the idea of my being here?"

"I have no opinion on that."

"What's this latest news of Mr. Kyle?"

"A special-delivery letter, sent out from Oakville, arrived at the house an hour ago. It purports to come from David Kyle."

"You don't think it does?"

"Listen, Mr. Blue," he spoke through tight lips, "you'll find out shortly that I am suspected of being behind this disappearance. I am not going to make any statements of opinion. I am not going to place myself in the position of appearing to point out any line of investigation for you. When you have seen the situation at the house, if you want to ask me any questions I'll be glad to answer them to the best of my ability. The letter is indescribable and I will not attempt to summarize it for you."

We swung off the narrow road onto a graveled highway. The speedometer started mounting.

I let a minute or two go by. Then I tried: "Mr. Kyle was pretty wealthy, eh?"

"He was wealthy, yes."

There was finality to it. But I've handled tougher ones than Crane. "Big establishment, is it?" I said.

His eyes got a little narrower. "There is Mrs. Kyle and a son and a daughter. Besides myself there is one other guest at the moment, a young man named Menocal. He is a friend of Miss Kyle's and was a former neighbor. There are only three servants—two maids, one of whom cooks, and an outside man. It is not a large house. I would suggest that you keep the rest of your questions till later."

I let it go at that. The powerful car was eating up the miles. I'd get going at the house.

CHAPTER TWO

House of Hate

IT STOOD at the top of a long, winding rise. In the fog, I couldn't be sure, but it seemed that we practically circled a hill. There was a bank of trees around the house, but not close to it. The house itself squatted there blackly, unlovely in outline as far as I could see it, turreted and cupolaed. There was light from windows on the ground floor, and from a single pane on the second. A veranda stretched across the front, ending in three steps down to the driveway. Crane brought the car to a halt by the steps. The headlights glared into a frame two-car garage, its front set flush with the rear of the house.

"I'll run it in, if you don't mind," Crane said.

I got my bag out. He pulled forward into the garage, snapped the lights out. He swung the door of the garage to with much creaking, then emerged from the gloom, mounted the steps beside me. For a minute he hesitated, seemed about to say something, but didn't. I followed him along the veranda and he opened the door.

We passed through a vestibule and into a carpeted hall. On the left, just opposite the foot of a flight of stairs, was an arched opening. As Crane closed the door, a woman appeared in this arch.

Crane said: "This is Mr. Blue, the detective, Martha. This is Mrs. Kyle, Mr. Blue."

She looked me over searchingly. "How do you do?" she said without enthusiasm.

I said I was pleased to meet her. She was a striking-looking woman. Her eyes were dark blue—strained and red right now; her hair was coal-black. I suspected a touching-up. A soft oval face, crow's-feet around the eyes and two lines from nostrils to mouth corners. She was tall, and I got the impression of a very youthful figure. She carried herself like a queen, even in a jersey suit, unadorned with any jewelry—not even a wedding ring. Her eyes shifted to Crane.

"I think it's important that you see that letter at once, Mr. Blue," Crane said. "Its nature is such that we decided it would be best to have you see it when all of us are there. Will you step into the living room?"

I put down my hat and bag. The envelope I'd gotten at the bank was still in my topcoat, so I just kept that on. I followed him in.

I don't know why, but I'd expected a crowd. There were only two other people in the room.

Louise Kyle was about eighteen. She had curly brown hair back over her ears

à *la* Garbo. Ordinarily, she would have been a dream. She had a complexion like cream satin, a soft, mobile red mouth, and big brown eyes, a slender figure. Now her eyes were hard, hostile, strained, like her mother's; her jaw was set hard, drawing the mouth into a straight little line and adding lines around the chin. She stood at the far end of a long mahogany table, one tight-clenched little hand resting on it; there was a cigarette in her other hand. She acknowledged Crane's introduction of me with a curt nod. Menocal did little better. He was a slender-hipped young Spaniard. He had black eyes and black hair, and a black double-breasted suit; an orange silk tie and black-and-white sport shoes. His skin was swarthy. He had one foot up on a chair in the corner of the room. He grunted something, made no move to shake hands.

I looked at the table. In the center of it was an ordinary sheet of notepaper that had been folded once. Crane said: "That's the letter, Mr. Blue."

I looked round the room. Four set faces were turned toward me. Four pairs of defiant eyes were on mine. There was dead silence as I stepped over and picked it up.

THE paper was heavy, porous—no fingerprints. The writing was small, crabbed, almost all angles. And it was a brutal document.

To the Kyle family, and others:—
Seventeen years of hell on earth for me come to a close tonight—seventeen years that you've all had a hand in building, in stoking the flames. You think I'm a fool—all of you. I'm not—not such a one as you believe. I've seen it—seen you gradually closing in on me, silently, getting as close as you dared in your dirty hearts, to what was in your minds—to kill me—to get rid of me—to get your greedy hands on my money —to grind me out. I've read it in your eyes—in your silky voices. You all hate me —have hated me for years. Well, I hate

every damned last one of you. My family —my devoted ones—that would give an eye to drive a knife into my back—if they thought they could get away with it. Well, here you are—you snarling fools—here you are—I'm finished. I'm at the end of my string. And I'm going to snap it off myself —if I can. If I can make it in time. I'm going to kill myself—unless one of you— or that other one—happens to strike first. And the one who knows doesn't dare to tell.

I'm beating you to it. I know every one of you has it in your minds to do it—now —tonight. Even you, Crane—you'd breathe easier, wouldn't you? And you, my chaste wife—now you can have your slinking lover —if you can get him! And my son—my dutiful son—how you will enjoy throwing my money to the four winds. Do you think you'll get it?

Good news! I'm talking from the brink of hell. Another hell—a different one from that I've been in. But that one will go on too, my charming people—it's boiling under you now. And you—you fools—you think that you'll be free! What a joke! I'll watch you, from the pit as you squirm and writhe and take up the torment I've escaped. I've stood it off—protected you from it, for seventeen years. Until finally I began to have to protect myself from all of you, too—behind my back—and it's too much. I've had to watch you day and night— and all the while, being hunted by this other thing, like a wild beast. Now you can take your turn.

How you have longed to have me out of the way! How you have all tried to whip up your courage to get me—to shove me off your shoulders! And now it's done! You're free of me. I'm no more than rotting flesh now. You can follow your own will—not mine! Isn't it glorious? Well, see how you like it, you fools, see how you like it!

David Kyle.

P. S. (For Blue, the detective): Maybe I'm not going to kill myself, Blue; maybe somebody is making me write this letter. Who knows? It's up to you to find out. That's what you're paid for, isn't it? And don't forget—whatever my plans might have been, I could have been interrupted—I could have been forestalled. I had to jump before they did it. The way I have it planned is pleasant, easy. I tell you it was

the only course. They were all at the point of doing it—and their ways would not be pleasant. Find out, Blue—and make them sweat blood—and watch your back. As well as anything else I left word for you to do.

D. K.

I laid down the letter, put my thumbs in my vest pockets. I didn't want to meet their eyes for a minute. A grandfather clock in the corner tick-tocked, tick-tocked.

Finally I said: "Is this Mr. Kyle's handwriting?"

"Of course it is," Louise Kyle said in a hard voice—and I saw her teeth. They were tiny, white, pointed.

I coughed politely. "I don't suppose there's anything in all this—I mean about all you people hating Mr. Kyle—"

"Of course you do!" The girl rapped out. "You suppose that every one of us loathed and detested him. And you're damned well right. We do—did. That letter—"

"Be quiet, Louise!" Menocal shot suddenly.

"That letter is practically—"

"Be quiet!" the Spaniard roared. I turned and looked at him. His eyes were blazing; his fists were clenched at his sides.

"What's the matter with you?" I said quietly. "Did you kill David Kyle—or anything?"

"No, I didn't—but understand this, Blue—we none of us relish having a cheap snooper like you wished on us to pry into our affairs. I know how your kind works —and I warn you—try any of your cheap intrigue here and you'll be sorry."

I let my eyes narrow. "I place you now. You're the friend of Mrs. Kyle's that's mentioned, eh?"

HE WENT white to the lips; his fists clenched, unclenched; he took a stumbling step toward me. "Why—why you cheap, rotten—"

"Mr. Blue—Mr. Blue!" Mrs. Kyle said suddenly, shrilly. "Wait—stop—you're making a terrible mistake, Mr. Blue. Mr. Menocal is engaged to my daughter—engaged to be—"

"The hell with that stuff!" The girl's voice cut like a knife. "Do you two think I'm blind? Tell him the truth!"

Menocal's face was livid. "Why you little hell-cat! You—"

"I'm not a fool!" the girl cut in. "Go on tell him—tell him why Martin cracked you in the jaw this morning. Tell him where—"

"Louise, Louise—that's not fair!" Mrs. Kyle blurted out. "You don't know anything about that. Martin was drunk—he misunderstood. You know Martin is—"

"Sure. I know he's a drunken swine," the girl cracked at her. "What of it? He found you—"

"That's a damned lie!" Menocal shouted.

I stepped in. "Stop it!" I rapped. "Where is this Martin Kyle?"

Menocal snarled: "Upstairs in his room—dead drunk, like the beast he is."

I looked at Crane. His eyes were on the floor. "I'd like to see this Martin Kyle," I said, "drunk or sober."

He looked up with a start, not realizing that I was talking to him. His eyes were haggard. "I—I am afraid—you see, it was necessary for me to put him to bed before we left."

"I can sober him up," the girl said harshly. "I've done it plenty of times before. Give me ten minutes." She started for the door.

"Just a minute," I said. I looked them all over. "There's something I want to say to you all. I realize—now—that none of you want me around here. I can't help that. I can understand why you don't want me—because I'm working for a man none of you like. He may be dead. It looks as though he were. But I'm

going to find out if he is, and if so, how he died. And I can get the authority—in case any of you doubt it—and make it damn unpleasant if I want to. I don't want to—but I've got to have a little co-operation around here. Your private affairs are your private affairs—unless they bear on what's happened to Mr. David Kyle—then they're mine. Obviously, you're all under suspicion. Of what—I don't know, yet. I've got to make this investigation whether you like it or not.

"You've got a lot of quarrels among yourselves. That isn't necessarily important. Evidently every one of you has a reason for wanting to do harm to Mr. Kyle. I'll ask you to forget that end of it for the time. One of you must—or at least should—have seen something suspicious between the last time you saw Mr. Kyle and now. I want you to try to remember any little detail you might have overlooked. Mrs. Kyle, I'd like you to have everybody in the house—that is everyone who was here when Mr. Kyle left—including the servants, in this room in ten minutes. I hope that we can make this the last conference of the sort. I realize that you are all upset"—I looked hard at Menocal—"and I'm willing to overlook any hasty words that might have been passed. Miss Kyle—if you'd please get your brother—" She nodded, and went out into the hall. I said: "Just one more minute," to the rest of them, and followed her. She had one foot on the stair when I called, "Miss Kyle."

She swung round on me, said nothing.

"Will you please tell me why you hate your father so?" I said quietly.

HER eyes bored into mine. There was green in them. "I'll tell you," she said in a dull voice, "but you'll never understand. Listen—if your father started when you were about five years old to refuse you every single thing you asked him for; if he started when you were about fifteen to swear at you for asking, and threatened you with whippings if you did, till you dared not ask a thing; if he never let you spend any money—not one red cent; if he insulted, carefully, and calculatingly, every friend you managed to make; if he tried to keep you a prisoner—not a day or a week or a month—but day in, day out, every damned hour of your life. Then, on top of that, if he accused you of planning to kill him—planning to steal from him—over and over again—would you hate him? Would you wish him dead, too?"

I couldn't hold her eyes. I let mine drop. "I see," I said. "I see."

"You don't see," she said bitterly, "but that's how it is."

I couldn't think of anything to say for a minute. Finally I asked: "Has the sheriff been notified of this letter?"

"No. That's your business."

"Surely, but—would you mind showing me where the telephone is—or is there—"

She made an impatient sound, swung back from the stairs, went to the rear of the hall. I saw the wall instrument now. She jerked the receiver off, started to spin the crank on the side. It was that kind of phone.

I stepped back inside the living room. "That's all for now, thanks," I said.

Crane followed me out. "I'll show you to your room now, if you—"

"In a minute," I said, then to the girl, "Tell him he'd better come right over."

I turned back to Crane. He picked up my suitcase and started up the stairs. I noticed a label had come off and was sticking to the rug. I picked it up, and followed him. On the way, I happened to notice it wasn't one of the hotel labels at all. It was a druggist's—the kind they stick on bottles. It came from an Oakville drug store. I put it in my inside pocket.

As we reached the top I heard the girl swear viciously at the telephone. Crane led the way toward the front of the house, turned right. My room was apparently the lighted one I had noticed outside.

It was roomy, old-fashioned, with a fireplace and a four-poster bed. The furniture was solid, heavy. Crane put my bag on a luggage stool, went back and closed the door. I took my topcoat off, found a hanger in the closet and was just putting it on when he said suddenly: "Look here, Blue—in the letter"—his voice was clipped, almost violent—"he says about the one who knows—not daring to talk—to tell. I'm the one."

I stood still and looked at him. "Oh?"

He had his hands clasped behind him; his arms were drawn tight to his sides. There were white bumps at his jaw corners. "And I can't tell you. I don't know what conclusions you've come to. And I'm not trying to exonerate anybody of anything. All I want to tell you is this—that any explanation you may make has got to reach a long way into the past, Blue. Everything you've seen tonight—and more—is the climaxing of certain things that started from one single cause —twenty years ago. That's as far as I can go."

I looked at him searchingly. "Why can't you tell all of it?"

He put his lips together, shook his head.

"I'm not a policeman, you know," I said.

His eyes snapped back to mine. "What?"

"I'm not forced to repeat anything anyone tells me. I have the same legal privilege as a lawyer or a doctor, that way."

He eyed me hard. "Suppose you heard of a crime—committed many years ago—and in a foreign country."

"I would consider it none of my business," I said. "Unless, of course, it was directly connected with this investigation.

I am only interested in David Kyle's disappearance right now."

He started to pace up and down, then stopped and looked at me half over his shoulder. "If it turns out that you have to tell my story in court, will you give your word to protect me—to withhold any clue to my identity?"

"I will—unless you're guilty of something I'm investigating." Then I added: "Or at least something that happened in this country."

He held my eye for a long minute. "All right. Listen. . . . Good God!"

CHAPTER THREE

Brothers in Blood

THE scream came from directly over head; it put my teeth on edge. It was a woman's scream, high-pitched, and there was a quality to it I couldn't recognize. I sprang for the door, jerked it open.

The frantic scream came again. I saw the stairs at the end of the corridor and raced toward them. The scream suddenly died—then in its place came a peal of harsh, squealing laughter. It rose, grating and furious, again and again. I ripped open the door at the foot of the stairs, raced up them three at a time. There was a bump, just as I reached the top. On the floor, on her knees, in the doorway to a room twenty feet away was the girl, her arms over her head, great sobbing bursts of laughter racking her.

Crane was at my heels, white-faced. I called: "Look after the girl—she's hysterical!" Gun out, I hit the half-open door with the heel of my hand, slammed it back against the wall. The light was already on. I jumped inside.

Lying half on the bed, half on the floor, was a young man in golf trousers. His face was staring at me, upside down. It was black. His tongue protruded. His hands were grasping the shirt at his throat. His eyes were wide open.

I could hear feet clattering up the stairs outside. I called: "Stay out of here, everybody!" as I caught the bitter almond smell of hydrocyanic.

I hesitated myself for a minute, sniffed cautiously, saw the window was open a few inches. Most of the fumes were gone. I stepped over to the bed, grasped the boy's pulse.

The hand was cold. There was no pulse.

My eyes darted around the room. I thought of suicide—and that idea collapsed. There was a handkerchief, diagonally folded twice, its ends crumpled, lying against the wall—an improvised mask.

I thought fast. I wanted to go through that room with a fine-tooth comb, and do it then, but these rural coppers are hell if they think you're against them. I didn't want the sheriff's heavy hand on me the rest of my stay in Oakville. I backed from the room and closed the door.

One of the maids was half huddled on the top of the stairs, afraid to go down, afraid to come up. From a room at the end of the hall came the sound of muffled sobbing, gasping, and the terrified voice of Mrs. Kyle. "What is it—what's happened?"

"Go on back down!" I snapped at the maid on the stairs. "Tell everybody to stay down from here! Mr. Crane!"

He came hurrying out of the room where the sobbing was taking place.

"Phone the sheriff," I clipped at him. "Martin Kyle has been killed. Tell him to bring the coroner and if he has any fingerprinting outfit in this place, to bring it too. I want the rest of the household to wait exactly where they are—every soul in this house. Go on, hurry—before anybody gets up here!"

Crane looked dazed, hesitated, then hurried down the stairs, herding the frightened maid ahead of him. There was a key on the inside of the murder-room door. A piece of ice was melting on the floor where Louise Kyle had dropped it. I took the key out using my handkerchief, and locked the door.

The sobbing lost its violence. I eased along, waited a moment outside the door of a room, which was half open. Louise Kyle said in a voice so husky and grating that I hardly recognized it: "I'm—all—right—mother, now."

I tapped on the door. "It would be better if you'd go downstairs now," I said.

They went down. I started opening doors. There were only four of them on the third floor. One other room beside Martin Kyle's was habitable. The rest were unfurnished. I found no sign of any human on the third floor.

I WENT down the steps to the second floor, walked the length of the hall till I was at the top of the front staircase leading down but could still keep the upper flight in view. I called over the banister, "Mr. Crane."

He came out of the living room hurriedly, ran halfway up the stairs, then looked up. "I caught him before he left the house—the sheriff, Mr. Blue."

"Good. Will you come up, please," I said.

He came the rest of the way. I led him along the hall and back up to the third floor.

"The house will be full of cops in a few minutes," I said. "See how fast you can tell me what you were going to tell me."

"I—yes, I've got to tell you now. But you'll keep my confidence—you'll—"

"Yes. Go on."

"It happened twenty-one years ago—in Rione. Rione is a little town near Ortona, in Italy. We—David Kyle and

I—we'd been knocking around—various countries. We—well, you understand that I don't see things now as I did then. We were young, arrogant—we weren't very particular—about what we did. We were nearly penniless when we reached Rione, and pretty desperate. Somewhere we'd heard that there was a lot of money in Rione. You—you understand—money that belonged to somebody else.

"The reason we went there was to try to find it. It turned out that it was there all right—but not in the shape we expected to find it. I don't know if you know the history of Fascism in Italy."

"No," I said.

"It was a party formed partly by the army, but gaining its great strength from hundreds of local societies—secret societies, all over the country. In Nineteen Eleven these were all loosely knit together. These societies were a combination of trade union and radical political organization. The members were fanatical in their loyalty, both to the aims and secrecy of the organization. It served them half as a religion, half as a hope for salvation of the country.

"We know now that the treasure we sought was the secret store of wealth of the headquarters of one of these cliques. We didn't know it then. And you understand that the members of these societies were not necessarily poor people. Some of the richest men in the district belonged. They had been, for years, patiently gathering money together against the day of the party's bid for power.

"Naturally, the government spies were active, trying to ferret them out. The result was—deeper secrecy. At the time of our appearance in Rione, government activity was at its height in that district. I can only guess at the details of this—but I imagine that the treasurers of the local band had found the search too warm, and were forced to seek a hiding place for the really sizable amount of funds in their custody. They elected to open an ancient crypt in the local cemetery that had been sealed up for years, and deposit it there, then seal it up again, until the danger was past.

"The drunken stonemason that Kyle ran into—how I never did know—was the man who had been employed to open the vault, and to seal it up again. Kyle milked him of his information, got the location of the vault.

"We happened to know two brothers —their names were D'Aguido. They were stonemasons of a sort. They were not above—well, thieving—any more than we were. We induced them to help us for we had to have someone with us who could open up the place. Until the actual moment when they opened the vault for us, we managed to keep them in ignorance of what our loot was to be. Then Kyle turned his flashlight on inside the vault. By coincidence—or whatever you want to call it—the rays fell directly on a great heart-shaped ruby. The gem was called The Bloodstone. And the trail of trouble leads directly from it.

"I am sure the D'Aguidos didn't know that the treasury of the local society was where it was. But apparently every one knew that this stone was part of it. They, at least, recognized it at once. Had it been at the bottom of the chest—but no matter.

"We had made our mistake in not ascertaining whether these two were members of the society. We found out, only too terribly now. They were. And we had drawn them into committing what was, to them evidently, an unpardonable sin. They were wild with fury. They attacked us and set up a furious outcry. I managed to overcome one of them and ran to aid Kyle. There was a shot, then another. In the darkness and confusion I thought he had been killed. But it was

the other way around. He had slain the other brother.

"We escaped—somehow. Needless to say, we had no chance to steal the treasure. Literally hundreds of people had been attracted by the outcry and the fighting. They were almost on us when the shots were fired. Nevertheless we escaped, managed to make the coast, and shipped as seamen on an American boat.

"A year or two later Kyle came into a small legacy. He plunged on the Stock Exchange and made a fortune. I have patented one or two ideas that have managed to keep me.

"This—this is the part that I almost hesitate to tell you." He ran a finger inside his collar. His forehead was covered with little beads. "I am sure that I don't have to tell you that this man D'Aguido would kill us—both of us— if he found us. Personally, I have never seen nor heard of the man—except through Kyle—since the night we killed his brother.

"Kyle has told me—many times, that he has seen him. And each time Kyle has bolted, moved his whole establishment practically overnight. Twelve times, in eighteen years. Out of a clear sky, I'd get these telegrams. I got to know them for what they were. I didn't dare ignore them. I'd come—and always it was the same story.

"He'd seen D'Aguido. D'Aguido had tracked him down. All he could think of was to run—to find a new hole to hide in. He'd go—and I'd clean up after him, send his stuff to wherever he had chosen. He believed his family to be in the same danger as he was. And yet he dared not tell one of them what was behind these sudden moves, these tyrannical rules he laid down for them. He tried to keep them under cover in every way he could. You can see the result—on them. You can't see the result on him—now. He was a normal young man. Now he is a creature fit for the gutters. This fear— or conscience—or whatever the devil it is, has eaten away his mentality, his morality, and most of his body. He has made his family loathe him. He has let his diseased fancies fasten on them—you saw that letter. Maybe he has driven them to the point of murder—I don't know.

"As for myself, Mr. Blue—I have never seen D'Aguido, or heard trace of him, save from Kyle's lips. I have hired private detectives by the dozen, and I know he has, too. I have spent weeks of my own time trying to get on his trail. I have gone to every conceivable length to locate him. I—it seems impossible that the man could have absolutely vanished twelve times running from under our eyes. How he located Kyle in the first place has always been a mystery—if he ever did."

"You think Kyle just imagined him?"

"I—I don't know what to think. It isn't inconceivable. Kyle was a mortal coward, Mr. Blue. If he went about day and night, expecting to see D'Aguido, who's to say he did not conjure up his image out of a feverish brain? And now you see why I wanted to tell you this, don't you? You see what I mean—what I'm afraid of! Damn it, man—don't you understand—"

"You think it's finally been too much —that he's gone mad."

"Yes! Yes! And God knows what he'll do, with this fear and hatred cankered inside of him! He—"

The door at the foot of the stairs burst open, and heavy footsteps came up. I motioned Crane to silence. It was the sheriff and his party.

CHAPTER FOUR

Fingerprint Stuff

THE sheriff was named Marx, and he was so far out of his depth it was harrowing. He had a deeply tanned, outdoor face, thin black hair, oiled, and apprehensive blue eyes. He was about forty-five, wore blue riding breeches and boots. A heavy Colt swung at his hip. He had two deputies with him. One was a great hulk of a man, easily six foot five, with hungry blue eyes and big hands. His name was Ellison. The other was a little whiffet, with the narrowest face I'd ever seen, and tortoise-shell glasses. He hugged a big tin box under his arm. The county coroner completed the party—a Dr. Ease—believe it or not.

I introduced myself. The sheriff had read of me in the New York papers. I unlocked the door and Marx and the doctor preceded me in. The deputies waited outside.

The room was a block "L." The door to the hall was at the top of the "L"; there was a bureau in the angle. The window, open an inch or two, was between the bureau and the foot of the bed, and there was a table two feet or so out from the bed. The bed was against the outside wall. There were two whiskey bottles, one Dewar's, the other Hilltop, and a water glass on the table. The Hilltop was full. There was about an inch in the Dewar's. The coroner went to the body. The sheriff stood with his hands on his hips, watching him.

"Cyanide, eh doctor?" I asked.

"Yes, yes."

I touched the sheriff on the arm, pointed out the folded handkerchief, and he swooped down on it. "A mask, eh? A mask!"

The doctor looked round, then back again. I prowled around the room. The window was slightly open. I looked out. It was a sheer forty feet to the driveway below. No human could make it.

The doctor got up after a minute or so. He took out his watch. "This man died from a whiff of hydrocyanic-acid gas. He died—let me see—between five minutes to nine and ten minutes after. That is definite, sheriff. At the time of death, he was under the influence of liquor, too far, in my opinion, to admit of suicide. The nature of the poison is such that one whiff kills instantly. That's why I can time it so closely."

There was a waste-basket at the corner of the table. I went over to it. There were several crumpled pieces of paper— and a small glass bottle. I got out my handkerchief, removed the bottle. It still held the almond odor. The sheriff was at my shoulder when I straightened up. "Here's what the stuff came in," I said.

He looked stupid, put out a hand for it. "Lay off," I snapped. "Get your fingerprint man."

He walked over to the door and called "Hayes."

I saw I'd have to do his work for him too. "And I'd send a man down to take alibis and see that nobody goes away," I said, "and have Mr. Crane out there go down, too."

I looked at my watch. It was ten minutes after ten. The sheriff tried to glare at me, but did what I said.

The doctor closed up his bag. "Go ahead," he told Marx. "I'll send for the body when you're through."

Hayes came in and put his tin box on the table. I gave him the bottle. "Try that and the doorknobs and the whiskey bottles," I said. His eyes gleamed. He went to work.

Marx stood looking expectantly at me. "How—how did it happen?" he asked. I told him part of what I knew, why I was there. He nodded nervously. "Yeah. We've been lookin' for Mr. Kyle all afternoon," he said. "There's a posse out."

I handed him the letter. "Just came about the time I arrived," I said. "That's what the first call was about. The one the girl made."

He took the letter, stood spread-legged, read it through. The color went out of his face. He finished, looked at me, licked his lips, looked back down at the letter. "Gosh," he said in a dry voice. "Gosh." Then after a minute. "What—what do you figure, Blue?"

"About the old man, or this one?"

"Well—well, they're probably both tied up, don't you think?"

"Not necessarily."

"Well, the old man's dead now, surer than hell, eh?"

I shrugged. "Mr. Crane, who's known him for years, thinks he may have gone off his head and wandered off somewhere."

"But we've looked—as good as we can in the fog, anyway—all around here. I don't see—"

There was a queer sound from Hayes. He spun around, his eyes big with pleasure. "Got him!" he said excitedly. "Got a swell print from the poison bottle, Mr. Marx."

We moved to the table together quickly. There was the full print of a man's forefinger outlined in white powder, as well as several smudged ones.

"Photograph it," I said.

Relief spread over Marx's face. "We'll print everybody in the house!"

I said: "Are you through with this room?"

"Yeah. Let's go down and get the prints."

"Suppose we move the apparatus down to the library on the second floor," I said to Hayes. "We can close this room up, and you can have the wagon come and pick the body up, Marx."

Marx said: "Sure. Hurry up, Hayes," and went out. He had an ink tablet and a bunch of cards in his hands.

Hayes started putting things back in the box, frowning. I went over and picked up the whiskey bottles—and damn near let them drop again.

From below came a hoarse, startled shout, then a banging. Then Marx's hoarse voice. "Stop! Stop—or I'll shoot!"

I RAN out the door and to the stairs, skidded halfway down, caught myself, and plunged the rest of the way. I swung around the corner into the hall, one hand on a gun, and checked myself just in time to avoid crashing into the sheriff. He stood at the bottom of the steps, his Colt in his left fist. The tablet and the cards were sprinkled all over the floor.

His hands over his head, a stocky, short man with stiff red hair stood sullenly halfway down the hall, breathing fast. "Awright," he said. "I'm here. What's the idea?"

"What's happened?" I asked Marx. "Who is this?"

"I'm the gardener here," the sullen-faced man cut in. "I come out of my room, and he bumps into me, and—"

"Where've you been?" Marx barked. "You haven't been in your room!"

"The hell I haven't." He gestured toward the half-open door at the foot of the steps. "I been sleepin'—"

I stepped forward, stooped, and ran my finger around the sole of his shoe. I held it up so the sheriff could see the wet mud. The sullen one said: "Who the hell are you?" to me.

"Sleeping, eh," the sheriff snarled, "and got mud on your shoes? Or maybe you're a sleepwalker, eh? Search him, Blue."

Marx was on more familiar ground now, and he was blossoming. I took a 44 automatic from the red-haired one's pocket. He said: "Are you Cass Blue?"

"Yes. Why?"

"I—nuthin'. What—what's all the fireworks?"

"Murder!" the sheriff rolled out.

"Murder—that's what. And now let's hear where you were between five to nine and ten after."

"Who—who's murdered? David—"

"Never mind that! Where were you?"

The sullen face froze up again. He clamped his lips. "I'll do my talking later."

I went into his room. The window was open. I walked over and put my head out. The roof of the veranda was right outside. There were muddy footprints leading across it. From the light in the room I could see a coil of rope in the corner of the roof. I went back out into the hall. They were all looking at me.

"You'd better talk," I told the gardener. "You're in a tight spot."

"Maybe I'll talk, if somebody'll tell me what it's all about!"

The sheriff took a quick step toward him. I thought he was going to slam him one with the cannon. "You'll talk—you'll talk, all right! I'll—"

"Listen, Marx," I said, "you've got a clear path to an arrest if you can find anybody in this house that made the fingerprint on that bottle. This man will keep. If the prints don't click, then we can work on him. But take it from me—you've got to work fast, or there'll be more trouble!"

His jaw gaped open. "What?"

"Just get the prints," I said.

He blinked at me. "What have you found out, Blue?"

"Nothing you haven't. But for heaven's sake—don't waste time."

Marx whirled on the red-haired man. "Get into the library, there." To Hayes he said: "Hurry up and get your stuff."

Hayes went back upstairs. I called: "Lock the door and bring the key."

He came back a minute later and we all went into the library. The little deputy was a wizard with his stuff. It took him just two minutes to say positively that the prints on the bottle were nothing like the gardener's.

Before the sheriff could get started again, I suggested he lock the gardener up and proceed with the family.

It was not till they had gone out, and were on the stairs, that my apparently ossified intelligence jerked me up. I slapped a hand to my breast pocket and with a sick feeling remembered the letter from the bank. Remembered that the scream of the girl had interrupted me before I switched it from my topcoat to my jacket. I turned and ran down the hall, burst into my room, strode across to the closet and yanked it open.

The lapel of my coat was turned back over the hanger. The manila envelope, of course, was gone.

And I remembered without pleasure the fact that the entire household had passed the open door of my room while Crane and I were upstairs with the girl. Any one of them could have taken it.

I JAMMED my hands in my pockets and cursed. I felt my confidence slipping. It had finally penetrated my thick skull that I was up against something almighty damned smart. A man who could watch his opportunities closely enough to crash in on this one was bad enough. That he was getting all the breaks as well was beginning to rankle.

And I was a long way from sure that he was through. That was the real hell of it. For if there wasn't more murder in the air of this unholy household I was crazy. I set my teeth, snapped myself out of it. Outclassed or not, I was the only thing that stood between this clever butcher and the rest of the household. And he'd made one slip—or someone had. The fingerprint. I'd hang someone on that.

I went through the futile motions of looking around for the envelope. Then I went out and downstairs, and I won't say I wasn't pretty well geared up.

I kept trying to recall if the man at the trust company had said the girl would be expecting the envelope, and finally decided that he hadn't. If she asked for it —well, I hoped she wouldn't. As it turned out, she didn't. I got that much of a break anyway.

I could see the broad back of Ellison, the big deputy, in the archway as I came down. He jumped a foot when I pushed him aside and went in. Menocal, Crane, the girl, and Mrs. Kyle were standing in a semicircle around the far end of the table, staring at the fingerprint cards on the table, their arms held away from their sides. They all had ink on their fingers. Two frightened-faced maids were standing together in a door at the rear of the room, also with stained fingers. Marx was saying irritably to the red-haired man we had discovered upstairs: "All some mistake. Come on—put 'em down."

The red-haired one turned on me as I came in. "Blue—tell this guy to wake up. He wants to spend the day printing me!"

It wasn't my argument. I shrugged.

"All right—then will you tell me—is Kyle dead?"

"Martin Kyle is dead. David Kyle is still missing."

His eyes got like marbles. "Martin Kyle!"

"Come on, come on," the sheriff barked, "put—"

"Wait a minute!" The red-haired one swung on Marx. "Listen—and get this straight! My name's Pearson, and I'm an operative of the Corcoran Agency in New York, and I ain't any part of a gardener. If you'll look upstairs in my bottom bureau drawer, you'll find my shield and my papers. David Kyle had me come down here about three weeks ago. Nobody was supposed to know I was a dick. He fixed that rope stunt upstairs so's I could get in and out without nobody in the house knowin' it. And I got plenty to tell you in private. Send these people outside, and I'll give it to you."

The sheriff clamped his lips together, glared at him.

"All right," he said finally, "all right —but if you—"

"Just a minute, sheriff," I said. "While these people are together why not get them all placed between five to nine and ten after?"

"Eh? Well, yeah, yeah."

I took out my watch. "Mr. Crane picked me up at the flying field about one minute to nine. From then until after the time Miss Kyle discovered the death of her brother, he has been with me. Could he have been here at five minutes to, and at the field at one minute to?"

"How could he—"

"I'm asking you."

"Well, he couldn't. It's over ten miles and the roads are bad."

"All right," I said. "Now the rest of you speak for yourselves."

"I'll speak for them," Menocal's husky voice said nastily. "Mr. Crane left here at twenty to nine. We—Mrs. Kyle, Miss Kyle and myself, sat down right in this room, and none of us left it till you arrived."

I bored into his eyes. "You'll swear to that?"

"I don't say things I won't swear to."

I looked at Mrs. Kyle. "And you?"

"Yes."

"Miss Kyle?"

"Yes. It's true."

T HAT kind of cut the ground from under my feet. I'd expected alibis, but nothing so utterly straightforward

and final as this. I played with the idea that they were all lying. There was a minute's silence. Marx turned on the two frightened maids in the rear of the room.

"Where were you?"

They couldn't speak. They turned appealing eyes toward Louise Kyle.

"They were in the kitchen," the girl said, "all the time."

"How do you know?" I asked.

She took an exasperated breath, walked over and pushed the two maids aside. I saw through the door a butler's pantry, doorless, and had a clear view through that of the kitchen. There was a back staircase whose bottom end was a door, and a sink, in sight. Between them were two chairs, directly in my line of sight.

Louise Kyle pointed to a chair directly behind me. "I happened to be sitting in that chair the entire time. I could see them."

I looked back at the maids. "Could you see Miss Kyle?"

They nodded together hastily.

I threw up my hands, figuratively. It was rock-ribbed, all round. I looked at the sheriff, shrugged my shoulders.

The sheriff had kept one hand on Pearson's arm all this time. He called: "Ellison!" and the big deputy was again in the doorway. "Go up and look in the bureau in the room by the third-floor stairs. This guy says he has papers and a shield there. Bring 'em down." Ellison nodded, went out. "Now the rest of you—"

"Oh," I said, "just a minute. I'm not quite through." I looked at Menocal. "What did you do when you heard Miss Kyle scream?"

He looked me full in the eye. "I went to the foot of the front stairs, and maybe a few steps up. Then when Mr. Crane and Vokes," he nodded at one of the maids, "came down, I came back in here."

I ran my eye over the others. Crane, Miss Kyle, Mrs. Kyle—they had all come up—and one maid. I picked out the other maid. "What did you do?"

She managed to say she'd gone as far as the top of the kitchen stairs and stood there.

That was a break. I turned round and sat down in the chair Miss Kyle had said she had occupied. There were two others, close beside it. I said to Menocal: "When Miss Kyle was sitting here, were you in one of these?"

"Yes."

I looked out through the arch. The lower third of the front stairs was plainly visible. "Then," I said, still to the Spaniard, "since the time Mr. Crane went out to fetch me, the front stairs have never been out of your sight?"

He frowned. "No, they haven't."

"Has anybody come down those stairs that is not in this room?"

"What do you mean?"

"Don't waste time. You know what I mean."

"Well, no—certainly not. Nobody else came down the stairs."

"I presume you're willing to swear to that, too."

"I am."

I turned to the maid who had stood at the top of the kitchen stairs.

"Please try to think carefully. From the time Mr. Crane left the house, it seems as if you should have been in sight of the back stairs, right up till this moment. Is that right?"

She took her time to think, and I was glad of it. I was reasonably sure she'd tell the truth, and I didn't want a hurried statement. She finally said in a clear voice that she had been.

"And did anybody come down the back stairs—anybody that's not in this room now?"

"No, sir. I am sure they did not."

I turned to Marx. "The ground is soaking wet outside, sheriff," I said. "It should be pretty easy to find footprints. It's very essential to know whether anybody jumped out a second-story window, and whether more than one person used Pearson's rope exit from the top of the veranda. It's important enough so I'm asking you to check it up yourself."

He blinked at me, still not quite with me. "Well, why—"

"I'll look after things here."

He hesitated, frowning, finally acceded. He went outside. While he was gone, Ellison came down with Pearson's shield and papers.

"Hang on to them," I said. "Mr. Marx is outside."

CHAPTER FIVE

Murder Vigil

WE waited a full ten minutes. Then Marx came back in. "Only one man came down Pearson's corner and went up again," he said. "There isn't any doubt of it. And there are no fresh footprints around the house anywhere. Nobody came out of no windows here tonight."

"You're absolutely sure?" I said.

"Sure I'm sure. What of it?"

"Just this," I said. "The man that killed Martin Kyle has had no opportunity to get down from the second floor since the murder. Every means of getting down has been checked. Either one of the people in this room killed him—or else the killer is still hiding somewhere upstairs!"

"But—but—"

"On the other hand—every single person in this room has a shock-proof alibi for the time the coroner says the murder was done—except Pearson."

"I've got an alibi! I've got an alibi, too!" Pearson said anxiously. "You'll see—"

The sheriff grunted. "I bet you have."

"I'd get that rope taken away from the corner of the veranda roof," I said to Marx.

He started, went hurriedly out into the hall and called up to Hayes, the little deputy, upstairs, to get the rope. Hayes wanted to know where the fingerprint cards were.

THEN Marx came back in and gathered up the white cards on the table, gave them to Ellison. "Take these up and come right back down."

Ellison handed him Pearson's stuff. "Got this in the bureau drawer," he said.

"All right." The sheriff frowned at the police card. Ellison went out. When he came back, Marx was still trying to look judicial over the stuff.

I coughed. "Suppose everybody go to their rooms now," I said to Marx. "We can see what Pearson has to say for himself."

"Yeah." He swung round. "You can all go to your rooms—your own rooms," he amended. "Nobody is to move outside till we see what's what. That clear?"

It was. They filed out. I took a position from which I could keep an eye on both front and back stairs. Marx stood spreadlegged till the room held only Ellison, Pearson, himself and myself. When the last of the others had gone, he turned on Pearson. "All right. Let's hear you talk yourself out of this."

Pearson pointed. "You've got my papers there."

"These don't mean nuthin'. Anybody c'd have these."

Pearson's eyes narrowed. He looked at me. "You going to let him frame me for this, Blue?"

"Go ahead and talk," I said impatiently. "Nobody's going to frame anybody. What'd Kyle hire you for, anyway—and when?"

"He sent to the agency about three weeks ago. When I got there he said there was a Wop in the village named Ricigliano. He thought the moniker was a phony and he wanted me to find out if the real one wasn't D'Aguido. Seems this D'Aguido had a grudge against Kyle from away back, and Kyle thought he might try and bump him off. But that wasn't all. He thought somebody in his family was fixing to give it to him, too. So nobody was to know I was a dick, and he cooked up that rope stunt so's they wouldn't get wise to me coming in and going out. See what I mean?"

"Go on."

"Well, when I hear them say you're comin' out—" he looked at me—"I figure I better grab this D'Aguido—er Ricigliano—and freeze onto him. Then you and me could work on him together. See what I—"

"Where is he now?"

Pearson licked his lips. "Well, the fact of it is, he's lammed. The guy in the next house to where he was told me he seen him load up an old flivver late this afternoon, and put a trunk in it. Then clear out. The guy that told me 's named Tomaso. He's a Wop, too. He's my alibi. I left here just before Crane did tonight, and—well, I got in just when you glommed onto me."

"Alibi?" the sheriff snorted. "You call that an alibi?"

"Easy," I said. "You can't afford to take a chance, Marx. You better spread the word around for that flivver."

"I never heard of any Tomaso in Oakville."

"All right, all right—but if you're going to charge this man, you'll look funny in front of judge if you pass these things up."

He hooked thumbs in his belt, eyed Pearson hostilely a long minute. "All right," he snapped. "Ellison, take this guy and lock him up in the cellar or some place. Then go see if you can find any Wop named Tomaso in the village. He'll tell you where he's s'posed to live."

"Well, hell now——" Pearson started.

He could have saved his breath. Ellison marched him toward the back. Two lights arced across the outside of the windows, and the sound of an automobile came up the drive.

"Morgue wagon," Marx said.

"I'd get on the phone if I were you," I suggested. "That flivver might be real."

"Say—those fingerprints." Marx suddenly remembered.

"Sure. Do your phoning, and we'll go up and see."

THE white-coated boys from the county morgue came in with their grim wicker basket. I said to one of them: "See that the little fellow in the library takes the prints of the corpse before you take it away, will you?"

"Sure. Where is it?"

"Third floor. You'll find it."

They went upstairs. Ellison reappeared. When he saw that Marx was phoning, he hung around dubiously.

"Go on," I said, "what are you waiting for?"

He mumbled something, took another look at Marx, avoided my eye and went out.

Three minutes later when the morgue boys came down Marx was still phoning, I held the door open for them, then closed and locked it. I went out and made sure the doors in the rear were locked. I came back to the hall, just as Marx hung up, mopped his face.

"He won't get far," he said, "if there is a flivver. I've got a line out for a hundred miles all round."

"Nice," I said. "Let's go see what Hayes has got."

Hayes was sitting scowling at the array of cards, behind a big library table.

The bottle, a heavier coat of white powder outlining the tell-tale mark on it, stood in the center of them.

"Get it matched yet?" Marx asked.

Hayes grunted. "It isn't any of these."

The wind went out of Marx. He sat down suddenly. "It—it isn't any of them?" he said incredulously.

"No."

"But—hell, it must be! That bird Pearson—take another look at——"

"I did. I did."

"Well—well hell, Hayes——" He looked over at me absolutely bewildered.

I was standing just outside the doorway, where I could keep an eye on both sets of stairs—back and front. I said: "Don't get in a panic, Marx. We're no worse off than when we started."

He scrambled to his feet suddenly. "Listen—that killer must be hidden in this house!"

"Sure. Sure. But take it easy. Stand here a minute."

I went to the juncture of the front hall and the one I was in. The flight of steps leading to the third floor was placed right beside a small window that would look down into the driveway. I tried to figure the best way to cover the house for what was left of the night.

I went back to where Marx was waiting.

"Listen," he said hoarsely, "we've got to search this house!"

"Didn't you search it when you came in?"

"Well, sure, but not the third——"

"I searched the third floor. There's no one there—at least no one you'll find by an ordinary search."

His eyes got wide. "You—you mean you think there's secret rooms?"

"I don't know. It may be. If there are, they're almighty damn well hidden. You won't find them without taking involved measurements. Everyone in this household is frightened stiff, already. They'll be of no help—and it's still possible one of them is the killer. Get them wandering around this house—knowing that they are likely to see this murderer any minute, and you'll have them jumping out windows. The one place where the three of us can watch them, is where they are now—in their own rooms.

"We've got our man bottled up here, I think. The one thing that's important is to keep him bottled up. I think his plans have miscarried somehow. I'll tell you frankly, I think there's something in Pearson's story. If we find that Italian, you'll have the key to this thing. Meanwhile—we've got to keep what advantage we've got. Turn these people out of their rooms, and there'll be so much confusion that the killer's bound to make a break for escape. And if you don't understand what that will mean, I'll tell you, it'll mean more killing, because I don't think he'll be taken alive. He's got everything to gain by killing everybody in the house, rather than that. They only can hang you once."

"But—but what'll we do?"

"One of us can stay downstairs and watch the bottom of the stairs. The other two can watch this hall. In the morning, if there's no news of this D'Aguido, or Ricigliano, you can get a posse of men here to surround this house, and we'll go through it right. I'm telling you—smoke this killer out now—even if you could—and you'll make a slaughter house of the place!"

Marx swallowed twice. "You think it's that bad?"

"If it isn't, we can't lose anything by preparing for it to be," I said shortly. "Has Hayes got a gun?"

"Yeah, sure, but—"

"O. K. Now, you go downstairs," I told Marx, "and get a spot where you can watch the bottom of both pairs of stairs. If anybody—anybody at all—

comes down, without Hayes or me telling you it's all right—kill them—and do it fast. Don't get soft-hearted and start talking—or we'll bury you tomorrow."

Strong? Sure, I made it strong. But the extra set of nerves that any good dick develops was clamoring inside of me to be careful. I didn't think anybody'd get by me, but if they did—then nothing I could tell Marx would be too strong.

HE went downstairs. I posted Hayes with his back to the door of the third-floor stairs. I got a chair from David Kyle's room, set it against the banister right at the top step of the front stairs, opposite Menocal's room. I put cigarettes and matches and a gun on my knees, and settled down to the long wait for dawn.

Gradually, the household quieted down. And after maybe an hour my nerves relaxed a bit.

Hayes had a pipe going. I could catch an occasional whiff of smoke from around the bend of the hall. And more often, Marx's restless tread downstairs. After a while the clock in the living room boomed out hollowly, twice.

And then Menocal's door swung open a foot.

I was on my feet in a flash, swung myself aside and covered the pitch-black aperture. "Stand still!" I snapped in a low voice.

"I'm standing still," Menocal said. "Don't point your damned gun at me."

"What do you want?" I snapped.

"Nothing—nothing. Just wondered what was going on, that's all."

I cursed him. "You get to hell back inside, and stay there," I said. "You're lucky I didn't throw a bullet at you."

He said something inaudible, and closed the door.

For a minute, I stood frowning at his door, trying to figure him out. I couldn't, but I didn't like it much. I sat down again, but I wasn't relaxed any more.

I let fifteen minutes go by.

Then I started humming. Not loudly, but so that if Menocal happened to be standing with his ear against the door, he could hear it. Then I got up, and walking slowly, went casually to the turn of the hall, swung round, stopped humming, and swung right back again. I caught a glimpse of Hayes' baffled face at the end of the hall. I stood silent, waved a hand behind me to warn Hayes to silence.

And Menocal's door came slowly open again.

I'D HAVE given a lot to swing back around the corner, and watch where Menocal was trying to go, but to do it, I'd have to lose sight of the two staircases. I didn't dare do that. I've found it doesn't pay to lose sight of what your main object is. My main object at present was to keep anybody from getting down those stairs. I just stood there till Menocal stepped cautiously into the hall, and stopped in mid-stride as he saw me looking at him. His face got red.

"I thought I told you to stay in your room," I said.

"Damn your snooping soul!" he burst out surprisingly. "I'm entitled to look around and try and protect myself. I heard what you said to Marx. This killer is in this part of the house, and I'm not going to lie quietly and be murdered! Who are you to—"

"Listen—" I reversed my gun in my hand, put the butt under his nose. "How would you like that across the teeth?"

"Why—why, you—" His face got white.

"Whatever you're trying to pull, we'll investigate in the morning. Right now you get back where you belong, and if I catch you moving around any more, I'll make it good and hot for you. Now, get inside!"

He jammed his hands in his bathrobe pockets, cursed me under his breath as he turned back. I slammed the door on him and started pacing up and down the hall.

Hayes was blinking anxiously at me, each time I came in sight. I finally halted, shrugged, and grinned, to relieve his mind. He grinned back, sat down, and I turned away—and then I saw it from the corner of my eye. . . .

Through the window behind Hayes an angry roaring sheet of flame was beating against the window pane!

He saw it the same second I did. He leaped up, his chair toppling over, and almost ran backward toward me. He swung round. His face was bloodless, his eyes wide. "Blue—Blue—Fire!" he croaked wildly. There was a queer feeling in my stomach. I rapped: "Shut up!" and ran down the hall. I slid to a stop, flung him out of my way, dropped my gun, and started to raise the window. It stuck. I jammed both palms upward again, and again. Finally it gave, slid up with a screeching sound. The flame swayed inward, but in the first glance I saw the wide sloping sill outside and the source of the fire.

Involuntarily, I'd ducked back. I sprang forward again, cursed, and shoved the wadded-up newspaper off the sill, still blazing. It fell to the driveway beneath. Then I noticed five other little balls of fire around the driveway.

I looked along the row of dark windows—the library, Menocal's, David Kyle's, Crane's. And they were all open except the library. It might have been possible to land a missile on the sill of the window where I was, from anyone of them. Menocal's was the best bet. But then there was David Kyle's room, supposed to be empty and finally Crane's. Anyway whoever it was had had five misses.

Hayes was beside me. I swung round.

"Phony!" I snapped. "Stay here a minute."

I scooped my gun from the floor, raced back down the hall, keeping to the small rugs which were scattered along its length. Just as I came to the corner, I heard a door close softly. I swung round, one hand on the wall angle, and I was wild. I don't relish being tricked—and I got madder when I realized that whatever it was Menocal had been trying to do, he had undoubtedly done now. I took one step toward his door and checked myself, my eyes nearly popping from my head.

CHAPTER SIX

What Mad Hands?

THE chair I had been sitting on was a heavy one. Unconsciously I had placed it on one of the small rag rugs. The corner of the rug was turned back, and protruding from under it, its corner evidently held down by the leg of the heavy chair, was the manila envelope I had received from the trust company.

I had been too fast for him! He hadn't been able to retrieve the envelope from where he had hidden it when he snatched it from my pocket! And was I pleased to see it?

I dropped to one knee, tugged gently at it, found it stuck. I lifted the chair with one hand, eased the letter out with the other, took one hasty glance at the envelope and saw it was the right one. I slipped it into my side pocket, let the chair down, got up and whirled toward Menocal's door. . . .

A black velvet hand whipped over my shoulder with the speed of a snake, smothered my mouth, jerked me off balance. I fell back against a body; the point of a long gleaming knife flashed down— and stopped—an inch from my throat.

Grunting breath was in my ear; the knife pricked me. I was as utterly helpless as a baby. My gun was useless; the safety catch on, and before I could move it anyway, the knife would be coming out between my ears. I know death when I see it, and this was no counterfeit. I froze. We stood like that for seconds, the only sound, the other's tense breathing. Then he eased his hand slowly off my mouth. Little good it did me. That knife couldn't miss by a miracle, the way he had me.

His hand slid down to my gun wrist. He took the gun from my fingers, tossed it onto the top step of the stairs where thick carpet swallowed the sound. Then he knocked my arm impatiently upward, from underneath. He had to do it twice before I got what he wanted. I wasn't even breathing till then.

I raised my hands slowly, and my nerve started coming back. By putting my throat deliberately against the knife as my arms raised, I made him let me get my balance back. My heart was going good and fast, and I was sweating all over as the knife made little pricks in my throat. I had to do something. My mind was racing, looking for a tenth of a chance, but the smooth, deadly efficiency of the devil left no opening.

Then he plunged his hand into my left coat pocket. I felt him pulling the manila envelope from my pocket. Then I came out of it.

In one motion, I hipped him, spun myself to the left. He made a muffled, furious sound, tried to drive the knife home as I whirled, but his hand, imprisoned in the pocket, jerked him just enough. There was a flaming line across my cheek as the razor-edge slashed me—and then I was around, diving for his wrist with both hands.

I caught it, threw my whole weight on it, dragged to get it down. I got the surprise of my life at his strength; he practically held me up on his forearm.

His free hand snatched the knife from the imprisoned one, flashed upward. I remembered to shout. I let go his wrist suddenly, kicked his legs viciously from under him, and threw myself wildly aside. He collapsed. I caught a glimpse of flaming eyes through slits in the all-over black hood. I threw a look for my gun, saw it on the top step, and dived for it as he scrambled up. I clawed behind me for the gun, missed it, had to look again. In that second he was on one knee. A sixth sense jerked my head back round as my fingers closed on the gun. I saw flashing steel almost in my face and flopped wildly aside. The knife thudded into the wall. I couldn't catch myself. I swung my gun around, fired wildly, and plunged head foremost down the stairs, rolling, flopping, till I hit the landing with a crash.

DOORS started banging; there were screams through the house. Marx came running from below, his face white as a sheet, as I picked myself up. He cried: "Good God!" when he saw the blood streaming from my face. I roared over my shoulder: "Watch those stairs!" Then pounded back up, three steps at a time, swung round the banister—and saw Hayes appear round the corner, his gun up, his eyes just closing to take a shot at me.

I called: "Stop, you fool!" just in time. He opened his eyes in utter astonishment.

"Get out here, everybody!" I shouted. "Fast! Come on, move!"

Doors burst open. I backed to the banister at the front, both my guns in my hands. "Hurry up!" I raved.

Doors stopped opening. I ran frantic glances around. Louise Kyle stood white-faced in the opening of her door. Crane, a heavy Colt in one hand, was fumbling with a dressing-gown cord. His eyes were haggard. Mrs. Kyle, looking as though she'd seen a ghost, clung to the door jamb of her room. The two maids hud-

dled together; one of them was sobbing.

Menocal's door was open an inch. It was black within. No one came out.

"What is it—what's happened?" Louise Kyle blurted.

"Be quiet!" I snapped.

I had my eyes on Menocal's door. "Watch them, Hayes!" I said. I stepped forward, kicked the door open. "Come out, Menocal!" I barked.

There was no movement. I stepped through, fumbled for the light switch and turned it on. There was no one else in the room, but a tremendous black cloak, fitted with a hood for the head, and a pair of black velvet gloves lay on the floor beside the leather couch. I snatched up the cloak, stretched out the arm. There was wet blood on it. My blood!

I heard a banging downstairs. I threw a quick glance around inside Menocal's room, then went out into the hall. I looked over the banister, saw Marx at the door, unlocking it. I waited long enough to see Ellison come in. I called out: "Come up, and leave him there, will you, Marx?"

He came running up, calling instructions over his shoulder. When he was at the top, I shushed him with a motion.

I called in a loud voice. "If you're hiding in one of the rooms, Menocal, you'd better come out. We're going through them, and shoot you on sight if you—"

Menocal appeared at Mrs. Kyle's door, behind her. "All right," he said sullenly. "Here I am."

"Put your hands up!"

He put his hands up.

"Come out of that."

He came. I stepped forward, held a gun against his middle, ran a hand over him. He had on pajamas and a dressing gown. There was nothing on him but a handkerchief.

"Where's the envelope?" I said.

He looked at me through narrowed eyes. "What's all this about?"

I checked myself. I had forgotten my own peculiar status in regard to that envelope. I turned to Marx. "I want to question this man alone a minute. Do you mind?"

"Well, hell—what's happened, Blue—what's—"

"I was attacked by a man wearing that hood; he gave me this." I touched my cheek. "I'll just be a minute. Get in there, you." I jabbed him with my gun. "Just keep the rest of them where they are a minute," I said to Marx.

Menocal went into his room; he eyed the hood as though he had never seen it before. I closed the door behind me.

"All right, greaseball—where's the envelope you stole from my pocket while we were scuffling?"

"Are you crazy?"

"I'm just crazy enough to give you a dose of this," I erupted, and took a step toward him. I had every intention of pistol-whipping it out of him, too.

"Wait—wait!" He backed away, real fright in his eyes. "Listen—you've got this wrong, somehow, Blue. Take your time, will you? Listen—when you went running down the hall, I ducked into Mrs. Kyle's room. I—I had something I wanted to ask her. I was trying to get to her all evening. You—you can ask her!"

I HESITATED. And I'm damned if I wasn't even now, half convinced that he was telling the truth. I clamped my lips. "All right," I said. "You keep your mouth shut when I open this door. I'll give you a chance."

I went out into the hall, just in time to hear Hayes' voice say excitedly: "Another print! Clear as day!"

I had to look round a minute to locate him. He was crouched by the top of the stairs, a tiny flashlight in his hand, looking through a magnifying glass at the knife that had been thrown at me, imbedded in the wall.

"A print?" I said.

"Yeah. Yeah."

"Take the knife out and see if it matches any of your collection."

Marx said: "For Heaven's sakes, Blue—what happened? And listen—"

"Save it—just a minute!" I said. "I had a scuffle with a masked man. I'll go into it in a second." I turned and faced the panicky crowd. "Everybody turn their lights on and leave their doors wide open."

They did it.

I took Marx by the arm and stood him in front of Menocal's door. "Watch this bird every second. He's got a hell of a lot to explain."

Menocal's insolence was back in his face. He was sitting on his bed lighting a cigarette. "Don't waste any time looking for the real murderer, by any chance, Blue," he said bitterly, and reached for a magazine.

I figured I'd take all that out of him later. I turned and started toward Mrs. Kyle's room. Marx grabbed my arm. "Listen, Blue—"

"I'll be with you in just a second," I said, and shook clear. I said to Mrs. Kyle: "Inside, please."

I followed her in, and closed the door. Her lips were trembling; her eyes were terrified. I guess I didn't look any too sane myself, with the blood all over me. I said: "If you lie to me, Mrs. Kyle, there's going to be more trouble than you'll care to cope with. When did Menocal come into this room?"

"Just—just now," she said weakly.

"When, just now?" I rapped. "Just after the scuffle in the hall?"

"I didn't hear any scuffle. The doors are thick—"

"Did you hear me run down the hall a while ago?"

"Yes. I heard your boots on the bare floor."

"How long after that did he come in?"

"Just—just then. While you were running."

I cursed under my breath. Had she just guessed it right, or was she telling the truth? I tried a new angle. "What did he come in for?"

"He—he wanted to ask me a question," she said.

"Why didn't he ask you before?"

She swallowed. "He—he said he wasn't quite sure before that I—I hadn't anything to do with—with David's disappearance."

"What was the question?"

"He—he wanted to know if I had ever heard David—heard David mention a bloodstone."

"A what?" I almost shouted at her.

"A bloodstone."

"What did he know about a bloodstone —I mean Menocal?"

"Oh, I don't know. He didn't tell—"

I DIDN'T wait for the last of it. I jerked open the door, strode into the hall. Marx came toward me, gesturing with both hands. "Blue—listen just a minute—Ellison says there ain't any such guy as this Tomaso. The house next where this other Wop lived has been vacant for months."

That stopped me. "What?"

"This Pearson's a fake! The Wop he said would prove his alibi—Tomaso—is a fairy story. Nobody ever heard of him, and the house Pearson said he lived in has been empty for months!"

"Well, get Pearson up here and see what he says now."

"Yeah." Marx leaned over the banister and called: "Ellison!" I took two steps toward Menocal's room. The little deputy, Hayes, suddenly emerged from the library, his face alight.

"Hey, Blue—Blue—what do you think?" he said excitedly. "The prints on the knife match up!"

Marx and I spun on him. We spoke in unison. "With what?"

"With the prints on the poison bottle!"

I just gaped at him; so did Marx. Hayes stood there, looking as though he thought he was pretty bright.

Then from below came Ellison's anxious voice. "You want me, Mr. Marx."

Marx spun round impatiently. "Get Pearson up here!" he called down.

And I got an idea that I should have had hours ago. My eyes went to the door next to Menocal's. "Get your glass," I said to Pearson, "and come in here."

I had the door open and the lights on in the room, when he came hurrying back. It was a larger room than mine, more modernly fitted up. There were bookcases and a leather couch, a dark mulberry rug, a couple of heavy leather chairs, as well as bed and dresser. "See if you can pick up the prints of the man that lives in this room," I said.

He went to work. He found a silver hairbrush, got one from the back of that, and another from a whiskey decanter. A third from a polished mahogany cigar box on the table. They were all the same.

"This is it, all right." he said.

"Take the cigar box, and try it with the poison bottle and the knife," I suggested, and we went out again.

I stopped at Menocal's door, as Hayes went back into the library. I couldn't make up my mind whether to wait and see if the prints matched, or question Menocal now. He was lying on his bed, his back turned to the door. Over his shoulder I saw a magazine. I hesitated—and there was the sound of running feet down below. Marx bent over the banister. Ellison came running halfway upstairs, panted out: "He's gone, Mr. Marx—he jerked the staple out of the door of the cellar!"

Marx made a hoarse bellow in his throat. He spun on me. "He's escaped!"

he croaked. "Pearson's escaped—Blue—damn you—you made me keep him here! I would have—"

We both turned toward the library, as Hayes, his eyes flaming behind his spectacles, burst through the door. "Blue—you've got him! The prints on the cigar box match the ones on the poison bottle and the knife! Whose are they?"

I felt a chill in my stomach. "They're . . . David Kyle's," I said.

MARX'S face went slowly white; his jaw hung open. Hayes stared from one to the other of us.

"You—you mean—", Marx gasped.

"I don't mean anything!" I burst out. "The prints on the poison bottle and the knife belong to the missing man, David Kyle." I clipped myself short, suddenly remembering the open doors around us, but there was no sign that we had been heard by anybody. I sank my voice. "Go put out the alarm for Pearson!" I said to Marx quickly. "Whatever this mess is, we've got to have Pearson. Send Ellison up, and phone round an alarm like you did for the car. Hurry up!"

Marx licked his lips. "That letter, Blue," he said in a hoarse whisper. "David Kyle's gone mad! He's hiding in this house!"

The blood was pounding in my forehead. "Go on and phone," I roared at him.

He went down, sent Ellison up. I set Ellison between the two staircases. Then I turned to Menocal's room. My patience with the Spaniard was at an end. It was clear he knew something. The fact that he didn't trust me or Marx with his information was no longer of the slightest consequence. If I had to beat it out of him, I was prepared to do it. I stepped into his room.

"Get up, Menocal!" I rapped at him. He made not the slightest sign that

he heard me. He was still lying on his side. The magazine was no longer visible over his shoulder. I saw red. I reached the bed in two strides, grabbed him by the shoulder. Asleep, I thought. The damned nerve of . . . I shook him hard. "Get up, you—"

His shoulder was limp in my hand. His head flopped over toward me. His eyes were wide open; his face, putty-colored. A gasp smothered itself in my throat.

I plunged my hand under his dressing gown, felt his heart; then his pulse.

It was no use. Menocal wasn't asleep. He was dead—stone dead.

And I caught a faint whiff of bitter almonds.

I felt panic racing over me. Five minutes before Menocal had been fully, insolently, alive. Since then he had not been for one instant out of sight of either Marx or myself. He had been murdered while in plain view of either one of us!

There was sweat on my forehead. I stood staring down at the dead face, almost in a daze.

Then something glistened on his cheek. I snapped myself together, leaned down. There was a tiny piece of glass imbedded in the dead flesh.

Hastily, I lifted the corpse to a sitting position. More faint slivers of glass lined the edge of the pillow. I turned back the pillow, held my breath, and jerked my head back as a smell of the hydrocyanic came up at me. After a moment, I looked again.

It was all too apparent what had happened. Somebody had put one or more fragile glass globes of the deadly poison under Menocal's pillow-edge. As he lay down, the weight of his head was more than enough to shatter them. The amount of gas instantly released would have killed three men. Somebody had been in Menocal's room while he was in Mrs. Kyle's!

Involuntarily my eyes flew round the

walls. They seemed solid, ordinary. If there were a secret entrance to this room, it was concealed with the devil's own skill.

The idea had been in my head for hours. Now, at this moment, I was driven absolutely to it—David Kyle, a raving maniac, was hidden, somewhere in the house and the disease in his brain had turned to murder madness!

But where was Pearson? Where was D'Aguido?

I laid Menocal back on the bed, walked out the door and closed it behind me. The big ox, Ellison, looked at me, and his jaw fell. I guess I was looking pretty queer. I said nothing to him, walked downstairs, and told the sheriff.

CHAPTER SEVEN

Phantoms of the Fog

IT WAS no longer possible to spare the feelings of the people in the house. We didn't tell them Menocal was dead, but we went through every room on the second floor with grim, deadly earnestness. I told Marx nothing about the manila envelope, but I followed him on the search, and if it had been in any of the places we looked, I would have found it, but it wasn't. And I didn't really expect it would be.

We found nothing. Inch by inch, we tapped the walls of Menocal's room, Kyle's and even Crane's, but nothing came of this effort. In the morning, with measuring instruments, we might do better. Tonight, till dawn, there was absolutely nothing to do but stalk silently up and down the hall, praying that no more tragedy would strike.

Five o'clock came, and with it, the coroner again. Then it was no longer possible to conceal from the others what had happened. Mrs. Kyle collapsed. Dr. Ease gave her a shot in the arm. With every ounce of will power we possessed, Marx

and I fought down hysteria in that house, as the frantic fear of death turned everyone half insane.

The morgue wagon rattled up, performed its grisly function, went away again.

Then the dawn—at six o'clock. A cold, wet dawn, the fog still rolling dismally, obscuring the sun with a faint gray haze.

At ten minutes to seven the phone rang for Marx. Someone had located the flivver in which the Italian, Ricigliano was presumed to have escaped. It was turned over, wrecked in a ditch, about twenty miles the other side of Oakville. There was no sign of either occupant or trunk.

At eight the coroner called, to say he would hold an inquest on both Martin Kyle and Menocal at ten o'clock, in his office, and would we all please be there.

That finished Marx. He tried to argue with the coroner, to get him to hold off the inquest. I guess Ease made some nasty remarks about Menocal's murder under our very noses. Anyway, he made it plain that he wanted to get the case into the hands of the county prosecutor's office as soon as possible, and that the inquest would be when he said it would, and that was all there was to it.

Marx came to the foot of the stairs and in a dull, dead voice asked me to come down, and told me about it. He sat on a chair, licked to a splinter. There was more of a problem in this than appears at first. Ellison was the only one in the house that wouldn't have to go. Marx was faced with either leaving the house in care of the one man, or else locating some new deputies by telephone—an almost impossible task at this hour. He thought it was impossible at any rate.

"But I'm afraid I'll have to do it," he said. "I guess maybe Ellison can handle it."

I went on back upstairs to my post. While I was talking to Marx, I had touched the druggist's label in my inside coat pocket. I hadn't forgotten about it, but from the time it had started seeming important, till now, there hadn't been any opportunity to check up on it. I took it out and re-examined it. It was the most important lead—the only one, as a matter of fact—that I had. There were a few figures and meaningless letters in the upper corner. It seemed a strong probability that the druggist would be able to name both the purchaser, and the contents of the container from which the label had come.

And there was no doubt in my mind as to where I had got the label. It had been lying in the rumble seat of Harold Crane's car when I had put my bag in there, and it had stuck to my bag when I took it out.

If that label should prove to have come, say, from a bottle of hydrocyanic acid, it would be something that could not be explained away. Who had bought it? Crane, was the most logical guess. Was Crane's the diseased mind behind all this wanton killing? Reluctantly, I had to admit that he could hardly have done the murder of Martin Kyle—yet that did not clear him of Menocal's death. And, like every single one of the possible suspects, he had had the opportunity to be the black-hooded one that attacked me and retrieved the trust company's envelope.

Mrs. Kyle? Louise Kyle? The maids, even? In cold hard fact, there was nothing to say that one of them had not been the person beneath the black hood, save my impression of more than normal feminine strength. And any one of them could have set the death trap for Menocal.

But every one of those people had what looked like an unshakable alibi to clear them of the death of Martin Kyle.

Any of them could have killed Menocal. None of them could have killed Martin Kyle. Any of them could have made the original theft of the trust-company letter from my pocket. Any of them might have donned the black hood, and made the attack on me, to recover the letter a second time.

Then the question rose: were both Martin Kyle and the Spaniard Menocal murdered by the same person? And the answer was: there isn't a shred of evidence to show that they were.

Allow the idea of secret rooms, secret passages in the house, and it opened up two very clear lines. Pearson, for one. For the second, that which led to a homicidal maniac, hidden in his home, slaughtering, one by one, his family, whom he hated—the line that led to David Kyle.

And then of course there was the Italian, D'Aguido. If there were secret rooms, if the bottle could be traced to the Italian—

I jammed my hands in my pockets, and went downstairs. I smelt coffee and went out into the kitchen and got a cup. There was breakfast served, a little later for those that wanted any.

AT about nine, Mrs. Kyle and Miss Kyle, their faces pasty against their black clothes, came downstairs with their suitcases. The little deputy Hayes was to drive them to the hotel in the village, where they were to stay, under his guard. Marx had decided to get them out of the house and keep them out. Marx himself was taking the two maids, and the bundle of fingerprints and other evidence. Crane seemed to be left to me. That suited me all right.

Hayes and the Kyle women left first. Then the sheriff and the maids. Then Crane and I.

Oakville was the other way from the air field. Crane drove quickly, silently, along the sticky road. He only spoke once before we reached Oakville. "What —how are you going to handle it after the inquest?" he asked.

I said I didn't know—it was up to the sheriff.

We rolled into the outskirts of the town in about fifteen minutes. I looked at my watch. We'd made just a little too good time, for my purpose. The sheriff wouldn't have had time yet to sit down in his office. I made excuses to keep Crane driving me around for five or ten minutes. The fog was so thick we could only see the stores directly abreast of us as we passed. I had the label in my hand in my pocket, and I was squirming with impatience. I didn't want to ask Crane to drive me directly to the drug store. If he *had* been the purchaser of the bottle of acid, it might give the whole show away. Finally I asked him to drive me to the sheriff's office. He seemed to know where it was.

The sheriff's car was parked in front of a grocery store. "I think it's upstairs over that store." Crane said.

I got out, and he did, too. I looked questioningly at him, was going to tell him to stay there, but he waved toward the store. "I'll get some cigars. Will you be long?"

I said I didn't think so, and we split. He went into the store and I ran up a flight of wooden steps. Marx and a couple of men I hadn't seen before were there. Marx was fussing with the evidence. A conversation stopped as I went in.

Marx said: "Hello."

I handed him the druggist's label. "Do you know the man that runs that store?"

"Sure. Charley Rouse. Why?"

"Can you phone him right now and ask him what that label was stuck on, originally? Also who bought it—whatever it was, and also whether he has sold any other—that is, any hydrocyanic acid in the last few months?"

His mouth opened. He looked respect-

fully at the label. "Where'd you get this?"

"Found it. Call him in a hurry, will you?"

He reached for the phone, called the number from memory. When he got an answer, he held a short conversation, read off the hieroglyphics on the label, then put one hand over the mouthpiece. "He's looking," he nodded quickly. "He says he can tell. Where did you find this?"

"At the house," I said.

"Who had it? Say, this will tie somebody into the . . . Hello, Charley. Yeah, Who? . . . Oh, yeah, yeah, I know. Crane. Sure, sure, but what was in it? Was it hydro . . . what? Oh, hell, wait a minute." He put his hand over the mouthpiece, looked at me disgustedly. "It was a bottle of alcohol for Crane's car."

And that cleared the boards. My last piece of evidence had blown up in my face.

I mumbled something or other to Marx, and my face was red as a beet. I backed out, closed the door behind me, went slowly down the steps, my hands in my pockets. Licked? No, I wasn't licked, but I don't mind admitting I was stumped. There wasn't a cursed thing to get your teeth in. The whole gruesome affair was like the rolling fog—melting into nothing whichever way I turned, yet full of very real and ugly menace.

CRANE emerged from the grocery store, as I crossed the sidewalk. We both consulted watches. Mine showed twenty-five past nine. We climbed in the car. Crane asked, "Coroner's office?"

I shook my head. There were still about twenty minutes before we had to start for the coroner's. "Just sit here a minute." I said.

Somewhere in my head, there was one of those ideas floating around that you can't quite put your finger on. I sat there, trying to get it. Something I had seen, or maybe heard, trying to blossom. And I couldn't quite catch it. I racked my brain to locate some angle I'd overlooked. But it just wouldn't come. I tried a dozen lines of reasoning, but they all led back inevitably to the house on the hill. Slowly, but with maddening certainty, I was backing into the theory that the house must be honeycombed with secret passages. It was a pill I didn't want to swallow, but damn it, I had to! Why didn't I like it? Well, for one reason —it smacked too much of crime plays and motion pictures.

I asked Crane: "How long have the Kyle's been living here?"

He looked surprised. "About a year, I guess. Maybe a month more."

"Where were they before that?"

He mentioned an address in New Jersey.

"Did they own the house in New Jersey?"

"No, they had rented it from some people named Davidson."

I chewed on that. I didn't quite know what I was driving at, myself. "How long did they live in that house?"

"About eighteen months."

"When they came here, did Kyle have any alterations made in the house?"

Crane frowned over that one. "It seems to me he did," he said finally. "As—as I told you. he moved very suddenly. I went to New Jersey and cleaned up after him, so I'm not sure, but I believe he had Mrs. Kyle and Louise stay at the inn here for a while, while he got the house in shape."

I knew now what I was driving at. And it seemed kind of feeble at that. I asked him: "Were there any secret passages in the house in New Jersey—or secret rooms, or anything of that sort?"

His eyes widened. "Why—why, I don't know, I'm sure. I didn't see any."

"Would you have seen them, do you think, if they were there?"

He hesitated. "Well, that's hard to say. I was there alone for nearly a week, but I wasn't looking for anything like that, of course. I—well, I don't know. No, I guess."

"Is there a telegraph office near here?"

"Why, yes. We wired you from—"

"Let's go there. It's a long chance," I explained patiently, "but I'm going to wire these people Davidson and see if they found any secret construction in the house after Kyle left there. I don't know much about insane people, but I do know that they repeat themselves over and over again in things like that. It's worth the price of a telegram, anyway."

Crane located the telegraph office in the fog. We went inside. I wired my office girl, Tam Cotter, giving her the address which Crane wrote out for me, and asking her to find out if any secret chambers of any kind had been discovered in the house after Kyle had vacated it.

As we went out again Crane gave me a worried look that said as plainly as words that he thought I was slipping.

We opened the car doors together, and my eyes popped open. So did his.

On the seat lay a dirty white envelope. Scrawled in pencil was: "To the detective from New York."

I turned it over. On a plain white sheet of paper inside, in the same scrawl, I read: "If you want Frank Ricigliano, look in the old church by Marsh's corners." The note was unsigned.

CHAPTER EIGHT

Satan's Sanctuary

I FELT a warm feeling run through me. I said, "Saved!" and handed it to Crane. I was already thinking miles ahead. A trap? Of course it was a trap! How the man who wanted to trap me had managed to drop the note in our car at the right moment was one of the things I didn't worry about. He had long since proved himself the master opportunist of all time.

When Crane read the note, he went white as a sheet. When he looked up, his eyes were saffron. "This—this must be D'Aguido," he said, hoarsely.

"Sure," I said. "Where is a hardware store—fast?"

"Wait—wait—the sheriff, Blue. We'd better get the sheriff, at once."

"Why?"

He licked his lips. "Listen, Blue," he said desperately, "if this is D'Aguido, he's—he's a dangerous man—a killer, Blue. I tell you, I know him better than—"

"Where is this church? Do you know?"

"No."

"Where can we find out? Or wait—is there a hardware store around?" My mind was racing now.

"There—there's a hardware store, yes. But—"

"Get there—in a hurry!" I snapped at him.

He started to speak, caught my eye, swallowed, and drove down the street.

The hardware store was a ramshackle ex-barn, fitted with glass show windows. There was a confectioner's on one side of it and a public garage on the other. As I sprang out I pointed to the garage. "Go and see if they know where that church is," I snapped at him.

The old man that ran the hardware store was polishing stock on a shelf. He looked at me over glasses, inquiringly.

"A box of thirty-eight automatic cartridges—blank. Pistol." I said.

He wrinkled his forehead. "Blank?"

"What I said."

He produced them.

While he was in the rear of the shop making change I took one of the two guns from under my armpits, ejected the bullets from the clip, and filled it with blanks. I dropped the gun in my side-coat pocket. The rest of the blanks I deposited in a barrel of nails by the counter. When he gave me my change I asked about the church but he was very vague about it.

Crane was still talking to the garage men as I got into the car again. I took my second gun from my armpit holster, slid it down behind the upholstery of the seat. Crane finally left the man he was talking to, came slowly toward the car.

"You get it?" I asked.

"Yes, I—yes, I got it, but—"

"Climb in."

He got in heavily, hesitated. "Damn it, Blue," he blurted, "we're supposed to go to an inquest. We'll both get into trouble—even if we don't get our heads blown off. Why, in the name of Heaven, won't you get the sher—"

"Start this car," I said grimly, "and drive to that church. Never mind any more conversation. I'll look after you."

He flushed, opened his mouth, closed it again, banged the door. He let in the clutch, swung back toward the Kyle house, put on speed, and we rolled through the fog-laden town, in silence. When we hit the gravelled highway, I said: "Step on it."

WE rolled and bumped over the uneven road. The speedometer steadily climbed. Crane sat tight-jawed, looking straight ahead. I sat on the edge of my seat, smoking a cigarette, a mounting excitement in my blood.

A trap! Queer as it may seem, the thought sent a warm glow through me. Why? Because it meant that I was treading on the killer's heels. There could be no other answer. Just how, I didn't know. But I had forced his hand, had forced him in some way to change his plans.

That it was his intention to murder me was beyond doubt. How, I didn't know, and I made a guess that he didn't have the details planned either. That wasn't his style. He had proved himself a Simon-pure opportunist. All right. I'd give him an opportunity he couldn't resist. I'd give him a chance to add to his murders. In short, if he wanted a crack at Cass Blue, Cass Blue would give it to him—in exchange for the one thing I had almost despaired of getting—contact with the murderer of Martin Kyle and Menocal. In the desperate frame of mind in which the note had caught me, the thousand-to-one chance it offered had seemed like a gift from the gods. Any chance would have. I wasn't fooling myself; I knew that he'd start with a deadly advantage—but whether he could hold it or not was something else. Maybe two could play at his game of opportunity.

Presently we slowed down. Crane peered to the left, looking for a side road that led to the church. We were almost by, before we saw it—an arrow sign that said: "Marsh's Corners." Crane turned in. It was a bumpy dirt road, past an occasional meadow, and an occasional clump of trees. We drove for three or four minutes. Then Crane cleared his throat. "We—we must be near it. Shall—"

"Drive within fifty yards of the church, if you can," I said, "and don't take the keys from the ignition when we get out."

We puttered along. The fog hid everything at twenty yards distance. Finally Crane came to a sudden stop. He pointed to a footpath leading from the road. "I think—we must be here," he said in a husky voice.

I got out quietly. He hesitated, then got out, too, stood with his hands in topcoat pockets, shivering. His face was almost saffron. I took the gun from my side-coat pocket. His eyes fastened on it, and he licked his lips. I said: "Come on," and started up the path. He grabbed at my arm, checked me.

"Mr. Blue—" he said desperately, "if —if that is the man I think it is, he— he's been searching for me, too—for twenty years—to kill me . . . I am unarmed. If—if—"

"Take it easy," I said. "All I want you to do is stay away from the car. Just do as I tell you and you won't be hurt."

We went silently up the path. I tried to peer through the rolling fog, but it was too heavy. And then suddenly the wooden frame of the long-disused church loomed out of the fog right in front of us. I stopped.

It was square, crumbling, with a pointed roof and a little belfry. Once there had been white paint on the walls, but now not much of it remained. The outside gleamed with moisture; the windows were board-covered. I said quietly to Crane: "Go round to the back. If there is a rear door, you can keep an eye on that and shout if anyone tries to get out. But whatever you do—stay where you are until I call your name. Things may happen. They don't concern you. If you feel too alarmed, go for the sheriff, but don't break in on my party. Is that clear?"

His eyes were bewildered. He nodded. "Go on, then."

HE turned and groped his way out and around the church. The fog swallowed him. I waited two or three minutes, then closed in on the little building. At the top of the rotting steps was a vestibule. The outer door was closed, but the latch had long since fallen off. I went up the steps, got my fingers on the edge of the door, pried it slowly open. The inner door was closed too. I slipped inside, drew the outer one carefully to behind me, putting myself in pitch blackness. Carefully, I made the inner door, put my hand against it. It was unfastened. I eased on pressure slowly. It creaked once, then swung easily inward. I dropped to my knees, crawled carefully through into the musty church.

There wasn't a sound, and the inside was as black as the vestibule for a minute. Then my eyes got accustomed to the gloom, and I made out objects. A row of fat white pillars down the center of the church. A broken chair to my right. An accumulated pile of dirt to the left. And high up in the back of the one-room building, a faint patch of luminosity that might be an old stained-glass window.

For a long minute I crouched there motionless. I couldn't hear a sound. Then, as I started to get to my feet, someone moved, far to the right, and ahead of me.

Feet moved across the floor. I was astonished. Anything that smacked less of a trap was hard to imagine. Automatically, I was on my feet, darting noiselessly toward the front of the church, in the shadow of the pillars.

A match rasped, burst into flame, and I flattened myself. The flame moved directly toward me. Still puzzled, I sidled round the pillar to try and keep in the shadow. The flame became stationary, brighter. I risked a look.

A gaunt, stocky-looking Italian stood before the remnants of the altar, setting a candle upright in its own grease. His face was covered with a black beard, his hair was unkempt and dirty, under an old hat. There was a dirty bandanna around his neck. His eyes were wild, the candlelight catching leaping glints in them.

I couldn't make myself believe that the tip-off had been on the level. Neither could I believe that this giant was playing a part. Either way, the die was cast. There was only one thing for me to do, and I did it. I stepped silently into the aisle and rapped: "Reach, D'Aguido!"

He made a queer sound in his throat as he whirled on me, one hand diving for his waistband. I leaped forward, jammed the muzzle of my gun into his face, clamped down on his wrist, hard.

"Steady!" I clipped. "I'll take it."

He stared cross-eyed at the gun against his face. His grip on the knife relaxed. I whisked it out, threw it clattering into a corner. "Now get your hands up!"

I stepped back as his hands went slowly upward. "What you want?" he threw at me hoarsely.

"I want you, D'Aguido, for murder."

Fire sprang into his eyes. For a second I thought he was going to jump me, and then his eyes flickered. "Come on!" I snapped. "Get going—out!"

I stepped back, to leave him room to pass me, started to gesture with my gun. And then I felt a hand suddenly snake up under my armpit, clamp up and around the back of my neck, jerking my gun muzzle skyward, and—for the second time in twenty-four hours—the razor-edge of the killer's knife was against my throat. A tense, hoarse voice hissed in my ear: "Drop the gun, Blue! Quick!"

I dropped it. D'Aguido's hands came down. He burst into a torrent of angry Italian. The black-hooded one snapped a sentence at him, and he paused. The hooded one clipped in my ear: "Raise your hands."

I raised them. The Italian burst out anew. My captor rapped a few words back at him. D'Aguido came toward me, scooped up my fallen gun, and stuck it in his waist, then searched me quickly. He collected my meagre belongings, stepped back and held them up, for inspection. They spoke a few sentences back and forth. I had my eyes on the Italian's face. This was the touchy point. If they decided to kill me here—I'd die like a dog, and there was nothing I could do about it. But they didn't. The Italian stuffed the contents of my pockets in one of his, stepped back—and his eyes winced, just a little. He might as well have written me a letter. I loosed my knee joints, relaxed my neck muscles, in the instant that the blackjack crashed down on my skull from behind.

There was a blinding flash of light in my brain. I let myself sag, sway forward, and flopped on my face and lay still, groggy, but not quite out.

I KEPT my eyes closed. D'Aguido said surprisingly in English: "What's happened? How did he—"

"Grab him—I'll explain later. There's a car at the road with the keys in the ignition; we'll use that. Get out of here as fast as you can with him. I think there's someone else around. Hurry it up!"

I felt myself lifted, swung over the Italian's shoulder like a bag of flour. As though the thing had been rehearsed a thousand times, we marched quietly, quickly to the door, out, and along the path. We came to the car in a minute or two. The hooded one opened the door, and I was pushed into the seat. A hand grabbed me and held me upright, till they got in, one on either side of me.

"Jerk the hat down over his eyes."

D'Aguido performed that function. The car started. We rolled away quietly.

"Who is this?" D'Aguido asked.

"A private detective. Blue his name is. He's the one I told you was coming."

"How in hell did he get into the church and you right behind—"

"The idiot stumbled onto something—the one thing that would give the show away. I had to get him out of the way somehow. It's bad enough as it is. I left a note where he'd see it, telling him you were hiding in the church. I knew he couldn't resist it. Then when he came in, stuck right behind him, and when he held you up, I took him. He's got to

be put away—put away right now."

"You mean—" I couldn't see the Italian's gesture but I knew what it was all right.

"Yes. I've phoned for a plane. It'll be at the air field in half an hour. There's a hornet's nest going to break open in about an hour, and we've got to get the stuff and get out. The other plans will have to go by the board."

"What's the program?"

"I'll let you off by the rock. You can dispose of this dick—put him in bed with the other one. I'll go on up the hill and get the stuff—"

"How? I thought you said—"

"The hell with what I said. I've got some nitroglycerine in my bag. If I have to, I'll blow the whole damned house to hell. Get it into your head, D'Aguido—we're on the run—due to this damned Blue. If we move like lightning, we'll be over the border in an hour, with the stuff—and then we're all in the clear. If we don't, we'll both hang. That's all there is to it. As soon as you've finished with—him—you come up and wait where the private roadway joins the highway, and I'll pick you up as I come out. And don't waste any time, understand?"

"How long will you be?"

"Not more than ten minutes in the house. I may have to shoot my way in. Here—" he handed something to the Italian—"throw that in with his body."

The car suddenly slackened speed. Then we turned to the left, slushed into trees, stopped. "Get going!" the hooded one clipped.

The Italian opened his door, dragged me out, and once more threw me over his shoulder. Without another word, he turned and started at a dog trot through high, wet grass.

The gun from behind the upholstery in the car was now resting snugly in my hip pocket.

CHAPTER NINE

The Man in the Hood

A MINUTE later I caught the sound of running water. I had my hat worked pretty well back off my eyes by now. I took a look. We were beside the bed of a small stream. Twenty yards farther on, without any warning, D'Aguido suddenly let go of me. I nearly bit the end of my tongue off as I flopped to the ground. For a second he stood still, breathing heavily, then spat in my face and stepped over toward the stream. I opened my eyes. Where we were the stream was not more than twenty yards across. A few yards upstream there was a huge bowlder. D'Aguido made for this bowlder.

I watched, puzzled. The rock was of such size that it seemed impossible one man could budge it, but some trick of balancing made it movable. As D'Aguido put his shoulder to it, it swung out hinge-like, quite easily, till a two-foot gap was opened between it and the bank.

D'Aguido looked down the crack, then wiped his forehead on a grimy sleeve. I rose silently to my feet. When he turned, he looked down the barrel of my gun. I said: "Just hold it, D'Aguido!"

For a split second, he stood as though paralyzed, one foot uplifted. Then he blurted *"Madre!"* and with a single, lithe, twisting motion flung himself into the shelter of a tree trunk, his hand diving for his waistband. The gun flashed out—the one I had so painstakingly planted on him—and almost in the instant he leaped, it roared. Three blasting reports stammered out before he took his finger from the trigger. I roared: "Stop it, you fool! They're nothing but blanks in it . . . " and with an angry snarling curse, his other hand came up and over, and I caught the flash of light on the hissing knife blade as it streaked through the air.

I threw myself awkwardly to one side. The knife flashed past; my foot slipped on the slimy grass, and I lit on my back. I roared: "Stop—or—" but there was no stopping him. When he was ten feet away—I was up on one elbow—I let him have it in the shoulder.

Thirty-eight slugs aren't heavy, but at that distance they hit like an express train. I whirled him completely around before he fell. I was on my feet in a minute. I leaped forward, slashed him with the muzzle of my gun, hard, across the head. He shrieked a curse at me. I hit him again. He groaned. I hit him once more and he lay still.

I grabbed up the gun he had dropped, jammed it into a shoulder holster and ran for one look at the crevice between the rock and the bank. I was pretty sure by now, what I should find there. And I was right. I turned away, sickened by the smell, stepped over D'Aguido—and stopped. There was a small black ball a few inches from his hand. It struck me that this was probably the object the black-hooded one had told him to drop in with my body. I picked it up. It appeared to be a length of black fishline wound on a small rubber cylinder. I had no time now to figure it out. I dropped it in my pocket, took a quick look at the ground, located the tracks we had left on the wet grass coming in, and broke into a run.

I WAS halfway across the clearing, feeling damn pleased with myself, when the silence split open with the crashing report of a gun. A red-hot cannonball burned through the fleshy part of my leg, and I dived headlong into the ground, my face plowing up a furrow. I spun like an eel, threw up my gun—and saw nothing. A stentorian voice from the fog shouted excitedly: "Drop your gun! Put your hands up!"

If I could have seen him, I would cheerfully have pumped my gun empty into his imbecile carcass, but I couldn't. I roared: "You damn fool, Pearson. This is Blue!" and he came stumbling into the clearing, a look of frightened astonishment on his bovine face.

"Blue—my God—how—where—"

"Don't stand there you fool!" I yelled in fury. "Come here! Give me your handkerchief!"

He stumbled toward me, fishing in his breast pocket. "God Blue—I'm sorry! Cripes, listen—Blue—you know yourself Marx was out to frame me. I didn't have a chance. I bust out an' I happen to think of this place. I tailed D'Aguido here once. I been waitin' here—then I hear gun-play, and how was I to—"

I had my trouser leg rolled up; the slug had gone right through. It was painful but I can take it—when I have to. "Give me a piece of stick!" I clipped at him.

I made a combination tourniquet and bandage and tightened it around the wound. It stung like fury. I got up, walked around a little, hastily. "All right," I said, "you wait here—and watch the Dago—over there! And don't you move out of here or I'll have you lynched. You get it?"

"Yeah, yeah," he said anxiously. "But listen—I tailed this guy here—I would of caught him if you hadn't come. You'll —you'll gimme a break on the reward, huh Blue?"

I couldn't think for a moment which I'd rather do—stay here and murder this guy or go after the triple killer. I howled: "Reward! Why, you blithering fool, if I hear another peep out of you about reward, I'll jug you for obstructing justice, accessory after the fact and about a dozen other charges that'll hold you in the local can the rest of your life. You stay here —and thank God you're alive!" And I turned and ran.

He shouted after me: "Hey—where you going?" but I didn't take time to answer.

I CAME out on the gravelled highway. For just a minute I was stumped. A bank of fog ended my line of sight in both directions at about twenty yards. Then I realized the slope of the ground. It was upward to my left. I jogged along that way, found myself making a wide spiral, and gasped my relief. I was less than a quarter of a mile from the Kyle house!

It was a tough run uphill, and with a wounded leg. The bandage slipped twice but I fixed it and increased my speed to make up for it. Then, as the bulk of the house loomed, through the fog, I stopped. I saw Crane's car in the driveway, and went over and ripped the ignition wires loose. I stood there a minute, panting, till I got my breath back.

I hurried to the porch, listened. I could hear no sound. On tiptoe, I hastenend along the porch to the front door. It was swinging open. And from the arched doorway of the living room, protruded a foot!

I was inside in a second. Ellison was lying unconscious on the living-room floor, blood from a scalp cut staining one side of his face. He was breathing regularly. I left him, crept to the foot of the stairs, undecided.

Then from underneath my feet came a *clank, clank!*

I said "So!" to myself, and shot like a cat toward the kitchen, my rubber-soled shoes noiseless.

The door to the cellar was ajar an inch.

Carefully, I eased it fully open. The clanking sound went on for a minute, then ceased. I stood tense, my hand on one of the guns in my shoulder holsters, afraid I'd been heard. Then came a grunting sound, and a scuffling footstep from below.

I reached for the first step with a tentative foot. The scuffling continued in the cellar. I tested the top step for creaks, found none, went down another, then another. I crouched down, tried to peer between the steps of the stairs. I could see a dim filtration of light, and that was all. The furnace bulged out near the top, and that cut off my view.

Halfway down, I could just see a black foot—and the bottom of the black hood, moving in and out of view.

I was two steps from the bottom before I could actually see what was taking place. There was an immense pile of vegetables of all kinds strewn around the floor. There was dust over everything. A light shone out from a small closet-like room. The vegetable cellar, I concluded.

And on a table was a coil of insulated wire, on a small drum, and a queer plunger-like instrument that I could not identify at first. As my eyes got keener, I saw that the other end of the wire ran into the vegetable cellar. And at that moment, the man in the hood emerged from the closet-like room. In his hand was a portable electric lamp. He set it high on a window ledge and suddenly I realized what the plunger signified.

Amateur-like, he had rigged up a device similar to that used for setting off dynamite in mines! Apparently, he was going to blow the house up! And then two things checked me— the memory of his mention of nitroglycerin in the automobile—and his declaration that he was seeking certain stuff in the house and that if he had to, he would blow the house up to get it. There was only one answer to that. The "stuff" whatever it was, was imbedded under the concrete floor or in the walls of the cellar.

THE man in the hood had picked up the plunger, was backing toward the door that led to the yard, the wire from the drum slowly unwinding in his hand. I shot a hasty look below me, found that what I had thought was the bottom of the stairs was only a supplementary landing—the stairs turned at right angles and continued down for another few steps. There were half a dozen empty packing boxes around the foot. I started down, slowly, cautiously—and the man in the black hood turned toward me, set the plunger on the floor, fussing with it.

I didn't think he had seen me and I saw no reason to wait any longer. I grabbed a gun out of my shoulder holster, jumped lightly to the landing—my foot suddenly crunched fragile glass, lots of it, and in one flash I realized what it was.

The man in the hood, the cyanide killer, had distributed a quantity—probably all of his remaining supply of the glass globes of hydrocyanic gas—on the landing of the stairs. I had a tenth of a second to act before the fumes reached me—and I acted blindly. I leaped—as far to the right as I could—and landed squarely on a packing box that was lying upside down.

The thin wood gave way with a cracking and a rending, and I hit the floor—up to my knees in the box, but I had a gun trained on the man in the black hood. And in that moment, he leaped too.

"Raise 'em," I snapped, "I'm not fooling with you. You stand a better chance with a judge and jury and a lawyer than you do with me. Get 'em up, or—"

"Notice where I'm standing, Blue!" he cut in, coolly. I did. He was standing crouched over the plunger of the infernal machine he had rigged up. I'll give him credit. He was the fastest thinker I've ever seen. "Shoot me," he went on, "and I'll fall on this plunger—and the chances are that the whole house will come down on your ears. I've a charge of nitro in there and I'm going outside to explode it. I don't know—it may just rip out a piece of the wall. That's what I hope. But I haven't enough faith in my own judgment of the proper dose to stay here and take a chance. If you have—then shoot me! And understand—I'm desperate. There's nothing you can do to me as bad as what'll happen to me if I'm caught. You know that. I'm going through with what I say—you can bank on it. Now—throw me that gun!"

"What do you think I am—crazy?" I said, and jammed the gun into my armpit holster. I kept my hand inside my coat though.

"Throw it here—or so help me God—I'll touch this blast off!

Hurry—or—" and I saw his hand close down on the handle of the plunger.

"All right, all right!" I shouted, with as much terror as I could manage to get into it. "Don't—don't—"and I sent the gun skidding across the floor. It stopped twenty yards from where he was. He made a queer sound in his throat, darted for it—and left the plunger.

His hand was closing on the butt, when my finger tightened on the trigger of my other gun—the one with real bullets in it—the one I'd switched on him when my hand was inside my coat. I shot him through the right leg. He screamed with pain; his leg buckled and he slammed back against the wooden outer wall of the vegetable cellar. His gun burst into roaring flame.

I guess he must have thought a miracle had happened when I didn't fall. I let him exhaust the blanks. Then, as his hammer clicked on an empty shell, he flung it wildly at me and dived toward the all-important plunger.

I shot his left leg from under him. He dropped like a sack of potatoes.

"Just lie there," I said quietly. "Till Ellison comes round. He'll probably make a tour of investigation when he does. I won't kill you—I'm saving you for the hangman—but I'll shoot your

hands off if you try crawling. Now be quiet."

For the hell of the matter was that I was imprisoned as neatly as a fish in a net. Try jumping through the top of a thin wooden box. The damned boards go down with you, and form a nice little hedge around your legs. If you try to pull your leg up, particularly if you've got a badly sprained ankle, and I'd got one when I'd jumped—well just try it. I was wedged in properly.

So we just sat there.

A S a matter of fact it wasn't Ellison that came finally. It was the two strangers I had seen in Marx's office. He had been swearing them in at the moment I'd appeared to ask about the label. They arrived—it couldn't have been more than fifteen minutes afterward. The man in the black hood had lost consciousness. The knee joints are terribly painful places to be hit.

It was a blessed relief to me to hear footsteps overhead. I shouted and they came piling down the stairs.

"Careful!" I called, "there's globes of poison gas on the little landing there.

"Hell," one of them said, "it's that detective from New York. What's happened? What are you—"

"Help me out of this damned box, and I'll tell you everything," I said.

They came down, gingerly, fingering guns.

"It's all right, boys," I said, "the case is all washed up. Get me out of here and let me phone the sheriff."

They looked at each other, finally tore the box apart and let me out. I pointed to the dark blob on the floor that was the hooded man. "Just keep your eye on him," I said. "One of you can come up with me, while I phone, if you're still suspicious."

They were staring wide-eyed at the motionless figure.

"What—is it, a man?" one of them said inanely.

"Sure. It's Harold Crane—and he's got three murders against him. Come on upstairs."

I found my leg was practically numb, but I limped up, the shorter of the two helping me along.

"You know the coroner's number?" I asked him.

He did. I called it. When I got the coroner on the wire, I said "This is Cass Blue. I've got your killer here—and the whole story. Adjourn your inquest, and bring everybody here. Send some men to pick up that detective, Pearson—and another *corpus delicti*—David Kyle— at a spot about quarter of a mile east of here on the highway. I can't locate it for you exactly, but there's a stream . . . Eh?"

He said he knew where I meant.

"O. K. And bring a stonecutter with you with an electric drill. You might also stop by the telegraph office and see if there's any wire happened to come in for me yet." I hung up.

The deputy was staring at me in astonishment. "David Kyle—dead?"

"Yep," I said. "Let's go back down."

We went back down. Behind the table I found what I needed—an open gladstone bag. And its contents were considerable. Crane had evidently collected everything incriminating at the last moment and dumped it into this bag.

There was a bottle of hydrocyanic acid, nearly gone. There were two more extra black hoods and cloaks, and a couple of the long, blued-steel knives, and the big Colt revolver, but it turned out to be empty—it had never been fired. And most gruesome of all—a gallon bell jar of alcohol—and floating in it, a hand, severed at the wrist—David Kyle's hand.

"You fellows will back me up that I shot this bird down and collared the evidence myself, won't you?" I said.

They said they would.

CHAPTER TEN

The Bloodstone

WE stood or sat in the living room of the Kyle house. Crane, his legs swathed in bandages, his face the color of marble, sat on a couch, his feet on an improvised stretcher. Only in his eyes was there any sign of life. D'Aguido, surly and in handcuffs, stood between Hayes and one of the deputies by the fireplace. Marx and the other deputies stood around the room. Ellison had a bandage around his head. I had one on my leg. Dr. Ease had put in a busy hour. And in my pocket reposed the manila envelope that the trust company had given me. I had found a necessary moment to slip it out of Crane's pocket. It had been opened.

In the centre of the table lay a miniature magnesium-steel safe. It had taken an expert stonemason almost an hour to cut into the concrete wall of the vegetable cellar to get it out.

I took from my pocket the manila envelope. I looked at Louise Kyle. "I was supposed to give this to you, unopened," I said, "but it has somehow become open. I hope you will forgive me. It contains only information of value to everyone in this room."

She stood right where she was. "What —what is it?"

"The combination to this safe—and a description of where it was hidden in the vegetable cellar. Also, a suggestion from your father as to what to do with— the thing inside. That you can figure out later. Shall I open the safe?"

"Yes. Yes."

I did. In a box of green lizard skin, the size of a collar box, resting on a bed of white velvet was a ruby. I've never seen anything like it. It was the shape roughly, of a heart—of perfect color, flawless, and larger than a turkey egg. Pure pigeon-blood.

"This is The Bloodstone," I said.

Marx had his mouth open. They were all gazing at the stone, fascinated. The coroner cleared his throat suddenly. "And —what has this—what is the story, Blue?"

I turned and looked at Crane. His eyes were fastened on the ruby, burning, fiery, a hungriness of twenty years in his white face. I took the ball of fishline from my pocket, tossed it up and down, till Crane's eyes shifted from the stone to it. He drew in breath sharply, then a slow, bitter smile twisted the corner of his mouth. His voice was infinitely tired.

"So you got even that, Blue," he said. "You're a very thorough young man."

"Kyle double-crossed you, didn't he?" I said.

He nodded. "Yes, he double-crossed me."

I turned to Dr. Ease. "Years ago, David Kyle and Crane went in on a plot together to steal this jewel. "But Crane was under the impression that the attempt was a total failure. As a matter of fact, Kyle actually got away with it. He never gave Crane his share of it. Is that right?" I was facing Crane again.

He smiled faintly. "Yes, that's right. You needn't use your persuasive tactics, Blue. I'll save you the trouble of guessing. I'm waiting to be hanged." He moved his eyes to the coroner.

"As Blue says, Kyle cheated me of my share of this stone. He also cheated D'Aguido there—" he nodded toward the Italian—"of his share and he killed D'Aguido's brother. Mr. Blue knows the details. The story I told you, Blue was substantially true—with the exceptions you see here now. D'Aguido has spent twenty years tracking Kyle down, with the intention—not simply of taking a revenge in blood, but of recovering that ruby. If you know the value of stones, you know that one is worth anything

from a hundred thousand to a quarter of a million. To make a long story short— Kyle has lived the life of a hunted man. Since he returned to this country, twenty years ago, he has lived in constant fear of D'Aguido here. For D'Aguido knew that he had the ruby. I, of course, did not.

"Each time Kyle saw, or thought he saw, D'Aguido, he would move overnight. I would come and clean up after him— send his belongings on to whatever new spot he chose to hide in. He employed private detectives by the score, and so did I, unbeknownst to him. You can understand that I too was in fear of the vengeance of this man.

"The last place in which Kyle lived was in New Jersey. It was when I went to perform my customary services there that I finally did locate this D'Aguido. I caught him as he was boarding a train to get out of town.

"I TOOK him back at the point of a gun to the house in which Kyle had been living, and then he told me that Kyle had had this ruby all the time, and that he, D'Aguido, wasn't worried much about his revenge—he wanted The Bloodstone.

"Then things began to dawn on me. Kyle was supposed to have been left a small legacy with which he speculated to make his fortune. I checked up, and found that this 'legacy' was a loan he had obtained on the stone. All my life I've had only moderate means while he has had the cream of everything. And half of what he had was mine.

"I plotted with D'Aguido to kill him. I came here and did it. It was then that I found out that you, Blue, were coming. I had to stage my act well, for I didn't underestimate your talents. There was one flaw in the situation—young Martin Kyle had come in on a conference that David Kyle and I were having, the night

I arrived. Frankly, I was trying to induce him to come outside. He did, later, and D'Aguido and I killed him and put his body in the place where you found it. I cut off his hand and put it in alcohol, solely for the purpose of creating the impression that he was still alive. But that you know—how I put his fingerprints on everything, and so forth.

"Anyway, there was the problem of the boy, but there was no use to take chances. He was a young rotter—a drunken, blasphemous swine anyhow, and I took rather a pleasure in killing him. As a matter of fact, I might not have done it, except that the method I used should have—save for the acumen of our friend Blue here—definitely made me the one person not suspected. For the only logical assumption that could be made was that one person had abducted Kyle, or murdered him, and had also murdered the son. By putting myself in the clear on one count, I felt that it would remove suspicion on both.

"And also, I wanted to terrorize the household so they would get out, and let me search for the ruby in peace. I knew it was here somewhere. I knew it would be very difficult to find, and still more difficult to secure. I had to be alone in the house to do it. I had a hunch where it would be, for in the basement of the Jersey house, there was a tremendous aperture left in the wall of the vegetable cellar after Kyle left.

"Before we had killed David Kyle, I had forced him to write that letter. I included my own name, so that I might appear even more innocent by divulging the secret to the authorities that the letter said I dared not reveal.

"When I heard that Blue was coming, it crystallized all my ideas. I planned and executed the murder—the perfect murder, if I do say so myself—if I had only burned that ball of fishline that Blue has there."

"I'll tell them how you did it," I interjected, "in a minute. How about Menocal —why did you kill him?"

"BECAUSE, if you had ever disclosed the fact that the trust-company envelope had been stolen from your pocket, and questioned everyone about it, Menocal would have given the evidence that would have betrayed me. If you remember, he ran up the stairs when Miss Kyle screamed. I had seen this envelope in your topcoat pocket downstairs, and I guessed that the reason you didn't remove your coat was that same envelope. So when you rushed out of the room, I grabbed the envelope as I followed you. Now before I had gotten out of sight of the front stairs, Menocal was standing there. He could have testified that nobody went into your room from the time I left it, till we all went downstairs. That would have branded me as the thief. It was a break for me that you didn't say anything about it. I hid the envelope under that rug, on my way downstairs a little later, for I expected, of course, that you would have the household searched. Then when I heard Menocal making those repeated attempts to get out of his room —I just made it a little easier for him by throwing that burning newspaper onto the window ledge to attract your attention. When he rushed out, as I figured he would, I ducked into his room and laid the trap for him, under his pillow. But you came back too quickly—before I could accomplish my secondary purpose— to get that letter back. I was in the shadow in the corner when you got it out for me—and I jumped you.

"The letter, as you see, mentions the hiding-place of the ruby and the combination of the safe. I thought the jewel as good as in my hands when you had to go and get a hunch about a similar hiding-place in the last house Kyle was in. You sent a wire requesting the information.

I see you have an answer there. What does it say?"

"Just what you expected," I answered. "It tells about the hole in the vegetable cellar."

"There you are, then. I knew that when that answer came through, I was sunk—that you would beat me to the jewel. By getting you out of the way, I would prevent the information getting out for at least another couple of hours, by which time I expected to be many miles from here but—it didn't work."

Marx could contain himself no longer. "But Martin Kyle!" he burst out. "Blue says you were with him when the boy was killed! How in the name of—"

"I'll tell you that," I said, and I produced my fishline. "Here is the murder weapon—or the most important part of it."

They looked at it in bewilderment. I looked back at Crane. "Correct me if I'm wrong.

"Martin Kyle was a drunkard. It was an easy matter for Crane to get him drunk, just before he was scheduled to start for the field to get me. He took him to his room, laid him, unconscious, with his head near the floor. You will recall that the head of the bed is only a couple of feet from the edge of the table opposite it. The waste basket is at the corner of the table.

"Crane had a small vial of this hydrocyanic acid. He had it corked with a rubber cork, so that he could pull the cork almost out before the fumes would start to escape. He balanced the small bottle on the edge of the table, just over the wastebasket, and saw that Martin Kyle's head was close to it. Close enough so that as the vial spilled into the wastebasket, enough of those deadly fumes would reach the boy to kill him.

"The crux of the situation was—this." I pointed once more to the fishline. "The black, thin thread was attached to the cork. Crane simply set up his arrangement, and dropped the other end of the line out the window, which was open a few inches. Then he threw the mask, the wadded handkerchief, in the corner for stage effect.

"Then when he drove me up and let me off at the steps, he drove the car into the garage, turned off the lights, and as he walked back to join me, he grabbed the end of the string that was hanging against the wall, jerked it. The cork came out of the bottle upstairs, the bottle fell into the waste basket and Martin Kyle was killed. Crane simply pulled the cork out through the window and pocketed it as he came toward me. There he was with the perfect alibi—in my sight, practically talking to me at the moment of the crime. Am I right, Crane?"

He said I was. I beckoned Miss Kyle over and showed her the bottom of her father's letter. It said that she ought to send the ruby to a certain man in Rione, Italy, as treasurer of this society he had stolen it from.

She tore the letter to bits, angrily. "Fat chance!" she said.

Crooks Carnival

by

Erle Stanley Gardner

Author of "Forged Kill," etc.

Skarle's fists rained left and right.

The local magnate had been robbed and both he and the chief of police knew it was a carnival job. They wanted a fall-guy to pin it on and Dane Skarle, Master of Magic, was the one they picked. But it takes more than a hick cop and a village big shot to stack cards against a sleight-of-hand expert.

CHAPTER ONE

Skarle & Co.

VERA Colma came in to Dane Skarle's dressing room without knocking. He looked up at her moodily and said nothing. She walked over to the little table, propped one hip against it, then slid her leg on it until she was half sitting on the table top, and made a wry face.

"Well," she said, "I let him have it!"

Dane Skarle straightened in his chair. Lights glinted in the black depths of his eyes. He looked the girl over from head to toe. She met his gaze defiantly for a minute, then lowered her eyes and regarded the leg which swung back and forth from the knee.

She was wearing her costume, a very short skirt, black stockings, with a bit of a white, lace-trimmed apron. Dane Skarle was attired in trousers, undershirt and slippers. He gave the impression of limitless energy being held in leash. When he glanced up there was almost a physical shock to the impact of his gaze.

"Why did you have to do that?" he asked, tonelessly.

"He insulted me," she said.

Dane Skarle sighed. "You've been insulted by experts," he said. "Every stage-door Johnny from here to the Pacific coast and back again, to say nothing of the guys you've met on trains, in hotels and on the street."

There seemed to be genuine curiosity in his voice, as though he were interested in the psychological reactions of the girl.

"He was so damned persistent," she said, "and I got so tired of it!"

She looked at him, winked her eyes rapidly. Two tears glinted the surfaces then crept, unheeded, down her cheeks.

Dane Skarle regarded the tears. "Don't," he said.

She swiped the back of her hand across her eyes, regarded the make-up which had rubbed off. She frowned, took out a compact, regarded herself in the mirror, carefully touched up the spots where the make-up had been brushed off.

Dane Skarle watched her with his strangely bright eyes.

When she had finished she smiled at him. "Doesn't show, does it? I wouldn't want him to have the satisfaction of knowing."

He shook his head. "You look O. K., Vera."

She snapped the compact shut, looked at him, blinked her eyes, and suddenly burst into sobs that shook her shoulders. She jumped down from the table, walked to a little window, turned her back to Dane, placed her head in the crook of her arm, and sobbed unrestrainedly.

He got up, started toward her, paused, went back to his chair.

She whirled around at him, face streaked with tears, mouth quivering. "Go on! Say it! Cuss me out!"

He shook his head. "It's O. K., Vera," he said.

She ceased to sob, but made no effort to brush away the tears. She kept walking toward him, talking as she walked. "No it ain't O. K. You know what it means as well as I do. He'll kick you out of the carnival. There's no place else for us to go. This was our meal ticket! Now it's gone."

Skarle shrugged his bare shoulders. "Aw, maybe he'll be O. K. What'd you do, Vera?"

"I swung on him."

"Hard?"

She regarded the reddened fingers of her right hand. "Hard as I could, and I wish it had been harder! Damn him! I wouldn't mind if he'd been right out in the open. But it's that way he gets of sneaking up beside you, lowering his of the side of his mouth in a confidential voice, and speaking so damned oilily out undertone. He's a sneak. I hate him, the big slob!"

HE nodded moodily, said nothing. Only his eyes, restless, filled with some strange physical energy, stared at her, looked away, came back to her again.

"Oh Dane," she said, going to him, "I'd feel so much better if you'd cuss me out!"

"Keep to the subject," he said. "How'd he take it?"

"I don't know. He hadn't recovered. He was taring at me with his jaw sagging and a big red spot on the side of his jowl. I guess it was such a novelty to have a show girl resent his attentions that he couldn't get the idea."

She whirled, walked to the piece of cracked mirror which was held in place by nails on the wall, regarded her face, took out the compact again. There was a pitcher, a basin. She poured out some cold water, dashed it in her eyes, picked up a towel, regarded it critically, turned it over, then selected a corner.

"Gee," she said, "I feel better! Listen, Dane, you don't need to take this on my account. You can get another girl to help you and go on with the act. You can tell Bob Barclay that I was fired yesterday. He'll think that's why I jumped over the traces."

Skarle said nothing. He watched her with those strange, enigmatical eyes.

"Will you?" she asked, turning to regard him over her shoulder.

"No," he said.

She sighed, went back to the task of making her face presentable.

"We got other troubles, too," said Skarle. His voice was like the rest of him, vibrant with an energy that seeemd somehow restrained, held in leash.

She whirled around. "That detective again?"

He nodded. "He thinks we did it."

This news brought her hands down from her face. She stared at Skarle's poker face as though she would stare behind the mask into the man's mind.

"But how could we?"

Skarle shrugged his shoulders. "That's the point. He can't figure out how. He only knows he thinks we did it. He's one of those hicks that sit out front with their mouths open. Just because he sees me hypnotize you, draw rabbits out of a hat, lock you in a cage, bang off a pistol and show the cage empty, he thinks we can do any sort of hocus pocus. He can't figure where the gems went unless we got 'em. Every time he tries to figure anything he runs up against a brick wall. He thinks the whole thing is impossible. He sees us doing seeming impossibilities. Therefore he links us up with the crime because he links one impossibility with another."

The girl narrowed her eyes. "Did you tell him that?"

While Skarle had been speaking, his face was strangely lit with enthusiasm. Now it became wooden once more. Only his eyes, so filled with the mysterious energy that seemed to burn within his restless brain, livened his face.

"No," he said; then added after a moment: "What's the use?"

"Well—" she began, and broke off as the door opened.

THE man who walked into the room was massive, broad-shouldered, slightly bald. His face was flabby, and his shoulders sagged a trifle, as though pulled down by the weight of his abnormally long arms, which hung limply at his side. His eyes were bold and rapacious. His mouth had perpetual sneer lines grooved around it. When he spoke his voice was rasping.

"Well," he said, "you're finished. I guess you know why."

The girl glanced at Dane Skarle. Her face had gone white beneath the fresh make-up.

Dane Skarle got to his feet.

He was slender, wiry. He gave no impression of great strength, yet manifested resistless energy, a high-voltage current which could melt away all resistence if it ever started. He was like a panther, held in leash, and straining against that leash.

"Why?" he asked.

The big man lumbered forward. He did not once glance at the girl. His mouth showed the sneer lines more prominently.

"Because," he said, "I don't want crooks mixed up with this carnival. We got troubles enough already. You're slick, Skarle, too damned slick. You're a clever man with sleight of hand and with cards. You know how to handle audiences. You're too good for Bob Barclay's Traveling Carnival—and you're too bad. You're through."

Dane Skarle stood motionless. He was not relaxed, yet he did not seem to be tensed. He was like a man who is patiently waiting for something to happen, something that will call him into action so that he dare not relax, yet something which is remote enough to keep him from being tense.

"What do you mean about the crook business, Barclay?"

The mouth made an open sneer this time. "As though you didn't know! Fifty thousand dollars in gems gone from the Manning house; the papers yelling about the procession of crooks who always follow a carnival; the chief of police coming down and talking to you with every guy in the street knowing he came! Bah!"

Dane Skarle's voice was even, low, monotonous. "What have I got coming, Barclay?"

"Nothing! Not a damned thing. You can take your equipment with you, your personal stuff. The machinery for that divan trick, the cages, and the props for the pistol trick belong to me."

Dane Skarle took a deep breath. He was smiling now, a cold smile. "Barclay," he said, "you've got something coming! You know why you're letting us go, and I know why you're letting us go!"

Barclay turned then, for the first time and sneeringly surveyed the girl. "I'm glad you know it," he said. "Some folks don't know when they're well off. These are hard times. You'll find that it ain't easy to get placed these kind of times . . . what have I got coming?"

He made of the question a slow drawling insult. The sneering lines of his mouth broadened until the teeth showed. From the security of his huge bulk, he surveyed the wiry form of the slender man before him. His long arms raised slightly, and the huge hands made into fists.

"You going to get beat up," he asked, "on account of a common—"

Dane Skarle seemed suddenly to slip the leash.

There was explosiveness in his actions. His face twisted with emotion. The fires of the black eyes seemed febrile. His slender arms flashed out, in and out.

Bob Barclay took the first blow on the mouth, without giving so much as an inch. His long arms snapped out. The left grabbed Dane Skarle by the neck of his undershirt. The right whizzed up and across.

Vera Colma screamed.

Dane Skarle whipped back. There was the sound of rending cloth. He jumped forward. His fists pumped regularly. Then he ducked a blow, and came up, on the inside, face distorted with savage delight. His nose was bleeding, his lip cut. He rained left, right, left, on Barclay's nose and mouth, paused as the big man, beaten back, seemed slowly setting himself. Skarle smashed home a terrific right. It caught Barclay on the eye.

Barclay went down. His fall shook the floor of the tent house.

When he got up, Skarle was back once more into his expressionless reserve. "Get out!" he said.

Barclay got to his feet, walked uncertainly to the door, paused, took a quick breath, as though he were about to say something.

His left eye was swollen almost shut. His lips were cracked and torn, and the blood and saliva trickled down his chin to stain his collar, tie and shirt.

Skarle moved a quick step forward.

Barclay stepped out abruptly through the flimsy door and slammed it shut. Skarle sopped his nose with a handkerchief.

"Oh, Dane!" breathed Vera.

Skarle might not have heard her. He walked to a hanger, took down a shirt, put it on, looped the four-in-hand tie and examined it critically. He kicked off the slippers, put on shoes and socks. He put on his coat and vest, reached for his hat.

"Well," he said, "you can get out of that rig and into your street clothes."

She stared at him. "You going out, Dane?"

"Yes."

"Don't leave me alone. Stay with me while I change. What'll I do—suppose he should—"

Dane Skarle walked to the door. "He won't," he said. He didn't look back.

"What you going to do, Dane?"

He opened the door. "I don't know," he said, and walked out.

CHAPTER TWO

Little Puddle—Big Frog

THE carnival lot was shimmering in the sunshine. There was only a breath of wind. It wasn't yet one o'clock in the afternoon, but people were moving about, wearily getting ready for the afternoon opening.

Men looked curiously at Skarle.

"Heard you and Barclay tangled, Skarle," said a black-face who was adding the finishing touch to a wide red mouth.

"Yeah," said Skarle.

"You leaving?"

"Yeah."

"Got a tip for you," said the black-face, coming closer. "As soon as Barclay got his face patched up, he climbed in his car and drove to the police station."

"Uh huh," said Skarle and started walking away. After a moment he called back over his shoulder, without turning his head: "Thanks!"

He walked to the end of the carnival lot, out onto the hot pavements. The shade trees broke the white hot glare of the light. Birds were singing. An air of tranquillity hung over the country town. Here and there pedestrians moved with even-paced regularity. A car swirled past.

Dane Skarle turned to the left, walked a block. There was a double street-car track here. He waited and a street car came along running east.

He boarded it, felt of his sore nose to see if it had started bleeding again, explored the cut edges of his lips with a tongue tip, and caught the eye of the conductor.

"How far out is Shamrock Street?" he asked.

"Eighteen or twenty blocks."

"Thanks. Stop for me when you get there, will you? I don't know the place.

Manning lives somewhere on that street, don't he?"

"Yeah. Walk a block south, turn to the right. It's a big house with white-and-green trimmings. There's trees all around it and an iron fence. You can't miss it."

"Thanks," said Dane Skarle, and sat down.

The conductor watched him with obvious interest. Twice Dane looked up and the conductor tardily let his eyes slither away. There were only two other passengers on the car. The car rocked along past three blocks, came to the center of the business district, stopped half a dozen times in as many blocks, then gathered speed again.

The conductor reached for the stop cord. "Shamrock," he said.

Skarle got to his feet as the car slowed.

"Block to the south, then to the right," said the conductor.

"Thanks," said Skarle.

He hit the hot pavement while the car was still slowing. In a graceful curve, he swung to the sidewalk. The car gathered speed. Dane walked with quickly nervous steps, turned to the right at the corner and saw the house.

He opened a gate in the wrought-iron fence.

Inside the house a dog started to bark, a shrill yap-yapping which grew louder as some one opened a door. Dane Skarle walked up on the porch and rang the bell.

Foot steps sounded inside. The door opened. A tired-faced woman in an apron stared with lack-lustre, disinterested eyes at Dane Skarle.

"Mr. Manning," he said.

"Who shall I say is calling?"

"Tell him the man he suspects of having stolen his jewelry is at the door."

The lack-lustre eyes widened, showed expression.

"And tell him I won't wait," said Skarle.

The woman vanished, returned, beckoned. Skarle followed her into the house, across a library, into a study.

MR. George Manning was a big toad in a small puddle and showed it. He filled out a huge office chair, and made a business of pushing out his jaw to show firmness and decision. He stared at Dane Skarle aggressively. "What d'yuh want?"

Dane Skarle spoke steadily, without emphasis. "I want you to call off your damned detectives. I want you to call off that chief of police. And I want to recover your gems."

"You want what?"

"To recover your gems before somebody frames the crime on me."

Manning was taken aback. "You're that King of Magicians from the carnival, aren't you?"

"Yes."

"I didn't say I suspected you."

"Your men did. And Barclay is planning to make a fall-guy out of me because he hates me and is afraid of me."

There was a gentle knock at a door on the opposite side of the room. The knob turned almost instantly. Manning frowned, then erased the frown with an effort. The door opened and a woman who was beautiful, dark and slender, entered the room.

"May I come in, dear?" she asked, her eyes on Dane Skarle. "I heard . . . heard who it was."

Dane Skarle locked eyes with hers. There was in his eyes that suggestion of inner force, that leashed energy. The woman's eyes widened with startled appreciation, then dropped.

"He says he wants to recover our gems," said Manning; and then added: "to remove suspicion from himself."

The woman nodded, looked at Dane Skarle again. This time her eyes did not turn away.

Manning blew his nose loudly. "There's a reward," he said, "of five thousand dollars for the return of those gems and the arrest of the crook."

"Is the arrest a condition of getting the reward?" asked Dane Skarle.

Manning shifted his huge bulk to a creaking protest from the springs of the chair. "It is," he growled. "I won't temporize with a lawbreaker. Somebody broke into this place, did it deliberately, worked some sort of sleight-of-hand hocus pocus and walked out with fifty thousand dollars in gems. I'm going to smash him. He'll go behind bars and stay there for the limit. He picked the wrong nut to crack when he picked this house."

And he glared threateningly at Dane Skarle.

Skarle spoke patiently, almost, it seemed, wearily. "I got the details from the papers. You were having a wedding. Your eldest daughter. There were a lot of gems, all in a lot on display in a room where you had the gifts on exhibition. There was a detective in the room. You gave three pieces. They're supposed to have cost fifty thousand dollars. The detective swears no one came into that room save the guests, and that he watched the guests and checked up on the gems after they left. When you started to pack up the gems, the three pieces you'd ordered were switched for paste imitations, made in exact duplicate of the originals. Is that about it?"

Manning picked up a pencil in his pudgy hand, slid his fingers down to the bottom of the pencil, let it turn, then planted the point and repeated the process. His voice was rasping.

"Except for the fact that there was a ladder placed outside the house, near the window. It was a light ladder used for the high dive in the carnival act."

Dane Skarle nodded. "And the detective says no one came in through the window."

Manning grunted. "You hypnotize people don't you? Suppose the detective had been hypnotized?"

"Couldn't have been done," declared Skarle.

"So you say," remarked Manning.

Mrs. Manning made a remark, in a well-modulated voice. "Parks, the detective, just told me something rather strange. He says that after Grace got dressed for the motor, she came into the room for a last look at the presents. It seems strange that she'd have done that, but Parks is certain it was she. He says she had on the big fur coat with the wide collar, and had on her hat. He recognized both the coat and the hat."

Manning frowned at her, irritably. "What would Grace be doing . . . " He stopped.

Dane Skarle turned toward the door. "You can't go shouting accusations against carnival people unless you got more evidence than that," he said. "You're putting me in a spot, you and that boob police chief. You got to quit it."

Manning's lips trembled with emotion. "Yeah? Who says I have?"

"I say so. And the lawyer that'll sue you for malicious prosecution says so."

Manning made his face into a sneer. "Go ahead and sue. The whole town thinks you're guilty, you or some one connected with that carnival. Start something in court here in this town against George B. Manning, and see what a judge and a jury would do to you before you got finished!"

Dane Skarle seemed not to notice the gloating tone, nor the threat. "Maybe I will," he said.

THE door opened and the lacklustre-eyed housekeeper thrust in her face. "Chief Kling," she said.

And as the face removed itself from the door, Chief of Police Bill Kling walked into the room, on the heels of her announcement.

"Heard he was here, Mr. Manning," he boomed. "I'm looking for him. I think I got a case."

He was big, broad-shouldered, regular of feature. Only his eyes prevented him from being handsome. Those eyes were the color of watered milk. He shifted them toward Dane Skarle. "Come on, Skarle," he said.

"You again," said Skarle wearily.

"In person," agreed the chief, ominously. He turned toward Mrs. Manning. His face was suffused with pride of achievement.

"I've located the missing link," he said, "the woman accomplice. I've found out how the paste imitations were made. Gottfried's rang up when they read of the theft. They said they'd received a letter, purporting to be from you, saying that there were so many robberies around that you wanted to have paste imitations made of the three pieces and use them for display."

The surprise on Mrs. Manning's face was evident. "Why . . . why, I . . . "

"Exactly," boomed Chief Kling. "The letter said that the paste imitations were to be sent to Miss Purkett at general delivery, that your husband wouldn't approve of the idea if he had known. The post office remembers Miss Purkett. She was a young woman that had a swell shape. Looked like a show girl."

Manning lurched free of the chair, got to his feet. He seemed all chest, stomach and jaw. "Chief," he boomed, "that was fine work. That's just as good detective work as they'd do anywhere."

Dane Skarle spoke. "All he did was listen to a telephone conversation and go to the post office and ask a question."

Chief Kling whirled on him, face distorted. "Shut up, you. I'll put you where you won't be so free with that lip of yours!"

Manning added a rumbling word. "He had the temerity to threaten me!" he growled. "Actually stood in my own house and threatened me. Understand, chief, I'm not prosecuting this man. I've placed my case in the hands of the law. However, I wouldn't be surprised if he turned out to be the thief. In the meantime, I'm reporting the threat."

The milky eyes turned on Skarle with gloomy promise. "I'll speak to you, after I get you to the jail," said Chief Kling. "In the meantime I'm going to search your things, and question that tart that travels with you."

"She ain't a tart," said Dane Skarle savagely, his eyes blazing.

The pale milky eyes narrowed. The lips twisted in a sneer. "No? I s'pose she . . . "

"Gentlemen," said Manning, rumblingly, hastily," my wife's here!"

Chief Kling grabbed Skarle's shoulder, gave him a push. "Come on, you! No funny stuff or I'll snap the bracelets on you."

Skarle left the room. At the door he turned back. He looked, not at Manning, but at Mrs. Manning. She was standing, very erect, very beautiful, her head up, showing her throat to advantage. Her eyes locked with those of Dane Skarle for a long instant. Then Skarle was pushed into the corridor.

CHAPTER THREE

Empty Pockets

CHIEF Kling pushed Skarle through the door of the dressing room. Bob Barclay followed them in. Vera Colma was dressed in her street clothes, standing in a corner of the room. Her eyes stared at Dane Skarle purposefully. Then the right lid fluttered twice.

That fluttering of the right lid was a signal in their sleight-of-hand act. It meant "I have it, but it's not hidden yet, give me more time."

Dane Skarle's eyes snapped to sharp focus on her face. He slightly raised one eyebrow. The lid of the girl's right eye fluttered again, twice.

Dane Skarle started to spar for time. "Now listen, you guys, I haven't said much yet; but I'm going to say a lot. Bob Barclay had an argument with me, over a personal matter. He went running to the chief of police, bearing some sort of a tale of . . . "

Bob Barclay's voice sounded strangely muffled as it came through his cracked lips. "Watch him, chief. He's making a stall. That's the tone of voice he uses when he's handling out a line of patter. He's stalling for time."

Skarle caught the look of helplessness on the girl's face. He moistened his lips with the tip of his tongue. That was a signal which meant: "Give it to me."

She let her eyes widen. Skarle repeated the signal. She moved over a step toward him.

"And watch her," said Barclay. "They've got a whole code of signals they use . . . "

Dane Skarle made a leap toward the big man. "You mug!" he bellowed.

Barclay recoiled before the force of that attack. Chief Kling grabbed Skarle's shoulder. Skarle lunged, threw the chief off balance, lurched against Vera. He felt her fingers slide up underneath his palm, felt some hard object against the bottom of his hand. He instantly contracted the trained muscles of his palm. They closed about the object. The chief jerked him back and flung him around,

sent him spinning against the side of the tent house.

"One more crack out of you, and I'll bust your head wide open!" he said, ominously.

Skarle kept his eyes on Barclay's face. "Get that slob out of here, then!"

"It's my tent house," said Barclay.

Chief Kling crossed to the little stool upon which was the suitcase the girl had been packing. It was filled with make-up, costume stuff, miscellaneous clothes. There were two bags and a trunk on the floor.

"I want all that stuff searched, to protect the good name of my show," said Barclay.

Chief Kling nodded, started pawing through the suitcase.

"The first thing they'd do," said Barclay, speaking in that strangely muffled tone, "is to rip the stones out of the settings and conceal 'em somewhere in their baggage, and they're slick, these two. You gotta search carefully."

"Say," said Kling, raising his milk-blue eyes to Barclay's face, "I guess I've dealt with crooks before! I don't need you to tell me how to run my office."

Barclay attempted his oily smile, which he used to square things in the hick towns. The cracked lips made of the smile a dismal failure.

"No offense, chief, no offense!" he said.

Dane Skarle took advantage of that moment when the two men had their eyes locked, their attention distracted, to turn his hand, look at the object which had been thrust against the palm of his hand.

It was a bit of platinum which had been twisted and pried to make it disgorge the stones which had been set in it. One stone had not been removed. It remained clasped in the platinum teeth, as though the crook who had been ripping the stones from their settings had been interrupted in the very act. That stone was a diamond, big as a man's thumb nail. It seemed to spit out cold fire in a million tongues of congealed flame.

SKALE hastily turned his hand so that the platinum and diamond was concealed, held the hand close against his clothes. He caught the look on Vera's face. It was one of alarm.

Chief Kling was tossing out the articles, one at a time.

Bob Barclay was watching with interest.

The chief complete the search. "Nothing here," he said.

Bob Barclay frowned. "Better go through it with a fine tooth comb. They're slick. I don't want them to slip anything . . . Say! The girl was packing that when you came in. She could have seen you, and grabbed out anything that was incriminating! Search her! And she might have slipped it to him. Search him!"

Kling made no move to search the contents of the bag again. He moved toward the trunk and said: "Don't worry. I'll search everything. And I'll search him here, and I'll have her searched by the matron at the jail . . . "

"Barclay snorted. "That'd be duck soup for those two. I tell you they're clever. You've seen 'em perform on the stage. You don't need to have a matron search her. Hell, she ain't modest. She's just a show . . . "

Dane Skarle made a rush for Barclay. "I've warned you to keep your dirty tongue . . . "

It was as far as he got. The chief went forward like a football tackler, grabbed Skarle around the waist, slammed him to one side. Skarle grabbed at the chief, stamped down with his heel, missed the chief's instep and took a blow on the

chin. He staggered back. Chief Kling pulled out handcuffs.

"Just for that," he said, "you'll wear bracelets, both of you."

"They go through handcuffs just like you'd slip an elastic band off your wrist," said Barclay.

"Not these handcuffs they don't," said Kling. "Get your hands behind you, guy!"

Skarle held his hands behind him, fists closed. He was breathing heavily. The chief clamped the handcuffs to the wrists, pushed the ratchets home until the steel fairly bit into the flesh.

"That hurts," said Skarle, holding his hands closed.

Kling grunted. "What you want me to do, bust out cryin'?"

Barclay laughed.

The girl whirled on him, took a gasping breath, then said nothing. Kling regarded her speculatively, then jerked his head at Barclay.

"Telephone headquarters and tell 'em to send a matron out here. I'm going to frisk that jane."

"Without a search warrant?" asked Vera, her eyes staring, level-lidded into the milk-blue eyes of the chief.

"Without a search warrant," he said. "I can either book you on suspicion of vagrancy, take you to jail, and have you searched before you're put in, or else I can have it done here, and maybe not have to take you to jail. Which'll it be?"

She kept her eyes on his. "O. K.," she said. "I'll take it here."

Kling flung his voice over his shoulder at Barclay. "Telephone for that matron," he said.

Barclay looked once more at the things on the floor which had come from the suitcase. Then he turned reluctantly.

"Watch 'em!" he cautioned. "They're clever. You've seen 'em perform."

Kling said nothing. He pulled at the

catch on the trunk. The girl took keys from her purse, tossed them to him. Kling opened the trunk, pulled out drawers. He had finished with the third drawer when Barclay returned to watch him curiously. The search progressed in silence.

When he had finished with the bags, a siren sounded. An officer and a plump woman with hard eyes and loose lips came into the dressing room.

Kling looked at Barclay. "Got another room here?"

"Yes. Sure."

"O. K. Take the matron to it. You go with the matron, young woman. The quicker you start acting sensible, the quicker you'll have it over with."

VERA walked from the room, eyes disdainful. The fat matron waddled after her, eyes hard and appraising.

"Take off your clothes," said Kling to Skarle.

"Can't until you take off the handcuffs."

"You've got to watch him . . ." began Barclay. Kling whirled on him, furiously. "I've heard about enough of that. It gets like a phonograph record that runs round and round until your ears get tired. You've got no business sticking around here, anyway. Keep your trap closed. This looks like a carnival job, and these two are a part of the carnival, but only a part!"

Barclay pressed his bruised lips together. "No offense, on . . . "

"Shut up!"

Kling fitted a key to the handcuffs, his eyes still on Barclay. Skarle stripped off his garments. Kling took each garment, searched it thoroughly. When Skarle had completely stripped, he ordered: "Open up your hands, spread the fingers apart. Now turn around."

The milk blue eyes stared with opale-

scent malignity. "Okay, now you can dress."

Barclay said: "I know it's in here somewhere, that is . . . "

The eyes glared at him. He tried a smile and his cracked lips made it a grimace.

"One more word outa you," proclaimed Kling, "and I'm going to hang one on your sore kisser, just for luck!"

Barclay tried to make it a joke. "Ha ha," he said. "Well, the matron will get them. That girl . . . "

Skarle, struggling into his trousers, lurched forward. "Damn you, if you say another word about that girl, I'll . . . "

The chief stretched forth an arm that had lost much of its force. "Now, now," he soothed, grabbing Skarle's shoulder.

Skarle tried to shake himself free. He pulled the police chief off balance, caught another hand on his shoulder for his pains, and the milky eyes glared into his.

"Listen, guy, I didn't get anything on you. If the jane's clean, you're O. K. But you keep asking for trouble and you're going to get it, see?"

Skarle let himself relax. After a moment, Kling dropped his hands. Skarle was breathing hard.

Barclay said: "You can see what a murderous disposition he has, chief. As a favor to law and order will you throw them off the lot and see that they don't come back. That's their personal baggage. Make them move it and get out, and stay out!"

Skarle said: "You don't need to get a cop to make me get away from you, you big tub of lard! If I don't ever see you again that's six months too soon!"

Barclay laughed, a hard, rasping laugh. "Try and get another job," he said.

Skarle was repacking when the matron walked into the room, followed by Vera Colma. "She didn't have anything," said the matron in a tone that was as flatly heavy as her figure.

"Uh huh," said the chief, and looked meaningly at Barclay. "Somebody gave us a bum steer, I guess."

Barclay spoke rapidly. "Come into my tent, chief. I want to do something to make this all right."

Kling nodded. "That's better," he said.

"As soon as we get rid of these two," amended Barclay hastily.

K LING nodded again. In silence they watched the pair pack. When the bags were closed, Skarle said: "Would you mind having the officer get a transfer man and staying here until the stuff gets off the lot? I don't want some cheap crook planting any stolen stuff in our baggage."

Barclay twisted his bruised face into a sneer.

Kling turned to the officer who had stood at the door. "Get a truck, Sam. You stay with the stuff until it goes out. Where you going to take it, depot?"

"Yes."

The chief surveyed the baggage. "It'll be four dollars," he said.

"Shucks, what do you think I am? I can get it done for . . . "

"Four dollars," said the chief.

Skarle took three dollar bills from his pocket, made up the other dollar in small change.

"Take it, Sam," said Kling.

The officer took the money. Skarle touched Vera's elbow.

"All right, kid. Let's scram."

They walked out of the dressing room, out of the tent house, into the hot glare of the carnival lot, without looking back. There was a small crowd, gawking around. Barkers were handling out their mechanical patter without enthusiasm. Most of the business was being done by the spot-the-spots, the cane racks, and

the wheels of fortune. The side shows had barely a dribble of patronage.

As soon as they were free of the lot, Vera spoke without turning her head. "What happened to it?" It was planted in the suitcase I was packing. I just saw the glint of it . . . "

"In my pocket," said Skarle.

"Didn't they search . . . "

"Sure."

"Then how? You had the bracelts. God, but I was frightened! I saw your hands clenched . . . "

He laughed. "It was gone before that."

"How come?"

"Cinch. Every time I made a lunge toward Barclay, the chief would grab me and start to muscle me around. I counted on that. When I got caught with it, I started toward Barclay. The chief grabbed me, and I slipped it in his vest pocket. Then when it was all over, and we had a clean bill of health again, I made a lunge, and he did his stuff just like he'd rehearsed it for a performance. I slipped it out again."

She sighed. "That means that Barclay did the job. He planted it, of course."

"Sure. I should have suspected him all along. If he'd made the plant good and they'd caught us with that piece, they'd have railroaded us for twenty-five years apiece. This guy, Manning draws some water in this burg."

"Well," she said, "let's ditch that thing. Be careful how you do it, because that flatfoot is shadowing us, or trying to. He'll try to keep us under his eye until we get out. There's a train at three o'clock. Got any money?"

"No money," said Skarle, "and we ain't going on the train. Barclay can't hand us a package like that and not have us slam it right back at him. Besides there's a reward of five thousand dollars for the return of the jewels, and the arrest of the thief. Don't forget that."

She turned to stare at him. "You going after that five grand, kid?"

He nodded grimly. "And how!"

CHAPTER FOUR

Check-Girl Set-Up

DANE Skarle sat on the edge of the express truck which waited on the depot platform. His brows were level, drawn into a straight line. He held his knee in his cupped hands. Vera Colma stood on the hot asphalt, looking unwinkingly at him.

"There was a woman that turned the trick for him," said Dane. "Unless the detective that was watching the outfit was a crook, the thief couldn't have climbed through that window. That ladder was a blind."

"Why use a blind?" asked Vera.

"Because, at the last minute, they knew it'd look like an inside job. See the sketch? He wanted you. He figured he'd make a play. If you turned him down, he'd frame it on both of us. If you fell, he'd make me the goat."

She laughed, and there was bitterness in her laugh. "He's made plenty of plays for me."

"I know, but this was the final act."

"Well, he got his final answer."

Dane Skarle stared into the west. The rays of the sun, sliding down the afternoon heavens, illuminated the strong contours of his face, the rugged jaw, the sensitive mouth, showed, more than ever, the strange depth of those eyes of his, inky pools into which light could not shine, but from which a light seemed to come.

"It would have been the girl who was taking charge of the wraps," he said. "See? She could have picked out the fur coat and hat that belonged to Grace. She could have walked into the room and made the detective think she had a right to be there, looking the gifts over for the last time before she started on a motor trip. See?"

She stirred, moved her feet.

"Then she could have had the paste imitations made, as Mrs. Manning?"

"Yes."

"And Barclay got the ladder?"

"To direct suspicion our way."

She said, abruptly: "Dane, I'm afraid of Barclay. He's so hard and ruthless, and he seems to know all the little crooked ways of people. You notice him when he's handling the carnival in a graft town. He seems to know just who is entitled to the gravy, and who has to beg. Let's duck out of this burg and leave those jewels wherever they are."

Dane said, slowly: "You may be afraid of him. I'm not. To you he's a bold, bad man. To me he's going to be Santa Claus."

"The flatfoot's still watching us," she reminded him.

Dane nodded. "Remember that jane that wanted to join the carnival, back in Middleboro? Barclay picked her up. She travelled along with the outfit for a couple of jumps. Then she slipped out of sight."

"Uh huh. Only she didn't slip out of sight, Dane. She's here, at a rooming house. I saw her. She turned a corner when she saw me coming. But that's who it was all right. Poor kid. I was sorry for her. She didn't need to have run away."

Dane slid down off the truck, looked at his watch.

"Three quarters of an hour," he said. "Let's walk. I want to talk with that girl."

Vera's voice was sharp, almost rasping. "Dane, you don't think that she could have . . . Dane . . . "

He strode ahead, without even looking at her. "Come on," he said. "I'll want you to do the dirty work."

"But, Dane, she's just a kid! Just a little scatter-brained kid that had her head turned by the glamor of carnival life, and that line of Barclay's that the best road to Hollywood today was through the practical experience a girl gets on the road with a carnival."

Dane's voice was almost dreamy in its preoccupation. "Don't waste time telling me how young she is. She traveled from town to town with Bob Barclay, and I'm going to talk with her."

VERA kept silent as she piloted him to the rooming house. The register revealed a scrawled lot of nondescript names in awkward handwriting, told them nothing.

Vera smiled her prettiest at a sniffing woman in a loose-fitting wrapper.

"We're looking for a girl, a little shorter than I am, who's been here for six days. She's got dark hair and gray eyes, wears a checkered suit, and . . . "

"Stella Jason, the right-hand front room on the third floor," said the woman. "You friends of hers? She said she was twenty-five. She don't look it."

Vera continued to smile. "Yes. We're friends. We'll go on up."

The woman in the wrapper turned her ample figure without a word. She sniffed her way back from the little pine counter that served as a "desk" and through a door which banged after her.

"Shut up," said Dane. "You're too darned soft. I'm running this party."

He found the room, knocked on the door. There was the sound of scurrying motion from the inside. "Yes?" asked a voice which seemed a little nervous. "Who is it?"

Vera sucked in her breath to call an answer. Dane silenced her with a frown, knocked again.

The sound of motion came toward the door, a key turned. The door opened a bare crack. An anxious gray eye stared out at them. Then they heard a gasp. Dane Skarle leaned his weight against the door, pushed it open. He walked in. Vera followed him.

She had on a kimono and slippers. She was packing a suitcase. There was a trunk, already packed, in a corner of the room. It was a light trunk, one of the larger aeroplane trunks that can be carried as hand baggage.

Dane walked over to the bed and sat down.

"Why . . . why . . . it's Dane and Vera, from the show. Hello, folks. How'd you know I was here? I just got in yesterday."

Dane stared steadily at her. "And registered under the name of Stella Jason, eh?" he asked.

Vera said, gently: "Dane, don't!"

Dane Skarle did not look around. He continued to stare at the white-faced girl who wrapped the kimono around her, not as a protection to her modesty, but as against the force of his accusing stare.

"How'd you get the job at Mannings?" he asked.

She gasped, and the hands loosened their grip on the silk.

"You . . . you know about that, then?"

"Yes. How'd you do it?"

"I .. . I don't know. Bob . . . Mr. Barclay, you know. He got me the job. That is, he gave me the references. It was a mob, and they advertised for extra help. I used to be a check girl in Middleboro, and I never had to give out pasteboards, tickets, you know. I could always remember faces and things that went with faces, clothes and hats."

Dane spoke suddenly, fiercely.

"How did Barclay make you pull the robbery? Did he threaten you?"

Wild color leapt into her features. Then her face grew pale as the pillow on the bed. "I don't know what you're talking about," she said, in a voice that made it seem her tongue was cold as ice.

"No?" asked Dane.

He got up from the bed and walked over to the dresser. There was a framed picture on it, a snapshot that was a very good likeness. It showed Bob Barclay standing beside a rock on which the girl was seated. Their faces were about on a level. Barclay was smiling, that wolfish leer of self-satisfaction. The girl's expression was hungry with the yearning of ambitious youth.

Dane slipped the picture in his pocket. The girl watched him with her gray eyes wide, frightened.

"The post office authorities," said Dane, easily, "can probably identify that picture as the girl who called for the package that contained the paste imitations."

She flung herself at him, clawed at the pocket.

"No, no! Give it back! You can't! You don't dare!"

Dane tried to shake her free.

Vera came over to them, put an arm around the girl's shoulders.

"Listen, dear, we know how it was. I can understand. I ain't perfect, myself. Tell me how it happened, where the gems are, and we won't do anything. You can go."

She paused in her struggles, stared at Vera. Then suddenly let her hands free the coat. She started to cry. Vera gave Dane a significant look and piloted the girl to the edge of the bed.

"Listen," said Dane meaningly, "I don't know how you feel about this, but I want those gems, and I want a fall-guy. I want a case against Barclay. If the girl goes, she's got to leave the evidence behind her."

Sob-twisted words came bitterly from the girl's lips. "I didn't have any idea what he had in mind. He told me he was going to get me on in the dancing-girls' act in the carnival. Then I was to get training and go out to Hollywood.

"He paid my expenses at first. Then he said I had to earn something. He got me the references to apply at the Manning place. I talked with Mrs. Manning. She was awfully nice. She hired me and said I could handle wraps the night of the wedding.

"I don't think Bob had any plan at first that was definite. He intended to make me get the jewels all right, but he didn't figure just how it was to be done. I was to get him into the house some way, I guess.

"Then I heard there was a detective employed to watch the jewels. I guess everybody knew about the three pieces that the Mannings had ordered. Bob made me write the note for the duplication. Then I went to the post office and got the package. It was a perfect imitation. That detective bothered us. Then Bob got the idea of me putting on one of the coats and going in as a guest.

"I put on Grace's fur coat and turned up the collar a bit, and I put her hat on. I waited until the detective was over in the corner. I didn't have any trouble at all. I just nodded to him, and walked right over to the jewels. After I'd been there a second, he moved over a little closer, but the imitations were in place then. I ran out.

"Afterwards I slipped them to Bob. He put the ladder up so it would look like an outside job."

Dane Skarle's voice was hard as granite. "Write it down!" he said.

"Aw, Dane," said Vera, "the poor kid . . ."

Skarle's voice held a note of more savage insistence. "Shut up, Vera. Write it down, kid! And make it snappy."

Vera pushed the girl from the bed. She crossed to a desk and started to write. The cheap steel pen made scratchy noises on the white paper. There was no other sound in the room.

CHAPTER FIVE

Stacked Cards

ABRUPTLY, and without warning, the outer door opened. Bob Barclay's cheery voice boomed out with forced optimism: "Hello, little sunflower! All packed—"

He broke off as the opening door disclosed the bed, Vera Colma seated on the edge of it, Dane Skarle standing with his feet apart, braced.

He jerked as though he would leave the room, then came in and banged the door. His hand was tugging at his hip pocket. "So," he grunted, "you had to—"

Dane Skarle rushed. The hand came out of the pocket. The gun roared, once. The bullet ripped a pillow apart with a thunking sound like a muffled explosion. Dane Skarle grabbed the big forearm, twisted it.

The bigger man struck out with his foot. The foot caught Skarle above the knee, on the left leg, pushed him back, wrested Barclay's forearm from his grasp. Barclay pointed the gun. Skarle was on him like a tiger.

They locked in struggle, swayed to the bed, rolled from it to crash to the floor with a jar that rocked the house. The gun roared again. Skarle twisted, squirmed to the top.

Vera Colma had rushed to the girl. She had ripped the kimono from her, was pulling on a skirt, shoes, literally pushing her into her clothes. There were steps in the corridor. Then the door burst open. The officer who had been trailing Dane Skarle rushed into the room. He was holding a gun in his hand.

Dane Skarle brought up his fist, hard. Bob Barclay twisted convulsively, lay still, gathered his strength, made a sudden roll. The gun slipped from his hand. Skarle flung himself over, grabbed the gun. Barclay got to his knees swung his great arm in a terrific blow. Skarle ducked. He smacked the barrel of the gun down on Barclay's forehead.

"Here, here, you guys!" said the officer, rushing forward.

He grabbed Braclay by the collar. Dane Skarle slowly dropped the gun, got to his feet. Vera pushed the girl out through the door into the corridor.

"This man attacked me, and tried to kill me," said Barclay.

He spoke thickly. His eyes were moving about, the eyeballs unsteady in their sockets. He raised his palm to his forehead, brought it away red.

The officer stared at Dane, then at Barclay. "Who did the shooting?" he asked.

Barclay pointed to Skarle.

The door into the hallway was open. There were curious faces peering in at the occupants of the room. No one ventured inside.

A swirl of shoulders, a grunting, and the milky eyes of the chief of police stared at the occupants. He pushed his way into the room. "What the hell?" he said.

Barclay pointed to Dane Skarle and said: "He tried it again. Murder this time. He had a gun."

Dane Skarle laughed.

"How would I have a gun? I was searched, and the officer's been following me since."

"That's right," said the officer.

"He got it from his accomplice, the little lady here," said Barclay.

SKARLE walked to the writing desk, picked up the penned sheets of paper. He read through them rapidly. Then he folded them and thrust them into his pocket.

"What's that?" asked the chief.

"Five thousand dollars," said Skarle, "Five grand for me, and a ticket to the pen for Bob Barclay. It's the girl's confession; she tells where the stones are."

"Give me the confession, or whatever it is," said Kling.

Barclay raised his voice. "Don't let this guy fool you. He's the one that's got the stuff. He had an accomplice in this little girl here. You let her slip through your fingers!"

Dane Skarle continued to stare at Kling, paying no attention whatever to Barclay's statement. "When I get five thousand dollars reward money," he said, "you get the statement."

"That show where the gems are?"

"Yes."

"O. K. You recover the gems and hand them to me, and we split the reward money."

"How split?"

"Fifty-fifty."

"Don't be silly. I've done all the work. I'll let you have a thousand. I'll take four. You get your thousand not for what you've done, but because you can hold Manning to the payment. I might have trouble."

Kling fidgeted. "O. K.," he said, "I'll shoot. Get the stones."

"Don't let him fool you," said Barclay. "She was his accomplice."

Dane Skarle took out his knife. He approached the overstuffed chair, ripped the stitches along the back, took out some stuffing, then a wad of cotton. They opened the cotton. Jewels cascaded into his hand. Kling gasped. The officer caught Barclay edging toward the door.

"You've got nothing on me," said Barclay.

Dane nodded his head toward Kling. "You've searched everybody. Why not him?"

Kling nodded, moved over to Barclay. Barclay raised his hands.

"Certainly. Only too glad to oblige."

The chief's fingers moved about in the pockets, suddenly withdrew an object that glittered. He held it up. "One of the settings with a stone still in it."

Barclay shouted: "You can't pin that on me. He's a sleight-of-hand-artist. When we struggled, he—"

Kling set himself. He started his hand travelling from the hip. It caught Barclay flush on the jaw. The big man went over like a falling tree slowly at first, seeming to pivot back on his heels, then crashing to the floor.

Kling inspected his knuckles. "God, how I hate that guy's song! Hope I didn't bust a knuckle."

He pulled handcuffs from his pocket.

"We want that reward," said Dane, "in cash. We don't want to fool around here waiting for banks to open tomorrow morning. We're finished with this burg."

Kling might not have heard him. "Sam," he said, "go out and pick up the jane that had this room. She'll be hanging around town somewhere. She may try to make that train. Get on her trail."

They took Barclay to the jail. Kling went to Manning's.

"I'll handle this reward business," he said. "Your split's agreed on, so there's no need you worrying. I'll be at the depot."

Dane nodded. "Only let's see that there's no trouble about the cash."

"There won't be. There's an express out of here at nine-twenty. You can take that, and get a nice compartment on a through pullman."

Dane grinned at Vera. "In the meantime," he said, "we eat."

WHEN they had finished eating they strolled back to the hotel, then to the depot.

The train was whistling when Kling drove up. "Had a devil of a time getting the cash," he said.

There were two policemen with him, men who left the car and stationed themselves on either side of Dane Skarle. Dane noticed them and leaned slightly forward, his dark eyes glinting ominously. Kling took out a bill fold.

"Five thousand dollars," he said, "and your split was three hundred and fifty. Here it is."

He held forth three nundreds and a fifty.

Dane's face went white. "Say," he said, "what you trying to hand me?"

Kling stared steadily. "Your share of the reward," he said, "and you've got just ten seconds to take it in. If you don't take it then you won't get it."

Dane moved forward. "If you think you can pin a deal like that on me you big four-flusher—"

Men moved up on either side of him. Chief Kling shrugged his massive shoulders and pocketed the money.

"O. K., Sam," he said. "Get 'em tickets out of town. Hold the train a minute if you have to. We'll let 'em ride in state. Get 'em Pullman tickets. See that the baggage gets aboard."

Dane's voice was steady, ominous. "You can't pull a stunt like that," he said.

Kling grinned. "You mean you just think I can't. As a mater of fact, we couldn't catch that jane who was the accomplice. You helped her escape. If you so much as stick your nose in this town again I'll jail you as an accomplice, as an accessory after the fact, and for resisting an officer."

Vera Colma put her hand on Dane's arm. "Oh let's go, Dane," she said. "We can't crash this town. The deck's stacked."

Dane's arm was stiff, the muscles tense. Sam came up with tickets. The bell of the train clanged. "Their baggage is aboard," he said.

Dane snarled: "Try and put me aboard, you double-crossing skunk—"

Kling laughed gleefully. He rushed. The men closed in. Dane twisted, squirmed, was rushed aboard the train. Vera came scrambling up the steps. Vestibule doors slammed. The train creaked into motion.

"This way, Vera," said Dane, and started walking rapidly back toward the rear of the train. When he had gone through two cars he paused in a vestibule, kicked up the trap, swung open the vestibule door.

"Can you make it," he asked, "if I catch you?"

"Dane you can't go back there."

"Can you make it?" he asked.

"Yes."

He swung out into the night. She went down the steps.

"Let go," he shouted.

She let go. He was running beside the train. His arms gripped her, held her up. The lighted windows slid past them into the night.

"But Dane, you can't—" she began.

"Don't be silly," he said. "I tempted the chief to rush me aboard that train. He wanted to play with crooked cards, so I stacked the deck."

She gasped. "Dane! Don't tell me you picked his pocket!"

He laughed pulled out a leather wallet. "Five grand" he said. "Let's stop an automobile and head out in the opposite direction. We'd better go into this crook-catching game. It's fun!"

And for the first time, his voice rang out without that trace of leashed restraint which seemed ingrained in the man's nature.

Far down the track, the night train whistled for a crossing.

THE CANDY KILLER

A Cardigan Story

by

Frederick Nebel

Author of "The Dead Don't Die," etc.

Cardigan thought it was a swell break when he got slated to herd the lovely Marta Dahl and her $400,000 back to Poland. But there was more in store for him than sweet nothings and kisses on the boat deck. Murder, dope, and a suicide all had to come before "Bon voyage."

CHAPTER ONE

The Peppermint Kill

GEORGE HAMMERHORN, the head of the Cosmos Agency, was signing correspondence at five that afternon when Cardigan pushed open the glass-paneled connecting door and came in. Cardigan, whistling a tune from *Show Boat,* sat down opposite Hammerhorn at the large double desk, jangled keys, unlocked a drawer, pulled out a bottle of Scotch and poured himself a neat jolt.

"George?"

"Nope."

Hammerhorn's pen scratched across paper. He said: "Ever get seasick, Jack?"

"Me? Once—on a troop ship. It wasn't something I drank." He raised the glass. "Mud in your eye."

"Bon voyage."

Cardigan chuckled.

Hammerhorn finished with the pen, laid it down, tossed the signed letters into a basket marked "Out" and leaned back. "Jack, you're going places."

He yanked hard and Sam went backward mightily.

"Tiarri's for ravioli and steak. Want to come?"

"You're going on a long journey, Jack."

"All right, be funny."

Hammerhorn scratched a match, lit a cigarette. "Poland."

"Now I'll tell one."

"Get your passport fixed up tomorrow and pay any bills you have around town. You'll travel on B Deck on the *Magnetic*. She sails day after tomorrow. You'll be gone three weeks and you don't have to send any postcards."

Cardigan sat back, laughed. "Rave on, George, rave on."

"Ever hear of Marta Dahl?"

"Ask me a hard one."

"You're going," Hammerhorn said, "as Marta Dahl's bodyguard. To Poland. Yesterday afternoon, as Marta Dahl walked from a taxicab to the entrance of her hotel, the Gallice, an umpchay broke out of the crowd and began calling her names. He was a bum, a tramp, with ideas. The essence of it is this: the umpchay thought it was on outrage because these foreign actresses come over, make a lot of dough and take it back to the fatherland. The guy got pretty rough and nasty and some guy took a swing at him. A cop comes up and grabs the umpchay and is going to run him in when Marta Dahl intercedes. She says, 'Let the man go, officer. It is nothing.' The cop swoons —who wouldn't?—and lets the bum go and Marta Dahl goes into her hotel. Catch on?"

"No."

Hammerhorn interlocked fingers behind his head. "About an hour ago her manager, a nice little old fat fellow by the name of Adam Baum, comes in here all hot and bothered. No, he's not worried particularly about the umpchay, but that helped. He wants a bodyguard to accompany Marta to Poland. Why? The ump-

chay? No. Tomorrow Marta Dahl will draw four hundred thousand dollars from a bank—in cash. Get that, sweetheart— in cash. She will lug four hundred thousand dollars in cash back to her native Poland."

"Why can't she transfer it?"

"Don't ask me why actresses do things. Baum tried to talk her out of it, but it was no go. The money's in a checking account and maybe she thinks that while she's on the water something might go wrong with the transfer. All that concerns us is that she's toting four hundred thousand dollars and you're to see that she and the dough get to Poland together. Our fee for this is one thousand berries, exclusive of your expenses. There is a Santa Claus."

"And I'm the goat, huh?"

"What the hell are you beefing about? An ocean voyage with the screen's hottest mama! I'd go myself, sweetheart, but the wife wasn't born yesterday."

He leaned forward, unhooked the telephone. "Get me the Hotel Gallice." He looked across at Cardigan. "Shuffle board, deck tennis, real liquor—"

"And a knife in the back."

"Do you expect everything for nothing? Think of the moonlight!" He ducked his head near the mouthpiece, spoke into the phone, waited, then said: "Mr. Baum? . . . This is Hammerhorn of the Cosmos Agency. . . . My ablest man will accompany Miss Dahl. His name is Cardigan."

"Suppose this dame falls for me and I don't come back?"

Hammerhorn hung up, made a sour face. "M-m-m, don't you hate yourself!"

TIARRI'S was a noisy Village speak. It had a large, low dining room in which Tiarri had gone wild with plaster frescoes. The bar was better, though noisier; it did not look like a vain attempt to transplant an Italian alley to lower New York. Cardigan was rolling poker dice with Frank, the barman. One side of Frank's mustache was gone; he had promised to cut that side off if a local Dago boxer lost.

Angelo, a waiter, punched Cardigan in the ribs. "Ouch!" said Cardigan.

Angelo bowed. "Onna da tele-phono." He jerked an illustrative Sicilian thumb. "In-a da off-eece."

"Listen, Angelo," Cardigan said. "I'm not here."

"Uk-key, boss."

Angelo went away and Cardigan returned to the dice. But in a minute Angelo was back.

"Deesa gentelman say, 'Nuts to you, Dago. Tell-a dat gorill' to get-a hell on de tele-phono."

"Sounds like a pal," Cardigan said, and sloped off into the little cubbyhole behind the bar. He scooped up the phone there, said. "Who's a gorilla, you big stiff? . . . Oh, hello Garrity! How's your diabetes?" He stopped short, the laughter ebbed from his eyes. He said, after a minute: "O. K." And hung up.

He rolled out at the bar, lost, paid up. He went into the dining room, got hat and topcoat from a costumer, slapped the hat on his shaggy mop of hair and went out the front, up three steps out of the areaway and into a taxicab.

A man opened the taxi's door in front of the swank Hotel Gallice, on Park Avenue. The man looked like an Austrian general but was only the hotel doorman. Cardigan swung across the sidewalk, slapped his way through revolving doors and headed across the lobby. His coat was six years old and looked it and his lop-eared hat was faded from rain, sun and old age. His thick hair bunched around the ears.

A man headed him off.

"Hello, Yager," Cardigan clipped, and was on his way, long-legged.

But Yager caught up with him. "In my office a minute, Cardigan. I got a proposition." Yager was the house dick.

"Got no time. What suite?"

"Fourteen twelve. Now listen, Cardigan—my office—just a minute and—"

"While Rome burns?" Cardigan said and walked on into an open elevator.

Yager bounced in after him.

"Fourteen," Cardigan said. He stood on wide-planted feet, spinning his hat on a big forefinger while the elevator rose smoothly, noiselessly, to the fourteenth floor.

Yager got out with him. Yager was a pudgy short man with a bullet head, a squat hard neck and gimlet eyes. He said: "Now listen, Cardigan. There might be some dough in this for us. Baum, the dame's manager, said he'd pay five thousand dollars—"

Cardigan lengthened his stride, reached a door numbered 1412, knocked loudly. A cop opened it and said: "Hello, Cardigan."

"Hello, Swanson," Cardigan said; lifted his chin. "Hello, Garrity."

Yager pushed in behind him, looking abused and misunderstood. Captain Garrity, a bluff headquarters dick, was sitting on the arm of a chair swinging a foot.

"Thanks for coming, you roughneck."

A WOMAN sat on another chair. She was young and in black livery. Her eyes were red-rimmed and she clasped a crumpled damp handkerchief in her hand. A short, rotund man in evening clothes was pacing up and down, his eyes glued wildly on the floor. He kept muttering to himself, shaking his head, rubbing his palms together.

Garrity clipped: "Mr. Baum, this is Cardigan."

The fat man stopped short, rushed across the room, bowed deeply, shook Cardigan's hand violently and then returned to pacing the floor. The maid broke out crying again.

"In here, Cardigan," Garrity said, and

led the way into another room. He was a lean, hard-boned man with a good jaw, hard gray eyes. "What do you know about this dame, kid?"

"Not a thing, Pete. I'll give you the straight of it. The little fat guy dropped in on George this afternoon and hired a man to bodyguard the dame to Poland. She's drawing four hundred thousand dollars out of the bank tomorrow and lugging it home with her. George picked me to dry-nurse the dough home. Just what happened?"

Garrity scowled. "Well, a couple of cops heard shots in West Fifty-fourth Street at nine tonight. They legged it over and found a taxicab halfway across the curb. The driver was in the gutter with his belly all shot to hell. All they could get out of him for a while was 'Marta Dahl! Marta Dahl!' Like that— over and over again. They got an ambulance and went to a hospital with him. They didn't get much more out of him. Only that Marta Dahl was his fare. He must have recognized her. Who wouldn't? The cops tried to get out of him where he picked her up, but the poor guy was croaking fast. It gets down to this, near as I can figure it out. A guy crowded into the cab at a traffic stop and made the driver turn west. Another car followed. In West Fifty-fourth Street the guy in the cab made the driver stop. The other car drew up and they switched the jane over. Then the driver gets heroic and starts to fight. One of the eggs lets him have it in the guts. Now the taxi driver remembered one thing: he said he smelled the guys breath—he smelled peppermint on the guy's breath. Why he remembered that, I don't know. He didn't get the pad numbers. So Marta Dahl is kidnaped. The old boy outside—this Baum lad—is all smashed up. I tried to stop him but right away he phones the papers and offers five thousand bucks reward."

Cardigan said: "That dough of hers is still in the bank. Has her manager got power of attorney?"

"No. Technically he's not her manager anymore. She's through with the screen. But the old guy's built her up and the way I get it, he kind of worships the ground she walks on. If these mugs call for ransom—if the call's in her handwriting —that can be fixed at the bank."

"How about that five thousand reward?"

"Well, I could use half of it."

"How about the other half?"

Garrity said. "What's the matter, you gorilla—can't you use half?"

Cardigan chuckled. "Pete, for a cop, I like you."

"Don't get me wrong, baby. A swell chance I'd have of grabbing the whole five grand with you waltzing around. So I'd rather have you with me than against me. Not that you faze me, Jack—but you have a habit of falling smack on your face into the breaks. This job is a tough one to crack. The jane walks out of the hotel at seven-thirty. The maid says she has a habit of taking these walks alone. The maid doesn't know where she went—only out. Ten to one she walked till she got tired, then snatched a cab."

CARDIGAN shook his head. "If these mugs tailed her from the hotel they would have nabbed her before she got in a cab. What I'l like to know, Pete, is where she went. She might have started out for a walk, but I'll bet you she changed her mind and went some place. Then she took the cab from that place. It was at that place that these mugs started to tail her. How about the cab?"

"I checked up on that. I thought the driver might have been on duty at a hack stand. He wasn't. I looked at his meter and from the fare on it he must have driven three and half miles. So start from that and tell me when you go nutty."

Cardigan said: "How about the umpchay called her names outside the hotel yesterday?"

"Yeah," Garrity chuckled; "I thought you'd come to that. No connection. Hackett, the cop collared him, says he's a hophead named 'Chink' Wiggins."

"Chinaman?"

"No. They just call him Chink. He thinks everything's wrong with the world. Every now and then they collar him for making goofy speeches on street corners."

"Listen, Pete. Collar that bird."

Garrity threw up his hands. "Nix. I'm not going to make myself a laughing stock by grabbing that sap. I'm out to grab some guys for the murder of Jacobs, that driver, and the kidnaping of Marta Dahl—"

"I tell you, Pete, grab him. We may be wrong, but what the hell!"

Garrity tossed his chin up. "Listen, Cardigan. I'm not asking you to think for me. I'm out to grab some killers, I tell you; not to make news by landing on any guy I happen to think of." He strode hard-heeled to the door, added: "Or that you think of."

Cardigan sighed out loud: "You cops, you cops! I think I find a cop with brains and what happens? Why, I find a Brooklyn Hibernian who's so proud of his record he never pinches a guy till the guy says, 'I did it, officer—with my little hatchet'."

"Oh, yeah?" Garrity took his hand off the doorknob and came toward Cardigan with a mean glint in his windy gray eyes. He punched Cardigan on the chest. "Listen, Jack, you bum: I'm one cop they can't hang anything on. I follow the line of my thinking. If that's wrong, it's my tough luck. But I let no guy make my decisions."

Cardigan laughed with rough good humor, threw his arm around Garity's shoulder. "Good old Pete Garrity! O. K., Pete! If I need a battering ram some day I'll borrow your head."

He ducked a punch, yanked open the door and reentered the living room with a gust of laughter. Mr. Baum stopped pacing. He looked shocked. The maid, who had stopped crying, put her face in her hands and began again. Windy-eyed Captain Garrity stalked into the room, his chest out, his manner important.

Yager, the house dick, began crabbing: "O. K. I guess I see where I stand all right."

Garrity eyed him. "What's eating you?"

"Yeah, you and that big tramp going in a huddle behind the door and leaving me out of it."

Garrity twisted his neck and looked at Cardigan, jerked a thumb. "This house dick a friend of yours?"

"What's the idea of making a dirty crack like that?" Cardigan said, eating an apple he had taken from a fruit bowl.

Yager leveled an arm. "I've got as much right to that reward as anybody! Why leave me out in the cold?"

Cardigan assumed a mock-grave expression. "There you go again, Yager—thinking only of the money. Thought of that reward never entered my mind and I am sure—" he turned, bowed toward Garrity and lifted an eyebrow—"it never entered the captain's."

"Of course not!" Garrity said indignantly.

Yager reddened to his ears, spluttered, turned and thumped out of the room.

Mr. Baum raised his hands, shook with rage. "That foul person! Thinking only of money while my poor Marta is lost—lost!"

"And don't forget," Garrity pitched in, "the dead taxi driver. A wife and five kids in the Bronx."

CHAPTER TWO

Hophead's Hideaway

WHEN Cardigan went through the hotel's revolving door into the street, a taxi was emptying. When the "Vacant" sign was raised he climbed in, gave an address, and leaned back. He was as Irish as Garrity was, and in his own way quite as stubborn. When he became obsessed with an idea, a hunch, he had to play it even though realizing, in great measure, the futility of it. The cab was heading south. At Grand Central it weaved through pedestrians. In the morning, Cardigan mused, these people would read of the disappearance of Marta Dahl. There would also be a parenthetical note about the death of one Jacobs, a taxi driver, who had attempted, apparently, to save her. But the death of a taxi driver is not news. The vanishing of a famous screen actress is news—a final fling for Marta Dahl at the headlines.

Leaving the cab, Cardigan said: "Hang around. I'll be right out."

He passed between two green lights and entered the station-house door. A lieutenant wheezed out a matter-of-fact greeting. Cardigan spoke through cigarette smoke, leaning comfortably with both arms on the desk. He got what he wanted and swung out to the taxicab, climbed in.

The city swallowed him and he turned up again, fifteen minutes later, on a downtown curb where an east wind pushed river smells up a dark street. When the taxi moved off, he dug his hands into his overcoat pockets and got under way. The street was not noisy. The sound of the departing taxi's engine echoed hollowly in the narrow street; and when it had died down the sound of a not distant "L" train crashed over the roof tops. After that there was only the sound of his footfalls, or a cough from an open window, or the squeal of cats.

Where two streets and a crooked alley wedged into a kind of triangular plaza, there was the distinct sound of pool balls striking. Cardigan, hitting the plaza on the north side, gave it the once-over. It

was very dark, dismal—with a few window lights here and there looking like yellow moths. Across the plaza, at the mouth of the alley, was a gaunt brick house of five stories. From the street-level floor of this house issued the neat smacking of pool balls. The house itself was by way of being a beacon in an otherwise tattered, down-at-the-heel district. Crossing the cramped plaza, Cardigan could make out big letters on the broad plate-glass windows. The windows were painted a solid blue three fourths of the way up. The big letters said: "THE FRIENDLY CIRCLE ROOMING HOUSE AND RECREATIONAL PARLOR."

It was a dump.

Cardigan, opening the door, pushing in, prodding the door shut with his heel, was aware of noise, smells, and about two dozen arguments. There were many strata of tobacco smoke, lazy, sluggish, swamping drop-lights that glared without benefit of shades. Two pool tables; round card tables and other tables; scarred oblong ones, littered with papers, magazines, the heels of men who reclined in battered chairs. There was dust. There was the smell of the unwashed. There were bromidic legends tacked on the leprous walls. There was a high pulpit-like desk at one side where a fat man with a pitted face and a nose like a Brussels sprout, sat beneath the only shaded light in the place. Behind him was a rack of keys. Above him was a big sign: "Beds—Ten Cents and Up. Rooms—Fifty Cents and Up."

A man in a rushing, passionate voice was explaining his ideas of government. He had greasy stubble on his face and looked like a phantom. Others listened, nodded, burning-eyed—wild-looking men, foreigners. Cardigan found that his entrance created no interest. He moved through the sluggish layers of smoke. Some of the men had blackened eyes, bruised jaws. He remembered there had been a riot at Union Square the other day. Cops had been stoned—and the cops had got tough. Cardigan reached the desk.

"Plainclothes?" asked the fat lump there, bilious-eyed.

"Guy named Wiggins. Where is he?"

"Ain't he here?"

Cardigan said: "Is he?"

"You cops take a chance dancing in this place alone."

Cardigan shrugged. He did not say he was not a cop. The fat man was craning his neck, roving his eyes around the crowd.

"I don't see Wiggins," he said. "He's got a room upstairs. Maybe he's upstairs."

"What's the room?"

"Three ten—third floor."

CARDIGAN turned and made his way through the crowd to the broad stairway. He climbed on worn boards. The first floor looked like a dormitory. There were cots in endless rows. A few men lay on them all dressed, without covers. He took the next stairway up. Three droplights made a dim glow in a long, bare corridor. He found a scarred door with tin numbers nailed on it. He palmed the knob and turned it and the door opened and he walked in, closed the door.

A man sat up on a cot that creaked. His face looked like yellow parchment and his hair was mouse-colored. He wore a flannel shirt, trousers, and his eyes were abnormally large, protuberant; his ears stuck out from his head and looked like dead shells.

He cried in a hoarse whisper: "Who're you?"

"You're Wiggins, aren't you?"

"What d'you want here? Get out of here!"

"What the hell are you scared about?"

Wiggins cringed. "I ain't scared! Just what right you got busting in here?"

"Where were you at nine tonight?"

Wiggins' fingers crept to a blue bruise on his jaw. He rasped: "Here! Downstairs!"

Cardigan gazed around the room. "What was the idea of making that grandstand play yesterday in front of the Hotel Gallice?"

The charred eyes blazed. "I'll do it again!" Wiggins cried. "I'm a citizen! I got rights! Them dames come over here, take all our dough—"

"Since when did you have dough? Did you ever do a stroke of work in your life?"

"Ah-r-r, you're one o' them too! I told her what I thought of her. I guess she'll remember it."

"She was good enough to ask the cop to let you go."

Wiggins jumped up, shaking. "What the hell do you want here?"

"I'm trying to piece together a puzzle. I'm trying to find a connection." He suddenly grabbed the man, tapped the man's pockets lightning-fast, tossed him away, picked up the coverless pillow, threw it down again. The man cowered in a corner.

"O. K.," Cardigan said. "I just wondered if you were heeled." He turned, twirling a broad blue garter on his forefinger. He had taken it from beneath the pillow. "Nice," he grinned.

"Gimme that!" cried Wiggins. He leaped like a cat, clawed at Cardigan's hands.

Cardigan bounced him onto the bed. "I'd like to meet the lady," he said. He tossed the garter back to Wiggins. He was groping in his mind, feeling his way, determined to leave no stone unturned. "Put your shirt on."

"I ain't going!"

Cardigan showed a row of dangerous teeth. "Get your shirt on, sap!" He towered, his eyes dark and threatening, his shadow massive on the wall behind. He leaned forward, showing a big brown fist.

Wiggins scampered off the bed, flew to a corner, shrank there. "I ain't!" he cried. "I ain't going!"

Cardigan took three slow, heavy steps, caught Wiggins by the throat, lifted him off his feet, held him up and shook him. Wiggins grinned at him. It was a crazy, maniacal grin—and in it Cardigan read a wild, fierce challenge. In that split minute Cardigan knew that this man would not obey. He unloosened his fingers. Wiggins fell to the floor and lay there making idiotic sounds. It was business Cardigan didn't like. He stood for a long minute, pondering, while the figure panted at his feet. He looked down.

"I'll find her," he said in a low voice. "I don't need you, Wiggins. I'll go out and find her myself."

He said no more. He turned and left the room, went downstairs and stopped at the pulpit-like desk.

"Was Wiggins in here at nine tonight?"

The fat man nodded. "Yeah." He pointed. "See that big bird over there with the red beard?"

Cardigan nodded.

The fat man said: "Him and Wiggins got in a fight. They were arguin' since about eight o'clock and then they got in a fight. Over the Roosian situation. They always argue. I been trying to figure out should I pitch 'em out."

"Thanks," Cardigan said.

HE went out into the street, crossed the dark deserted plaza and dropped down into a shallow areaway. It was damp and cold but from it he could watch the rooming house. A stray dog came down in search of scraps, yowled and scampered off when Cardigan moved. A few minutes later the door across the way

opened; a figure slipped out and scurried past the alley in frantic haste. Cardigan gave it a head start, then rose out of the areaway, felt his way rapidly along the dark house fronts and caught a glimpse of the figure sloping beneath a pallid street light. He heard the frantic rap of heels. For seconds he followed this sound alone. Then there was a brief instant during which the figure sped past a lighted store window; then darkness again and then a momentary glimpse of the figure slanting beneath a street light. Alleys made shortcuts. Cardigan followed. He didn't bother with his gun. He somehow felt that this man was not a gunman. By profession perhaps a petty thief, a purse snatcher in crowds—stealing just enough to buy hop. A pitiful wisp of humanity. Maybe not even a petty purse-snatcher. Cardigan didn't know. The cops called him a nuisance. When he really got hopped up he criticized the government and created a disturbance, but he had no penal offense against him. Maybe he was a beggar.

In his haste, Wiggins fell. His heels rasped the pavement and he whined petulantly as he went down. But in a moment he was on his feet again—and running, skipping, through the dark streets, the back alleys. Until presently he fell against a wooden door and beat upon it with his fists. It opened and the house swallowed the man, and Cardigan, flattened in a nearby doorway, heard the echoes of the slammed door peter off in the silent street.

A minute later he walked on, spotted the house and counted the number of houses to the next corner. He went around the corner, found a board fence and scaled it, dropping into a yard. Moving through the darkness, he counted the houses and paused when he neared the rear of the house through whose front door Chink Wiggins had entered. It was three storied with a network of fire-escapes in back and the only light that glowed was one on the top floor, beyond a window whose shade was drawn down.

Cardigan put his hands on the rough metal of the fire-escape, took a few upward steps. He climbed in fits and starts, putting his feet down cautiously. He did not stop at the lighted window on the third floor. He went on up to the roof and then stood for a long moment among the dim shapes of chimney pots. The yard was a black well below and a damp breeze puffed from the river. Moving carefully, he found a roof entrance to the regions below—a door with a lock that answered to the fifth skeleton key he used.

Blackness yawned below, but he felt around with a foot, found a step. The narrow staircase was steep. He closed the door and went down slowly, making sure of each step before resting his weight on it. Then he was at the bottom. A door there opened at his touch and he found himself in a lightless corridor. The darkness enabled him, however, to place instantly the location of a door by the thin horizontal sliver of light visible where door did not meet flush with threshold.

Toward this Cardigan moved. For an instant he felt indecision of spirit, as though a large question mark had appeared in his brain to doubt, clerically, his movements. But he brushed it aside with a rough mental gesture. And then he asked himself why Chink Wiggins, yesterday, had chosen Marta Dahl as his particular target of abuse. A man who haunted the back alleys, the tawdry squares and shoddy streets of the lower city—why had he gone far afield, to Park Avenue, to abuse Marta Dahl in a public demonstration?

Cardigan stopped at the door. He heard the troubled whine of Chink Wiggins' voice. He noiselessly tried the doorknob and found that the door was locked. He waited until the whine abated a bit. Then he knocked. Instantly there was silence. Then a woman's voice, hushed, close to the panel. "Who is it?"

"A detective," he said in a low, casual voice. "Better open it, little one."

"W-what's the matter?"

"Open it, I said."

A bolt clanked. The woman opened the door on a crack but Cardigan punched it wide open and walked right in saying: "Now that's nice, that's nice, Chink!"

Wiggins almost fainted on the window sill. He had opened the rear window and now he crouched motionless in it.

Disgusted, angry, Cardigan snapped: "Well, get in or out. If you go out, you won't have to walk down but you'll be a mess when you reach the yard."

Wiggins backed into the room. Cardigan strolled to the window, closed it with a bang and yanked down the shade. The woman had closed the door. She wore heavy red lounging pajamas—the blouse was Russian, with a stand-up black collar, embroidered in gold. She had hair black as jet, smooth as an otter's back, with straight bangs in front. Her eyes were black coals, her mouth a red gash in an oval face, her fingernails were lacquered red. She looked exotic, hard, cruel, beautiful.

UNLIKE the outside of the house, unlike the neighborhood, the room was large, spacious, with heavy Oriental rugs, teak-and-ivory statues and ivory figurines; bronze lamps with parchment shades, severe mirrors, a cloying odor of perfume—an air of luxury and lavishness without foundation, a kind of stage set, a rare nightmare in a lean-flanked, hungry fag-end of the great city.

Wiggins didn't like the silence. He began blubbering and his lips got wet but no words came out—only flip-flopping little sounds.

"Oh, cut it out," Cardigan growled.

He was making certain, at the time, that broad sliding doors at the front end of the room were securely shut, and he did not look at Wiggins. Swift, silent,

Wiggins palmed a heavy bronze paper-weight. Fear, fright, drove him to it. He hurled the thing. But Cardigan's eye had beaten him to it. Cardigan raised his hand. The bronze weight made a loud slap in his palm, his fingers closed over it for an instant. Then he hefted it.

"Throwing things like that," he complained, and set the thing down on the long mahogany table. His grand unconcern struck terror to Wiggins' heart and Wiggins slumped into a chair like a balloon suddenly deflated.

The woman had not moved.

Cardigan eyed her. "I've walked into something that I get a swell kick out of."

Only her lips moved in a face that was like a mask. "What am I supposed to say to that?"

He picked up the paper-weight, grinned, said: "Catch!" as he tossed it lightly at her.

She twisted, raised her hands to cover her face. A small gun clattered to the floor from one of her broad blouse sleeves. She hissed, dived—but Cardigan's big foot landed on the weapon. He grabbed her, spun her away, picked up the gun, unloaded it.

He was grinning, but not pleasantly. "I thought so," he said.

She was mask-faced again, unemotional. Her voice was flat, toneless, measured. "What do you want?"

"I've found this out," Cardigan said. "That punk there lives at a cheap flop-house but he lives there only as a blind. A cheap punk wouldn't have an in to a place like this. I'm going to turn up something, little poker face, and you're going to help me. So is Mr. Wiggins."

"And what do you think you will turn up?"

"I've a strong suspicion that I'll turn up Marta Dahl."

Expressionless, the woman said: "You make riddles."

Cardigan went toward her with lowering brows. "When I told that bird over there that I was going out to find a woman, he left the flop-house like a bat out of hell and came straight here to warn you."

She mocked him with her flat voice. "Warn me about what?"

"That I was coming after you. Listen, sister; you can hand me all the crap you want, but I had this scatter figured out the minute I came in here. I've got you figured out. This place is lousy with hop. It's a hideout for the needle and the pipe and the sniffers. Wiggins is a contact man for the cheap trade. But this place right here—this room with all the fancy trappings—is a joy house for the swells."

"If all this is true," she said, calmly, "what connection has it with Marta Dahl?"

"That's a riddle you'll answer before you paint your lips again, honeybunch. There is a connection. I feel it in my bones. Wiggins didn't just wander up to Park Avenue yesterday. He—"

WIGGINS was on his feet, livid. He cried: "You leave her alone! You hear me, leave her alone! I went up there because I wanted to! I went up there to kill Marta Dahl!" He screamed it out; panted on: "But—but I didn't. So—so I got some friends—friends like me, that hate the rich, that hate these foreigners who come over here and take our dough back home. I got in a fight at the flop-house and Red hit me and I went to my room. But I didn't stay there. I had it all planned. I sneaked out, met my pals—" He stopped and shook an arm at Cardigan. "You leave this girl alone! I did it! Me and my pals! And you'll never know who them pals are! You won't!" he screamed.

He braced his arms on the table, his breath came hoarsely from his twitching mouth and his eyes rolled. Cardigan felt that he was looking at a madman, at a man whose brain was cracking, at a man whose brain was plagued by a dread disease.

He said: "Why did you come here?"

"To say good-by to—her. I knew you was after me. I wanted to say good-by. I—I killed that chauffeur. Me and my pals did away with Marta Dahl! I always hated her on the screen. She was rich, she took our money, hoarded it. Me—me—I did it!" He grimaced toward the woman. "I'm sorry I come here. But you was always good to me. I wanted—wanted to say good-by."

His eyes dropped from her face, bulged on space. He turned, sagging, and went toward the window. He pulled up the shade, opened the window. He turned and cackled.

"I'm going, mister. You know what to do."

Cardigan drew his gun. His brows were bent, his eyes glittering, his mouth tight.

Wiggins threw a leg over the window sill. His face was deathly gray but the crooked, unreal smile lingered. "I'm the guy you want, mister, but there ain't no cop taking me in for a shellacking—and I stick by my pals. Go ahead, shoot."

Cardigan was grim. "I'll give you till you get halfway down, Wiggins, to think it over."

Wiggins climbed out, disappeared. Cardigan, watching the woman, backed to the window, closed it, drew down the shade. "Now we can talk," he said.

"About what?"

"About who really killed that taxi driver and kidnaped Marta Dahl."

"You heard, didn't you?"

"I heard a poor little hophead. I saw a poor little hophead try to talk me into killing him. I'm not a killer, sister. The sap's in love with you. You've held him in the hollow of your hand. You've sup-

plied him with hop, kidded him, fooled around with him till he's nuts—till he'd die for you. There are guys like that. But he didn't pull this job. He knows all about it because he knows you. No papers would have it yet. It's not news yet. But he knew the details. The sap, sister, was a fall-guy that I didn't let fall. I want Marta Dahl."

There was movement in her face now—slow anger, frustration. Jewels sparkled on her fingers as her hands clenched. There was the faint sound of her breath escaping.

Then there were footsteps in the hall; a moment later a knock on the door. Cardigan shoved his gun into his overcoat pocket but kept his hand on it. He went close to the woman.

"Open it—and one false move and you get hurt."

He backed up beyond the radius of the bronze lamps. The woman went slowly to the door and opened it.

CHAPTER THREE

"I Hate Cops!"

A MAN in evening clothes came in, said: "Nita—" and stopped short. She had turned from him with lowered eyes. He was tall, middle-aged, with white hair carefully combed. He stammered: "I—I beg your pardon."

"Come in," said Cardigan.

"No, thanks. I—I'll come back later and—"

"Get in." There was a whip in Cardigan's voice. "If you're a customer here, it's your tough luck. Close that door."

The woman closed the door. The man fidgeted with a black velours hat, bit his lip, turned and looked quizzically at the woman. She drifted past him with her head lowered, sat down, fitted a cigarette into a long ivory holder and lit up.

The white-haired man demanded:

"What is this? What is this anyway?"

"It's a riddle," Cardigan said. "Sit down."

"But I tell you, sir—"

"Sit—down!"

The man sat down, his eyes wide and jerking from the woman to Cardigan.

Cardigan said: "I'm tailing down a little matter of murder. And kidnaping. I'm a private detective—"

The woman started.

Cardigan dipped his head toward her. "I forgot to tell you about the 'private' part . . . Stay put!" he barked at the man. "Murder—and kidnaping. I was engaged by Marta Dahl's manager to escort her to Poland, but before I can start any escorting she's kidnaped. By dumb luck I land here—"

The man was on his feet. "I tell you, sir, I can not afford to be mixed up with this. I came here for another purpose."

"I know what you came here for, You're a rich man with nerves and you need hop to keep you going. You crashed in here at a bad time but you're not leaving till I get things straight. The sooner this woman talks the quicker you go."

The woman said: "Of course, I am not talking."

The man said: "Oh, my God!" and patted his forehead with a handkerchief.

"There was a little sap in here," Cardigan said, "who tried to tell me he pulled the job. I had the choice of killing him or holding the woman. I held the woman."

The man raised his palms. "But why do you hold me? If you know what I came here for, and if it's not in connection with what you're after, why must I stay? Come, I can fix things with you. Surely a hundred-dollar bill—"

"Nothing doing."

The man groaned. "Then name your price!"

Somewhere a door banged. The woman started. The man with the white hair tensed.

"I've got to get out of here!" he cried.

He jumped up and made a blind dash for the door. Cardigan lunged after him. The man had his hand on the knob. He yanked open the door and spun around to strike Cardigan. Cardigan leaned with the blow and brought his gun down on the man's head. The man fell against him, a dead weight, slumping, and Cardigan tried to shove him off.

Something landed on the back of his head and he whirled around to find the woman there—her eyes staring fiercely, the bronze paper-weight in her hand, upraised again. She struck and he caught hold of her descending arm, twisted it. There was a rush of feet behind him. The woman bit her lips, buckled downward.

Cardigan pivoted, his lip curling—to find three men covering him with leveled guns. Their faces were granite-hard. Their guns did not waver. The foremost moved wide lips.

"What the hell's going on here? Drop that rod, you!"

CARDIGAN scowled at them. His gun lowered and he stood on wide-planted feet, his hat knocked awry and a tuft of hair sticking out over his left ear. The woman was sitting on the floor behind him, rubbing her wrist. The white-haired man lay at his feet, unconscious.

It was the woman who spoke. "He's a private cop."

"Oh, he is, is he?" snarled the man who had spoken before. "So you're a private cop, are you? Well, I hate private cops!"

Cardigan was more angry than frightened. "Maybe you think I get a thrill out of heels like you."

The big man came forward; his gun muzzle stopped against Cardigan's stomach. "Take his rod, gang."

The two men moved. One took Cardigan's gun, examined it, said: "Nice hardware."

The big man hit Cardigan a punch in

the jaw and Cardigan covered four feet backward and landed in an armchair. He rubbed his jaw.

"Geez, don't I hate private cops," said the big man.

The other two dragged the unconscious man from the doorway, closed the door and bolted it. They were quite young, wore snappy clothes, and seemed to enjoy the goings-on with a kind of satanic relish. They helped the woman to her feet and escorted her to a divan. She lay down. They propped pillows behind her head and she received these attentions matter-of-factly. She asked for a cigarette. One of the natty young men hastened to the table, brought back a box. She took a cigarette from it and the other young man was ready with a match. The big man who hated private cops turned and said: "Well, Nita—what went wrong?"

She inhaled, stared intently at Cardigan's profile for a long minute. Then she said: "This dick knows too much. Altogether too much. He fell on Chink Wiggins and it led here."

"Where's Chink?"

"He went out the back window some time ago."

The big man said: "Yeah?" He turned and stared at Cardigan. He hauled a paper bag from his pocket, drew out some flat, disc-shaped objects, shoved them in his mouth. He chewed industriously. He took two steps, leaned over Cardigan. "So you know too much, huh, baby?"

"I know more right now than when I came in here?"

"Oh, you do! Ain't that just grand?"

"It's the nuts. Or should I say the peppermints? A big smart guy like you shouldn't go around bumping off taxicab drivers."

The big man straightened, looked around the room.

The woman said: "See?"

She rose, cool, composed, and let smoke dribble from her nostrils. "There's noth-

ing else to do, Sam. This fellow knows too much and there is only one way out. You know what that way is. And see if you can do this job without bungling it."

The big man flushed. He started to retort, but the woman silenced him with a keen, steady look. She said: "And I want no arguments. If things had worked out the way we planned, I could have thrown Chink Wiggins to the cops. He would have taken it for me. The sap was dropped on his head when very young and he got an idea somehow that I was a goddess." She laughed coldly. "He was one guy would have taken the rap without a murmur. He took it tonight. But this cop was too wise. Well, mister private dick, you see what happens to wise coppers."

"You know," Cardigan said, "you're a dame I'd enjoy putting a bullet in."

"You should have done it when you had the chance."

"You're telling *me*?"

She turned to Sam. "I want you boys to take him out and polish him off somewhere." She indicated the man on the floor. "Take him in the other room."

SAM lugged the white-haired man into the room beyond the sliding doors. Returning, he closed the doors, ate more peppermints, looked at his watch. "We got to wait," he said.

"Wait!" snapped the woman. "I told you—"

"I know, Nita, but there's a cop comes through this street about now. We got to wait. Then we'll take him up in Harlem and let him have it. But I ain't lugging no guy when there's a cop around."

One of the natty young men picked up a banjo and began strumming it. The other hummed, kept time with his foot, rolled his eyes. The woman, seeming oblivious to the music, stared coldly, intently at Cardigan. Sam walked up and down heavily, munching peppermints.

Every once in a while he took a punch at Cardigan's head and said: "Geez, ever since I was a kid, I hated cops!" He seemed to feel a little better after each punch.

Cardigan was perspiring. He didn't talk, he didn't look frightened. Every time Sam hit him he tried to roll with the punch. The strumming sound of the banjo, the humming of one of the natty young men, seemed unreal in the room. The dark, slitted eyes of the woman never left him. He wondered about Chink Wiggins. Where had the hophead gone? He had expected Chink to turn up again. It didn't matter, though. But he was glad he hadn't killed Chink. Though he wished he had killed the woman. Sam, after an especially hard punch, swung across the room and added his clogged bass to the banjo music and the humming tenor. The tenor broke off long enough to do a snappy soft-shoe dance. Through it all the woman remained remote, masklike, with her cruel eyes fixed on Cardigan.

Presently she said: "Well, Sam?"

The music stopped. Sam looked at his watch, scratched his head. He said: "Listen, Bertie, suppose now you take a run downstairs and see if that cop's in this street."

The banjo player laid down his banjo. "O. K., old boy, old boy," he said cheerfully and pranced out of the room.

Sam came over to stand spread-legged before Cardigan and said, grinning: "I'm gonna like this, baby."

"Can I make any kind of a deal?"

"What, for instance?"

"Well, I'd keep my mouth shut."

The woman laughed flatly. The tenor laughed. Sam roared and said to the others: "Ain't he funny!"

"Honest," Cardigan said, wiping sweat from his face. "I'd keep my mouth shut."

"Yeah," Sam said. "Till you got to the first cop, you would."

The woman said: "Nobody asked you to come into this, mister. You asked for what you're getting. These men do as I say. And you heard what I told them to do. You had a chance to grab Wiggins. It would have been a snap. He confessed. But no, you had to act exceptionally bright and now you're holding the bag."

He said grimly: "I knew Wiggins was lying. I knew he didn't have a hand in it."

"What you didn't know," she ground out, "was that I told Wiggins the other day he ought to tell Marta Dahl what he thought of her. His brain's not right. Ten minutes later he thought the idea was his own. So he went up to Park Avenue and told her. That was not an accident. I put the bug in his ear. For a reason. So that he would create a disturbance, the cops would pick him up, release him— *but remember him.* I was never afraid of Wiggins squealing on me. The poor little fool had a crush on me. He was simple as a kid. I figured the cops would land on him when Marta Dahl disappeared. I knew he was a sap they couldn't beat the truth out of. He'd die for me. I had him—" she held up her hand, closed it—"like that. I wanted a fall-guy if something went wrong with the snatch. Something did go wrong."

"And you didn't have a fall-guy," Cardigan said.

"So I've got to get rid of you."

"Hey," Sam said, looking at his watch, "where's Bertie?"

Nobody said anything. Sam went to the door, opened it and listened. "I don't hear him," he said.

The tenor said: "Maybe he went around for a drink."

"Geez, it would be like that guy to do that. Listen, Arch—you go see. Go get him and come right back."

"Sure thing, Sam."

CHAPTER FOUR

Tickets to Poland

ARCH went out whistling lightly to himself and Sam closed the door again, took a mouthful of peppermints and sighted down along his gun. He twirled it carelessly in his hand, went over and sat on the edge of the table. He got restless there and stood up again, planting himself before Cardigan on one of the many small rugs that lay about the room. He regarded Cardigan after the manner of a butcher regarding a choice side of beef. He munched on peppermints.

"Have one," he said.

He tossed one and Cardigan reached for it, missed, and the peppermint fell to the floor. He bent over to pick it up. Sam laughed and took a lazy kick at his head. It might have been that that angered Cardigan beyond all endurance. It might have been the last straw, or the pain of the kick lancing his head might have snapped the idea to birth. But he followed out the idea.

His hand gripped the edge of the rug. He yanked hard. Sam went over backward mightily. Cardigan shot out of the chair as if a spring had driven him. The gun flew from Sam's hand, skated across the floor and disappeared beneath a divan. Cardigan's fist, traveling fast, crashed against Sam's jaw and banged his head back against the floor. Sam kicked up his legs and Cardigan went sailing over Sam's head.

The woman did not cry out. She dropped to her knees and tried to get the gun from beneath the divan. Cardigan bounced up from his knees, hurtled across the room. He got her by the back of the neck, swung her around and sent her flying away from the divan. She hit the table, knocked over one of the bronze lamps and tumbled to the floor.

She had not got the gun. Cardigan groped for it, but it was way back, and Sam was coming. Sam kicked out. His shoe grazed Cardigan's head and Cardigan caught the leg, rose with it and shoved Sam away. The woman leaped with a paper-cutter, a long, slim bronze blade. She was quick as a cat, but Cardigan had long arms. He laid the back of his hand across her mouth and this time she yelped and the paper-cutter spun across the room, flashing.

The sliding doors opened and the white-haired man teetered in like a man in a trance. He did not join the fight. He looked like a drunk who had entered the wrong house. He blinked, rubbed his eyes. A heavy book, flung at Cardigan by the woman, missed Cardigan and caught the white-haired man between the eyes. He fell back into the other room—patent-leather shoes flicking upward as his back struck the floor.

The hall door flung open and Arch appeared. For a moment he stood poised, then went for his gun. Cardigan leaped to the divan, hurtled over the back of it landed on the floor. His hand closed on the gun that had disappeared. The room thundered and a slug, tearing through the back of the divan, buried itself in the wall. Cardigan gave the divan a shove that sent it scooting out across the floor. It struck Arch, who had bounded forward, and knocked him over. But he was up in a flash, his thin young face white and murderous.

"Kill him, Arch!" the woman screamed.

It was Cardigan's gun that spoke. Arch made a sickly face, turned and fell against Sam and Sam ripped the gun from his hand. The woman leaped with the agility of a cat, with the swift ruthlessness of something wilder—fell on Cardigan's gun arm. His gun went off, not aimed. A bullet drilled a hole in a mirror—bits of plaster fell from behind the mirror. Cardigan cursed and swung her around in front of him, his left arm locked under her chin.

Arch crumpled in a lop-sided heap and Sam, swinging his gun down, made a shuddering sound with his teeth and shook his head—because Cardigan was using the woman as a shield. And sweat stood out like blisters on Cardigan's face.

He snarled in the woman's ear: "You asked for this, you mascaraed heel—and if this punk of yours wants to get me he'll drill you first! Maybe one guy gets out of this shooting-gallery and I'm chosing myself—"

"Get from behind her, you!" Sam roared.

The woman choked "Get—behind him —Sam. I've got his—gun hand—here—" With both hands she was gripping Cardigan's gun hand.

Arch, whom they all thought was dead on the floor, suddenly screamed. Then he died—rolling over. The scream seemed to shock Sam. He shivered.

The woman choked: "For God's sake —Sam—get behind—give this bird—" She kicked back at Cardigan's shins. He tightened his left arm. Her tongue stuck out, her eyes popped. Sam made a lunge across the room. Cardigan let the woman go and she slumped down, hacking.

The men's guns whipped toward each other. The two explosions interlocked. The wall shook. Plaster dribbled. A shot ricochetted and whanged into a porcelain vase and the vase went to pieces; flowers mushroomed upward and some fell on the back of Arch's neck. Sam flung backward with a look on his face that seemed like the beginning of an uproarious laugh. It might have been caused by the way the light and shadow networked the room. Sam's back hit the wall hard and then he stumbled forward. He fired with his gun pointing downward and a hole jumped magically into the carpet alongside Cardigan's foot. Sam went on stumbling and

then began turning awkwardly, like a man turning around in a great gale. Sam seemed to be crying now. His left hand jammed against the table. He hiccupped, braced himself, raised his gun.

Cardigan, brown-faced, tight-lipped, shook his head slowly. His gun was leveled. His gaze was rooted on Sam. The woman reached up—like a cat's paw her hand struck at Cardigan's gun. He ducked as Sam's gun went off. The woman set teeth into Cardigan's gun hand. Sam lurched forward, coughing, raising his gun.

There was a terrific blast from the doorway. Sam went down like a felled tree.

"Hey, Cardigan," Gerrity said, "what the hell do you think you're doing?"

THE skipper stood with a derby raked over one ear. His coat collar was up and there was a windy look in his eyes, a sidewise jut to his jaw. He snapped into the room after the manner of a man who knows his business.

"Hey, you gorilla, what are you doing to that woman?"

"Doing!" Cardigan exploded. "What am I doing! Don't I get a laugh out of that!"

Garrity went over, bent down. "Hey, lady, you're biting his hand! Don't do that!" He laid the flat of his hand across her face and she let go, flopped over. Garrity stood up, spread his palms in an explanatory gesture. "It's like you have to do to a drowning person."

Cardigan snapped his hand and blood flew from it. Gerrity jumped back, clipped: "My new coat, damn you!"

Cardigan pointed. "Look out for that dame, Pete. She's a female Dracula."

"Listen, you. Who's that I handcuffed to the stairway downstairs? Listen. I met him coming out the front door before. He stopped and then he decided to go for a walk. So I walked with him and then I asked him if he always walked with his hand in his pocket. So he was warming a rod. So I waltzed him back to the door. Who is he?"

"A heel. They're all heels."

"Well, I'm glad I know. When I came in here, I didn't know whether to shoot you or this guy."

"My pal!"

"Who's this guy I shot?"

"His friends used to call him Sam. He bumped off that taxi driver."

"Listen, *now* after I save your life are you going to hand me a load of baloney like that?"

Cardigan pointed. "Hold that jane. When I say hold her, I mean hold her. Put your foot on her neck."

He gripped his gun in his left hand, pushed back the sliding doors, found lights, stepped over the white-haired man and put his shoulder through the next door. He brushed splinters from the shoulder, turned on lights, stopped short.

A woman lay on the bed. He saw her eyes rolling. She was bound and gagged. He tore off the gag.

"Oh!" she cried. "Are you the police department?"

"The police department is in the other room. You're Marta Dahl. Listen, don't tell me you're not!"

"I—I—am Marta—"

"Swell! I'm Cardigan. Glad to know you, Miss Dahl. Now don't get excited. We're going to Poland together."

"But I have a husband in Poland—"

"What the hell—I mean, I would get a break like that—I mean, sure, that's swell!"

"But please—these ropes—they're cutting me— Oh, I'm so hopeless—so horrified—so tired—"

He got the ropes off, said: "Now rest here. Just rest here a little while. Everything's all right. Only—" he nodded toward the rear of the house— "I would-

n't want you to see what's in the other room. Just rest here. There's no danger."

SHE nodded, put her hands to her eyes. He spun on his heel, strode long-legged through the next room, stepped over the white-haired man and entered the rear room. Garrity had laid the woman on the divan and was stroking his hard jaw. He sighed.

"Pretty, Cardigan, ain't she?"

"Now I'll tell one. What I'd like to know, Pete, is how the hell you turned up here."

Garrity scratched the underside of his chin. "It sounds nutty. Yager busts into headquarters a little while ago hauling this hophead Chink Wiggins. Yager is all smiles and yelling for the reward. He says he nabbed this egg on the back fire-escape of this address. What does the egg say? 'I killed the taxi driver. I kidnapped Marta Dahl.' And Yager says, 'You see!' like that."

Cardigan snapped. "That dirty bum Yager tailed me from the hotel and he's been tailing me—"

"Yeah, what I figured. So the newspaper guys flock in. Yager grins and sticks his chest out. The hophead says he killed Marta Dahl too. Yager don't say anything about you. But I begin to figure. I know he's a lousy dick. I figure he couldn't follow a clue even if it was hooked onto his nose. But I remember you had your mind set on this Chink Wiggins. I figure you tailed Chink and Yager tailed you. But I don't say anything. I slip out of headquarters and fandango over on my lonesome. . . . Oh, young lady, are you awake?"

The woman stared at them. "I guess I'm done for, huh?"

"I'll say you are," Cardigan said. "With Marta Dahl in the front room."

"What!" exclaimed Garrity.

"Resting, Pete. Sit down and wait. This jane here is the head of it. She got all these bums to kidnap Marta Dahl."

"Oh, yes?" the woman said and chuckled brittlely. "And who got me to get these bums to do it? I'll tell you. I won't burn, smart boy. Not me! Do you know who's behind it? I'll tell you." She leaned back. "Francis K. Braun. Who is he? Marta Dahl's banker. The head of a small uptown bank where a friend of a friend told her to put her money. When she wanted the four hundred thousand grand the bank was in a bad way but they didn't dare tell her she couldn't get it inside of two weeks. Braun had been fooling around with the funds. If he told her she couldn't have the money it would have raised a howl. Bank examiners. Ruination. Penitentiary. So he came to me. Knew me well. I supplied him with hop. Sure, he was a hophead too. So Marta Dahl was to be kidnaped, held until he could replace the money, and then released. That's all there was to it. It would have worked. Only Sam there went hay-wire. It was a neat plan. It would have worked swell but things happened."

Garrity was stunned. "You mean to tell me the head of a bank would do a thing like that!"

"Listen, copper, when a big shot gets in a jam he'll do anything. He invited Marta Dahl to his apartment this evening—"

Garrity got up, crossed the room and picked up the phone. "I'll have some men pick that guy up. I'll—"

The sound of a gun rocked the room. Garrity dropped the telephone. Cardigan bounded to his feet and lunged through the wide doorway to the other room.

The white-haired man was turning over on his stomach, groaning. A smoking gun slipped from his fingers. He stiffened and then there was a dark splotch growing on the old rose carpet.

Cardigan turned him over. He heard a faint outcry.

Marta Dahl was standing in the doorway that led from the front room. Her hands were pressed to her cheeks.

"That," she said, "that is my banker! That is Mr. Braun!"

Cardigan rose, turned and went back into the rear room.

Garrity was tearing a gun from the woman's hand.

He said: "By God, Jack, if she didn't try to put a bullet in your back!"

"She just doesn't like me," Cardigan said. "It must have been something I did."

The Man in the Vault

by
Howard E. Morgan

Jigger Higgins was a clever crook—and he knew it. What he didn't know was that even the smartest thief can get caught when he talks too much. Particularly when it's someone else's words he's trying to steal.

SEVERAL people were interested in Mark Trice. Casper Marchmont, president of the Central National Bank, thought Mark Trice was a good accountant. That was why he liked Trice and had raised his salary. Moira Knapp thought Trice was a good accountant, too. But that wasn't the only reason why she liked him. "Jigger" Higgins didn't like Trice. He didn't like anybody except Jigger Higgins. And yet, Jigger's interest was no less active than Moira Knapp's or Casper Marchmont's. Jigger intended robbing the Central National and he had decided that Mark Trice should be the fall-guy.

Pinkerton operative "Arab" McGork told his chief: "Of course Trice lied to get his job in the Central National. But what the hell! He's earnest, hard-working, and all that. Old Casper Marchmont is boosting him. And Moira Knapp, Marchmont's secretary and an honest-to-God girl, is for him."

McGork's lean hard face was very earnest. But the chief wasn't impressed. "Trice is a crook," he said. "You're takin' Bill Caxton's place in the Central National Monday morning. And you're watchin' Mark Trice. If things begin t' look the least bit screwy, yank him in."

Trice had been convicted of a minor offence in Lynn, a town twelve miles from Boston. This was why Boston and Arab McGork knew all about him. Jigger Higgins hailed from the coast, Portland, Oregon to be exact. Boston had never heard of him. To Arab McGork—at first —he was just another electrician.

To give the cuss his due, Jigger was a good electrician. He had an ingenious turn of mind and was a valuable man on intricate jobs such as the wiring of the antiquated Central National Bank.

The job involved complete rewiring of the old bank including installation of an elaborate buzzer system. Jigger and his two companion mechanics were given the run of the place. They went in and out of cages where money was always lying about, at will; drilled for hours in massive vaults containing fortunes in negotiable securities. Nobody paid them any attention. It was a thief's paradise.

Jigger Higgins began to make plans. He was too old a hand to fall for the obvious. Almost any day for instance, he might have picked up a fortune and gotten away with it, temporarily. But, the moment the stuff was missed, the three electricians would be picked up. His, Jigger's fingerprints were on file in the Bureau of Identification at Washington. That would be enough. Even though they might not prove anything, he would never be able to spend the money. He knew the Pinkertons. There was one of these, a sleepy-eyed lug named Caxton, on constant duty in the bank.

Jigger had been working in the Central

National three days before he even saw Mark Trice. This was understandable. The latters' old fashioned roll-top desk was in an isolated corner, plunked up against a dark wall. The industrious young accountant seldom left it except to answer a call from Marchmont's office.

Trice walked with a curious sidelong gait which in itself reflected a sort of bashful uncertainty. He was characteristically diffident and shy, and unassuming almost to the point of self-effacement. In appearance he was long-bodied, lean and slightly stoop-shouldered; an unruly shock of corn-colored hair was always in his eyes.

Jigger Higgins was long-bodied too, and lean, and his hair was yellow and unruly. His shoulders weren't stooped and there was nothing shy or diffident about him—but these were minor considerations. With practice, Jigger knew he could impersonate Mark well enough for his purpose.

It was Trice's voice that proved the biggest stumbling block. During a week of constant watching and listening, Jigger did not hear Trice speak a dozen words. The accountant's voice was high-pitched, with a slight twang. So much Jigger gathered from listening at a distance while Trice, his back turned, spoke briefly over the phone. With this scant information the prospective thief had to be content.

AFTER the first day on the Central National job, Jigger Higgins brought his lunch and ate it in the bank. He soon discovered that outside of two tellers who remained on duty during the noon hour, most of the bank's employees went out to lunch promptly at twelve and returned at one. President Marchmont and Trice were the only ones who ever varied their routine: both of these usually lunched at twelve. But Trice was no clock watcher and there were times when engrossed in his work, he had no lunch at all.

Casper Marchmont was depending more

and more upon Mark Trice, hence one of the first features of the new installation to be completed was a call buzzer connecting Marchmont's private office with Mark Trice's desk. This made for efficiency but resulted in Moira Knapp seeing far less of the blond accountant. Before the buzzer had been installed Moira had been in the habit of personally notifying Trice when Marchmont wanted him. The girl was palpably in love with Trice, and he with her.

Jigger knew when Arab McGork replaced the lethargic Caxton. But he was not particularly interested. To him one flatfoot was pretty much like another. He would have been interested though, had he known that the keen-eyed McGork had spotted him instantly as having been in the penitentiary.

Jigger laid his plans with elaborate care. He spent a sunshiny Sunday at Revere Beach. While there he engaged a room in a low-priced hotel, paying two weeks' rent in advance. He saw McGork with a fat woman—probably his wife—and two redheaded kids, splashing in the surf. McGork saw him but apparently did not recognize him.

Monday, Jigger purchased a third-hand flivver for thirty-five dollars. This ramshackle vehicle, he parked in unrestricted space near the bank. That noon he bought a cheap blue serge suit like the one Mark Trice wore, a pair of white and tan shoes and a soft gray hat.

Early Tuesday while his two companion workers were busy in a remote section of the bank, Jigger tapped the private buzzer line between Marchmont's office and Mark Trice's desk. He ran a wire to a row of filing cases from behind which he could give the familiar signal which would take Trice to Marchmont's office. Twelve o'clock came and the bank emptied including Casper Marchmont himself. Trice, stooped low over his desk, worked on.

Jigger got a package out of his tool

chest and hurried out to the washroom. Five minutes later, he slipped behind the filing cases dressed in a blue serge suit, white and tan shoes and with a gray felt hat pulled down over his eyes. The wide, flagged floor before the cages was deserted. The two tellers on duty surreptitiously read magazines. Trice was engrossed in a mass of vouchers filed in a shallow tin box at his side.

Jigger pressed the improvised push button at the end of the wire lead. The buzzer rang three times. Trice jumped nervously. He came to his feet and sidled along behind the wire cages toward Marchmont's office on the second floor in the rear of the bank.

Jigger Higgins went into action. He circled swiftly about, bending low, and before Mark Trice had traveled half the distance to his destination, Jigger was coming back along the dark passageway behind the cages, one of those familiar tin filing boxes under an arm. He expertly unhocked the flimsy catch and slipped inside the empty cage usually officiated over by Frank Knowles, the senior teller.

BOTH of the magazine-reading tellers saw his stooped back as he fumbled in the cash drawer. Mark Trice often visited the tellers' cages. He always carried one of those tin boxes. Usually he filled it with vouchers which he took to his desk and checked at leisure. But it wasn't vouchers that were going into that box today. Jigger knew exactly what to look for. He filled the box with worn greenbacks of large denominations, and slipped out. He was just refastening the catch on the cage when a girl laughed.

There was the sound of leisurely steps approaching. Jigger glimpsed the two tellers, Knowles and Whipple, and Moira Knapp. They were returning, earlier than usual, from lunch. He was in shadow. They had just come in from the sun-bright outdoors. They hadn't seen him, yet. The open door of a big vault yawned before him. He slipped inside. With the tin box in shadow, he knelt and started pawing over a pile of dusty vouchers. The steps stopped at the door. Knowles laughed; asked, "Don't you ever eat, Mark?"

Jigger's heart jumped. He cleared his throat. Imitated Trice's nasal twang. "Sure," he said, "but this is my busy day."

"Busy day," Knowles snorted. "Every day is your busy day. Who's going to win at Fenway Park this afternoon?"

"Red Sox," Jigger answered unhesitatingly. "Danny MacFayden will be pitching. His last game for the Sox—"

Jigger stopped talking abruptly. Trice he knew was a baseball fan. So also was he. But he didn't want to get into a long-winded conversation. Neither Knowles nor Whipple answered. Jigger heard the mumble of their voices as they moved on. Moira Knapp apparently wasn't with them. Jigger would have given a great deal to have looked around. Where was Moira Knapp? Why hadn't she spoken?

Jigger jumped to his feet, looked out. Moira Knapp was nowhere in sight. Whipple and Knowles stood behind the latter's cage, talking low-voiced. Knowles would discover the robbery the instant he entered that cage.

Tightly clutching the square box, Jigger hurried back around the cages to Mark Trice's desk. He thrust the greenbacks into a big Boston bag, then slipped out a side door, clambered into the old flivver.

He turned several corners then stopped on a deserted side street. He transferred the money to a pasteboard box, which was already stamped and inscribed with his new Revere address. Then he dropped it into a parcels-post box, nearby. He slipped into the back of the car, stripped off the blue serge suit, changed his shoes, and two minutes later was driving by a round-about way back to the bank, dressed in the overalls of Jigger Higgins, electrician.

He met Jimmy Menlo, one of his fellow

workmen, outside the bank. They went in together. Everything seemed to be functioning as usual. Of course Mark Trice was absent, and Frank Knowles was not in his accustomed place behind the chief teller's cage. Jigger whistled a bar or two of "Paradise" and while Menlo was in the washroom quickly removed the wire leading behind the filing cabinets.

Menlo came back, walking fast. "Ed's in Marchmont's office," he said. "They want us in there, too."

Jigger stopped whistling. "We've probably balled something up," he hazarded.

Menlo grunted "Yeah" and preceded Jigger to the rear of the bank.

A rap brought Arab McGork to Marchmont's door. The detective didn't look at Menlo at all. His eyes seemed to fasten upon Jigger Higgin's face. Jigger sensed this regard and fidgeted uneasily. Had something slipped?

The office was almost full. Casper Marchmont, very white of face, behind his seventy-two inch mahogany desk, Mark Trice, Moira Knapp, Frank Knowles, and Ed, the other electrician, and Arab McGork. The two tellers who had seen "Mark Trice" open and enter Frank Knowles' cage were not there; apparently both were at lunch still.

TRICE was a pitiable object. His hands were shaking and his pale cheeks were wet with perspiration. Moira Knapp had apparently just finished talking. She was crying softly. Casper Marchmont watched her closely. Arab McGork's eyes were still all for Jigger Higgins. "I must confess, I don't quite understand, Miss Knapp," Marchmont said. "You claim Trice was in this office, in this very chair, when you came in immediately after leaving Whipple and Knowles in the lower hall. And yet you admit you saw him, Trice, in Number One Vault. Knowles and Whipple both saw him there. Knowles talked to him."

Then Mark Trice took purposeful steps forward. He began to talk and the world dropped away from beneath Jigger Higgins' feet. "I t-t-t-tell you, I w-w-w-wasn't in that v-v-vault," he stuttered. "Your b-buzzer r-r-r-rang and I c-c-c-came d-d-d-directly here."

Jigger Higgins' wet fingers clenched. Mark Trice was a stuttering fool! That was why he so seldom spoke; that was what made him so shy. Something seemed to collapse inside Jigger Higgins. His knees were rubbery. His mouth dry.

"—as I've already told you, Mr. Marchmont," Knowles was saying. "Neither Whipple nor I was sure that the man in the vault was Trice. Unfortunately, we weren't suspicious enough—"

"Just why didn't you think the man in the vault was Trice?" McGork interrupted.

Knowles looked unhappy, half apologetic. "Well," he said, "the man in the vault—er—ah—didn't stutter!"

For a moment there was complete silence in the room. Jigger Higgins mopped his face. Then Arab McGork laughed. He turned quickly, caught Jigger Higgins' nearest arm. "It couldn't have been this man you were talking to could it?"

Jigger Higgins gasped and stepped backward. "No, no," he heard himself protesting. "I didn't do it." He was excited, his voice high-pitched.

Relief flooded Knowles' face. He crashed his palm with his fist. "Absolutely," he almost shouted. "That's the man! Same build as Mark. Voice similar. Only —of course—he doesn't stutter."

Jigger Higgins protested volubly. But McGork knew him, knew all about him. "That money, now," McGork said. "Might it be Jigger, that you sent it to an address in Revere? No, no, of course you didn't. But we'll check up on it, just for the hell of it, eh?" He chuckled noisily as he led his prisoner away. "It's a smooth one you are, Jigger. But not quite smooth enough. Next time you pick a fall-guy grab one that don't stutter."

JUST IN CASE

IF THE readers of this department have come to think, during the past year, that its sole purpose has been to give the editors an opportunity to brag, about DIME DETECTIVE MAGAZINE; just in case you've gained the impression that this page is nothing more than a medium for self-congratulation and back-slapping (We realize that we have talked about ourselves a good deal) to correct any such possible notion which we have been guilty of fostering we're going to perform a right-about-face this month and talk about everything and everybody but ourselves. And that means our rivals—or at least one of them.

But before we start effacing ourselves, burying our light under the proverbial bushel, just a few words about a man who has done more than a lot to make that light shine as it has. Sorry! There we go forgetting ourselves again. Anyway, here's Carroll John Daly whose *The Red Death* you have just read, and been thrilled by, we hope, as we were when the manuscript came in.

He was born in Yonkers, N. Y., some thirty-odd years ago and has been writing fiction for the past twelve years. Before becoming an author he was interested in the theatre and owned and operated

Carroll John Daly

theatres in various places. He has traveled widely and only the fact that his wife feels his presence is needed at home, prevents him from continually embarking on strange ships for strange places. He is fond of camping out if there is a tiled bath and good bed close at hand; he has a highly developed sense of humor—too highly developed according to some of his friends; he does not believe in Prohibition and his main hobby is writing crime stories. (Boy, do we wish we could make our hobbies as profitable as Daly makes his!) Incidentally, if you happen to be a Daly fan you're in good company, for Dr. William Lyon Phelps of Yale thinks the creator of Vee Brown is the best writer of detective fiction working in that field today.

And now for those remarks we promised about our rival. Friendly rival, we should have said, for DIME MYSTERY BOOK MAGAZINE (Oh-oh! The secret's out of the bag.) is the new addition to the Popular Publications group and what an addition! For when the first issue appears on the stands November First you're going to get the biggest magazine thrill that's—But you'll find the whole story on the next page. Better read it!

The First Time In Magazine History!

A
TWO DOLLAR
Book-Length Detective Novel

for

10 CENTS!

In

this new, amazing

10c   DIME

MYSTERY

BOOK   Magazine

MYSTERY—
THRILLS—
Spine tingling SUSPENSE—

Served piping hot on this fiction bargain counter by the World's Best Writers of Detective Thrillers!

❖

Match your wits against the fiendish cleverness of men who kill for gain, for vengeance—and for pleasure!

❖

Ten cents, dropped on your corner newsstand, will bring you the best book-length murder-mystery money can buy—plus short stories, plus detective features, plus murder problems you can have a try at solving yourself!

❖

Selected novels, hand-picked from the season's best . . . . If you can lay one aside before the last clue's been followed up— the last shot fired—we'll eat the back cover!

126

128

www.ingramcontent.com/pod-product-compliance
Lightning Source LLC
Chambersburg PA
CBHW080911020726
47502CB00008B/2422